Grape Expectations

**Other Pennsylvania Dutch Mysteries
by Tamar Myers**

Grape Expectations

A Pennsylvania Dutch Mystery
with Recipes

Tamar Myers

 NEW AMERICAN LIBRARY

NEW AMERICAN LIBRARY
Published by New American Library, a division of
Penguin Group (USA) Inc., 375 Hudson Street, New York, New York 10014, USA
Penguin Group (Canada), 90 Eglinton Avenue East, Suite 700, Toronto,
Ontario, Canada M4P 2Y3 (a division of Pearson Penguin Canada Inc.)
Penguin Books Ltd., 80 Strand, London WC2R 0RL, England
Penguin Ireland, 25 St. Stephen's Green, Dublin 2, Ireland (a division of Penguin Books Ltd.)
Penguin Group (Australia), 250 Camberwell Road, Camberwell, Victoria 3124,
Australia (a division of Pearson Australia Group Pty. Ltd.)
Penguin Books India Pvt. Ltd., 11 Community Centre, Panchsheel Park,
New Delhi - 110 017, India
Penguin Group (NZ), cnr Airborne and Rosedale Roads, Albany,
Auckland 1310, New Zealand (a division of Pearson New Zealand Ltd.)
Penguin Books (South Africa) (Pty.) Ltd., 24 Sturdee Avenue,
Rosebank, Johannesburg 2196, South Africa

Penguin Books Ltd., Registered Offices: 80 Strand, London WC2R 0RL, England

First published by New American Library, a division of Penguin Group (USA) Inc.

First Printing, February 2006
10 9 8 7 6 5 4 3 2 1

LIBRARY OF CONGRESS CATALOGING-IN-PUBLICATION DATA:

Myers, Tamar.
    Grape expectations / Tamar Myers.
      p. cm.
    ISBN 0-451-21485-4
    1. Yoder, Magdalena (Fictitious character)—Fiction. 2. Women detectives—Pennsylvania—
Fiction. 3. Pennsylvania Dutch Country (Pa.)—Fiction. 4. Vintners—Crimes against—Fiction.
5. Wine and wine making—Fiction. 6. Pennsylvania—Fiction. 7. Mennonites—Fiction.
8. Cookery—Pennsylvania. I. Title.
    PS3563.Y475G73 2006
    813'.54—dc22   2005022627

Set in Palatino

Printed in the United States of America

This Book could not have been written without the inadverdent support of my three best friends. They are, in the order of helpfulness:

Pagan, my basenji dog, who spends her days lying on a blue chair, in a sunny spot, in my office. She is my constant companion. My rock.

Kasha, my Bengal cat, who has learned how to push the print button on my printer, and then jumps down to the tray to help the pages come out faster (although not always in great condition). He makes me laugh every day.

Catrina the Great, my F1 Jungle Cat hybrid, the newest addition to our family. Her majestic beauty (she is as large as our dog) reminds me that there is another world out there, a world beyond my imagination.

Thank you, all.

Acknowledgments

I am grateful to the Concord Grape Association for allowing me to use some of their recipes in this book. They may be contacted at the following address.

Concord Grape Association
5575 Peachtree-Dunwoody Road
Building G, Suite 500
Atlanta, GA 30342
404/252-3663
E-mail: info@concordgrape.org
Web site: www.concordgrape.org

1

Sturdy Christian underwear saved my life. I mean that literally. Once, in the concealing darkness of an abandoned mineshaft, I turned a brassiere into a slingshot, thereby enabling me to disable a giantess from New Jersey. On another occasion, my plain Protestant petticoat caught on a branch, preventing me from sailing over a cliff and thus becoming a buzzard buffet at the bottom. Sturdy Christian underwear, however, did not prevent my papa from doing the horizontal hootchy-kootchy with Odelphia Root. And if Odelphia had kept her sturdy Christian underwear where it belonged, she wouldn't have conceived Zelda Root.

It was Doc Shafor who knocked Papa off his pedestal with that bit of unsavory information, which could hardly be called news, given that it happened over forty years ago. At first I couldn't believe my ears. Then I got angry—not at Papa, but at Doc. I was still railing at him three months later.

"Doc, why tell me now? After all these years?"

Doc put another piece of warm pie on my plate and topped it with a scoop of freshly churned ice cream. "Dig in, Magdalena."

"I don't want more dessert. I want answers."

"I've given you answers. Now I'm giving you pie à la mode. Eat."

"Just one more time, Doc—please."

Doc sighed. "This is the last time then."

"Last time, I promise."

"I told you because Zelda is hurting. She could really use a sister."

"She's hurting because the man she worships—the man who just so happens to be married to my *real* sister—is being tried for murder. And while Zelda may not be guilty of aiding and abetting our erstwhile Chief of Police, she certainly turned a blind eye his way."

"She's still your sister. Your flesh and blood."

"Half sister. So just flesh—no blood."

"Why, Magdalena Portulaca Yoder, I must say I really am disappointed in you. I thought you were a bigger woman than that."

Doc Shafor is one of my oldest friends. Ever since my philandering papa and ill-tempered mama were killed in the Allegheny Tunnel, squished to death between a milk tanker and a truckload of state-of-the-art running shoes, the octogenarian has been my mentor. The fact that he finds me attractive in the romantic sense has so far been his problem, not mine.

"I'm sorry if I disappoint you, Doc, but this is all very hard for me to process. Three months ago I walked into this house with one sibling, sat down to eat, and walked out with two. I'm not going to leave with a brother today, am I?"

"Magdalena, sarcasm does not become you."

"I can't help it. Besides, you haven't told me yet how it is you know for sure that Zelda is my sister. And another thing. Did everyone in Hernia know except for me? And Susannah," I added, referring to my full flesh and blood sister. "Does she know?"

Doc chuckled. "If anyone else knew, do you think I'd be the one telling you? Magdalena, Hernia is to gossip what Milwaukee is to beer."

I don't drink alcoholic beverages, but I knew what he meant. Last year Kathy Baumgartner went to Bedford, our closest real city, to see a podiatrist about a bad case of toenail fungus. Tongues started wagging even before she left. By the time Kathy made it home—Bedford is all of twelve miles away—Kathy's fungus had progressed to the point that she was no longer among us, and her tootsies were pushing up daisies in Walnut Grove Cemetery.

"But Papa was such an upstanding man," I said stubbornly.

"Part of him was."

"You still haven't told me how you found out."

"Yes, I have."

"Not today, you haven't." To be honest, I was hoping that, in the umpteenth telling, the story would turn out to be a mite less horrid.

Doc sighed. "He told me. They both did. You see, Magdalena, they came to me one night asking if I could help them with a certain problem. This wasn't the first time a couple had come to me at night like that, and I knew right away what they wanted."

"An *abortion*?"

"Exactly. I told them—"

"You're just a veterinarian, for crying out loud."

"That I am. But they didn't know what else to do. I told them that even though I believed a woman had a right over her own body—therefore her own reproductive system—I believed a baby had a right over his, or her, own body as well. I know that's fence-sitting, but that's how I felt. I also told them that, my personal feelings aside, I simply wasn't qualified to perform such a procedure on anything smaller than a horse."

"So then what happened? Did Odelphia Root go off to stay with a distant relative until after the baby was born?"

"Magdalena, as you know good and well, Odelphia was Mrs. Angus Root when the affair happened."

I stiffened as the now familiar stench of hellfire filled my nostrils. "Papa slept with a *married* woman."

"I'm afraid so. The irony is that Angus was shooting blanks, and he never would have been a father if your Papa hadn't stepped up to the plate."

"Did Odelphia ever tell Angus who the father really was?"

Doc shrugged and scooped the melting ice cream from my pie into his mouth. "If she did, it didn't seem to matter to Angus. Believe me, I kept a close watch on that man, and all I ever saw was how kind he was to Zelda. The funny thing is, they even looked alike. Don't you think so?"

I nodded reluctantly. Angus and his assumed daughter were both built like plucked chickens. Skinny ankles, no waist, a meaty breast not delineated into bosoms—there was, in fact, an uncanny resemblance.

"Doc, if Odelphia was doing the mattress mambo with Papa, a married man, and she was married as well, who's to say the hooch wasn't doing the horizontal hootchy-kootchy with half the men in Bedford County?"

"I was waiting for you to ask that, Magdalena. To be honest, only a DNA test will prove conclusively who Zelda's biological father is—rather, was."

I stabbed at my pie before Doc got his mitts on that too. "So, what is it you want from me? To make like Papa never cheated on poor unsuspecting Mama?"

Doc roared with laughter, giving me back some of the ice cream in the process. "Now that's a good one—your poor unsuspecting Mama! Magdalena, what universe are you living in? When I said that no one else knew, I wasn't including your mama."

I couldn't help but grin. Even a weight-lifting sheep couldn't pull the wool over Mama's eyes. If it happened in Hernia, Mama knew about it—sooner rather than later. If Mama had come to terms with this disturbing revelation, why couldn't I? Zelda was six nuts short of bridge mix, but she wasn't a bad person.

"I'll try to be nice to her," I said.

"You'll do more than that," Doc said. "You'll succeed."

"Don't be so sure of that."

"If I wasn't sure of that, I wouldn't have told you."

"Life keeps throwing me curveballs," I wailed.

"You could use a few curves, Magdalena."

Doc was right. Here I am, in my late forties, and I have yet to develop a figure. I can eat all I want and not put on a single pound. Yes, I am aware of the fact that virtually every other woman in America would be glad to have my problem. What problem? they might even ask. But when you're pushing the half-century mark and lack ballast—both forward and aft—it isn't funny. Just the other day a busybody from church, who fancies herself a wag, said: "You know, Magdalena, if you drank tomato juice and wore nothing but a zipper, you'd make a pretty decent thermometer."

I've always been teased. When I was growing up my parents didn't believe in deodorant. If the Good Lord didn't want us to stink, He wouldn't have created armpits, they said. This philosophy works fine if everyone around you subscribes to it. But I went to a public high school, which included among its student body children of a more progressive society. It was only a matter of minutes before I was dubbed "Yoder with the Odor." It was soon shortened to just Odor. When the "in" clique wanted to get away from me, their leader, Mary Jane Yocum, would say in a loud voice, "Come on, guys, let's de-Odorize."

The really hard part was not being able to retaliate. You see, I am a Mennonite of Amish ancestry. My people have been pacifists for hundreds of years. We believe in turning the other cheek, even if that cheek is still sore from a previous assault. We love our neighbors as ourselves, although not all of us love ourselves very much. That would be too proud.

I put up with Mary Jane Yocum and her henchmen for most of my freshman year. Then came picture day. After attendance we were supposed to line up in the gymnasium and get photographed for the yearbook. I knew I was going to be right behind my tormentor and had prepared for the occasion. At the time I had a pet hamster, Willard, that was so sluggish he wouldn't even use his wheel. Willard rode to school in my otherwise empty bra that day, and as we students stood obediently, if impatiently, in alphabetical order waiting to be photographed, Willard somehow found his way into Mary Jane's beehive hairdo.

Yes, it was a cruel thing to do to Willard, and I have since repented of my sin: Mary Jane's shrieks caused the hapless hamster irreparable hearing loss. But as the beehive hairdo came undone, so did Mary Jane's status as leader of the pack. Much to my surprise, there were many students at Hernia High who felt the same way I did. For a brief period of time I was a heroine. Mary Jane, on the other hand, was known as Hamster Hair for the rest of her high school career. Today, I am told, she runs a beauty salon in Lawton, Oklahoma.

Not that it's any of your business, but I now use deodorant on a daily basis. And while I may not be the most popular woman in town, I am by far its most distinguished. I say that in all humility, a virtue of which I have an abundance. After my parents' death I turned the family farm into a full-board inn. The PennDutch caters to the well-heeled: mostly Hollywood celebrities and millionaire congressmen, all of whom are eager to fill my coffers.

The secret to my success is what I call the "squint when you travel" syndrome. Once on a trip to the wild and woolly state of Maryland (I carried my own provisions, of course), I realized that I was putting up with conditions I never would have tolerated back home in civilized Pennsylvania. Tourists, it seems, are quite willing to settle for less and pay more for it as long as they can view it as a cultural experience. The more abuse heaped on one and the higher the cost, the better. How else can one explain Paris as a travel destination?

Back home I applied this same principle to my inn. Although I make my guests pay through the nose, they get the option of paying even more if they agree to clean their own rooms and help out with the farm chores. I call this feature ALPO—Amish Lifestyle Plan Option.

At any rate, being a millionaire in a small town like Hernia (population 1,877, now that the Kreiders have had their baby) gives one certain rights and responsibilities. I'm the head of the town council because I pay the mayor's salary, along with a stipend to the other councilmen and -women. Oh, did I happen to mention that I *am* the mayor? This is a recent development that came upon us rather suddenly, when our Chief of Police, Melvin "the mantis" Stoltzfus, was arrested for murder, and his only deputy—the aforementioned Zelda—was sidelined for possible collusion and general incompetence. Our then mayor, Brenda Turweiliger, resigned from her post, citing paparazzi harassment, but everyone knew she'd been dipping into the town till to get her tooth capped.

I'd had three opponents in the mayoral race but won by a landslide—eighty-three percent of the forty-six votes cast. My first duty as mayor was to hire a new Chief of Police, which I did. Olivia Hornsby-Anderson was unanimously approved by the town council, as was her pick for deputy, a very handsome young man named Chris Ackerman.

Despite a major and humiliating setback, Hernia, Pennsylvania, was back on its feet again—until the day the vineyard came to town.

2

The mayor's office is a windowless cubbyhole behind the jail. It is so small a toad wouldn't hibernate in it, although it is a popular spot for old flies to go when they die. The only ventilation is a ceiling fan with a broken blade; the illumination consists of a fluorescent shop light that can't decide if it's off or on. I've heard my workplace described as an Episcopalian's version of Hell.

In winter this so-called office is heated by a radiator that is stuck on high, so that one is forced to either leave the door open or bake like one of Freni's cinnamon buns. Thus it was that I was thrashing my brains at my desk one morning, trying to make sense of the town's astronomical water bill, when Agnes Mishler darkened the doorway. So completely did she cover the space that I thought the door had blown shut.

"Magdalena, have you heard?"

"I've heard plenty, dear. To what, specifically, are you referring?"

"Sodom and Gomorrah. That's what Hernia is going to turn into if we don't put a stop to this."

"If you flee, remember not to look back."

"What's that supposed to mean?"

"Don't you read your Bible?"

"Of course I do. I'm a Mennonite too, you know. Just because I belong to the First Mennonite Church, and not Beechy Grove Mennonite like you, doesn't mean I don't read the Bible."

The First Mennonite Church is the most liberal branch of the Plain People in Hernia and its environs. The most conservative are the Old Order Amish, the ones seen riding horses and buggies. Then there are the Black Bumper Amish, who are allowed to drive black cars just as long as the chrome is painted black. I belong to a conservative branch of the Mennonite Church, the one to which the Good Lord would belong if He were living on earth today. I drive and use electricity but dress conservatively, like the Good Lord intended, and wear my braids neatly tucked beneath a white organza prayer cap. For the record, I do not consider myself better than anyone else in Hernia—even the Presbyterians.

"Agnes, dear," I said patiently, "when Lot's wife fled Sodom and Gomorrah, she turned around to look at the burning cities, and God turned her into a pillar of salt. I was only thinking of your health. Aren't you on a sodium-restricted diet?"

"Magdalena, you obviously haven't heard."

"Enlighten me, dear."

"Well, Ed Gingerich—"

"No, I meant that literally. Please step in all the way. You're blocking my light."

She squeezed into the space not occupied by my desk. "Like I was about to say, did you know that Ed sold his farm to those folks from California?"

"Yes, for the experimental fruit farm."

"Experimental, my asterisk. There'll be grapes on that farm."

If only I had the freedom to swear like Agnes. "There's nothing wrong with grapes, dear. They're mentioned many times in the Bible."

"And so is wine. You're not suggesting that wine is okay too, are you, Magdalena?"

"Heavens, no. But what does wine have to do with the farm Ed sold?"

Agnes leaned forward, the better to emphasize her coup de grâce. Her wispy hair, unrestrained by any sort of covering, fluttered dangerously near the fan blades.

"The Californians intend to build a winery."

"Oh my."

"*And* a hotel."

I leaped to my feet, taking my temper with me. "A *what*?"

"Not just any hotel, Magdalena, but a five-star luxury hotel.

They'll have one-thousand-thread-count sheets on the beds—like 'butter' the brochure says. And gourmet meals prepared by French chefs. Oh, and a spa with mud treatments and hot stones. What's the deal with hot stones, Magdalena?"

I hadn't the foggiest. Once when I was a child at Lake Wanna-makya church camp, Johnny Armbruster told me to lie still on the beach while he covered me with pebbles. But then Johnny started getting careless where he put his hands, so I told him to get his rocks off and play by himself. Those stones had been lying in the sun, and thus pretty hot, but it was not a pleasant experience by any means.

"Do you have this brochure?"

Agnes fished around in a pocketbook large enough to contain Richard Simmons. "Here," she finally said, and handed me a wrinkled but very classy brochure.

My heart sank as I flipped through the glossy pages. Grape Expectations, the new enterprise was calling itself. Prizewinning wines grown on the premises. Food and lodging fit for a king. Even horseback riding. And a gift shop offering authentic Amish arts and crafts, as well as Amish cheese and a "dazzling variety of home-canned treats, such as pickles, apple butter, and jams."

"I'm ruined," I wailed.

"Magdalena, this is no time to focus on your indiscretion, not when our entire way of life is at stake here."

Give me mad over sad any day. "I wasn't referring to my inadvertent adultery," I snapped. "I'm talking about my business. Who is going to want to sleep on burlap sheets when they can get butter?"

"You give your guests burlap sheets?"

"Only if they pay extra. Besides, burlap is exfoliating. No need for loofah when you loaf in my beds. Still, I can't compete— Wait just one Pittsburgh minute. Maybe I can compete! I can add a gift shop, and I already have a barn, so horses are not a problem. As for mud and stones, I'm sure I can come up with plenty."

"How about a French chef?"

I sighed. My cook is Freni Hostetler, an Amish woman in her mid-seventies. Freni quits every other whipstitch—at last count it was ninety-eight times—but she always comes back to rule the roost. Besides being a dear friend and a mother substitute, she's a passable cook. But Freni would quit for the last time if I brought in a French chef.

"I'm ruined," I said again. "Well, at any rate the PennDutch will be a thing of the past—unless I cut my prices drastically. Then there goes my Hollywood crowd. You know what they say: If it's cheap, it can't be trendy."

"Who says that?"

"Don't bother me for details, dear. Where did you get this brochure?"

"From my cousin Martha, who sometimes does alterations for a lady out on Hungry Neck Road. Can you imagine someone not knowing how to sew, Magdalena?"

"Where did Martha get it?"

"She says there's this billboard next to Ed's drive, and there's this plastic tube, or something, with these in it. It says to take one, so she did."

"One must never disobey the tube."

"Huh?"

"Never mind, dear. I want to know how this could happen. How could the Bedford County Planning Commission let this slip by them? Wait!" I jumped to my feet, the top of my noggin just missing the ceiling fan. "Ed Gingerich's land is within town limits. He's got to get permission from the town council, of which yours truly is not only a member but its president. Bye-bye, Grape Expectations."

Agnes Mishler was irritatingly unmoved by my decisive victory over one-thousand-count-thread sheets. "Sorry, Magdalena, but you're wrong."

"I am *so* president of the town council; that's part and parcel of being the mayor."

"You're wrong about the town limits. Remember about fifteen years ago when Ed and some other folks out there on Hungry Neck Road petitioned the town to extend its limits so that they could hook up to the water and sewer lines, but yous voted that down on account that it would cost more to run the lines out there than yous could collect in revenues?"

"Don't you 'yous' me, dear. I wasn't on the council then."

"You are now. So what are you going to do about it?"

"What can I do?"

Agnes toyed with a chin hair. "Well, you could bully Ed. You've always been good at that."

"I have not!"

"Remember the time—"

"No time for memory lane," I sang, and squeezing past my desk, pushed Agnes gently out into the light.

I drove straight over to the Gingerich farm. Ed's wife, Fiona, has been dead for forty years. They never had children, so up until his retirement last fall, Ed worked the farm with hired help. This is an unusual situation in these parts, where families tend to be large and there is no lack of capable hands into which one can leave the family enterprise. Although Ed belongs to my church—Beechy Grove Mennonite—and I see him nearly every Sunday, I had no idea he was planning to sell the farm to winos—or would that be vintners?

At any rate, Hungry Neck Road dead-ends five miles out of town, so unless one has a specific reason to go out that way, one rarely does. Therefore I cannot be blamed for having no prior knowledge of the huge sign at the end of Ed's gravel drive.

COMING SOON—GRAPE EXPECTATIONS!
A world-class resort for the lover of the grape. Visit us at www.grapeexpectations.com.

"Well, we'll just see about that," I said aloud, and unwisely pushed the pedal to the metal. Even though I had traded in my sinfully red BMW for a more modest Crown Vic, the gravel was none the less punishing to my car's exterior. It didn't do much to improve my mood, either.

Ed was sitting on a rocker on his front porch, looking for all the world like the retired man I thought he was and not the sneaky, backstabbing real estate mogul that both Agnes and the sign made him out to be. The morning paper lay in his lap unopened.

"Hello, Ed," I said, after having scrounged in the basement of my emotions for some false cheer.

His Adam's apple bobbed. "Hello, Magdalena."

"I suppose you're wondering why I'm here."

"Nope."

"Were you planning to share this bit of news, or were we supposed to guess once the limos started streaming into town?"

"It's not what you think, Magdalena."

Lacking an invitation from him, I invited myself to sit on his steps. "I think you made a bundle on this transaction."

"You know my roots in this community go back as far as yours. I love Hernia just as much as you do."

"So what was it? A cool million?"

"Nope."

I'd only been joking when I named a figure that high, but I breathed a sigh of relief anyway. At least for a little while more I wouldn't have to share the title of millionaire.

"Well, whatever it was, dear, I hope you got your money's worth."

"Thirteen."

"*Thousand?* Look, Ed," I said, trying to suppress some of the glee in my voice, "we're not exactly on the same side here, but I got to tell you—you've been had. Taken to the cleaners, as they say."

"Million."

"Ha, ha, very funny."

"I don't joke, Magdalena. You should know that as well."

He was right about that. Neither Ed nor I has a funny bone in our body.

"But, Ed, you can't be serious—"

He nodded somberly. Somewhere between the house and the barn a rooster crowed. Meanwhile, I felt like I'd swallowed a gallon of molten lead.

"They misrepresented themselves, Magdalena. First they said they wanted to grow grapes and produce jelly—you know, like Smucker's. Then they said something about grape juice. I didn't hear anything about wine until it was too late."

"Wine, swine. Get to the part about the luxury hotel and the spa. When did they mention those?"

"At the closing. I swear it's true, Magdalena, and you know I don't use that word lightly."

We Mennonites, along with the Amish and Quakers, have historically held that our "yeas should be yeas, and our nays, nays," just as the Bible commands us. Ed Gingerich had less personality than a bowl of congealed oatmeal, but he wasn't a liar.

"Why didn't you back out then, Ed?"

"Well, you see, I'd already signed some papers that I hadn't read too carefully—you know, the small print—and because, uh . . . let's face it, Magdalena: thirteen million dollars is a lot of money."

"Indeed it is."

"All I wanted was to be able to retire to Sarasota. Maybe do some saltwater fishing—I hear it's a lot of fun. And play shuffle-board. You ever play shuffleboard, Magdalena?"

"I've shuffled while bored, but I don't think that counts. Ed, how long before you move?"

"Tomorrow."

"Get out of town!"

"I beg your pardon?"

"That's just something my sister Susannah says. I think it's Presbyterian. Anyway, I'm in shock. I really am. I just found out about this a few minutes ago, and tomorrow you leave."

"I feel sick about it, Magdalena."

"Funny, but money seldom does that to me."

"I'm serious. I wish I'd never signed those papers. I would give it all back, if I could."

"Money definitely doesn't do *that* to me."

"I tried to, you know. After I got home and had a chance to think about it some more. But the real estate agent just laughed. She wouldn't even give me the telephone number of anyone connected with Grape Expectations. She said I could give the money to charity if I felt that guilty, but no way was I going to get the farm back."

"So what *are* you going to do?"

He stared over my head at the bottomlands of Hungry Neck Creek. The Gingerich family had been farming the land since 1805, when a Delaware chief by the name of Hungry Neck sold the land to Isaiah and Beverly Gingerich, fresh off the boat at the conclusion of a journey that began in Switzerland. A man still has a right to do as he pleases in this country, and that includes playing shuffleboard. It was clear to me, however, that Ed Gingerich had not intended to sell his heritage along with the land. Yes, he was guilty of greed but not betrayal.

"Ed, as it just so happens, I've got a vacancy at PennDutch this week. Why don't you come and stay with me a couple of days. Maybe I can help you sort this out."

When, after a decent interval, Ed failed to respond, I spoke into a closed fist. This is another worldly trick I learned from Susannah.

"Earth to Ed, Earth to Ed. Come in, Ed."

"They're coming, Magdalena."

"Yes, and so is tomorrow. The Grape Expectations folks will be here before we leave, if you don't give me an answer soon."

"They're coming now."

I turned. A shiny limo was creeping up the long gravel drive.

3

If it would have done anyone even just a smidgen of good, I would have taken off my bra, gathered some choice pieces of gravel, and slain the advancing motorized beast. But neither fantasy nor sturdy Christian underwear was going to get Ed out of this pickle.

First, I ordered him to get off his rocker. Then I climbed up on the porch and we stood shoulder to shoulder. I even reached for his hand but dropped it shortly thereafter; farmers have hands that range in texture from rough sandpaper to cheese graters.

"United we stand, divided we fall, dear."

"Tell that to the walls of Jericho," he muttered.

When Joshua fit the battle of Jericho, he didn't have to contend with Grape Expectations. Soon after the limo stopped, a beautiful young woman with sinfully long legs emerged, unfolding in the process like a butterfly emerging from a metal cocoon. Everything about her reeked of money and, of course, power. She also reeked of an expensive French perfume. The best perfumes, by the way, contain an oil derived from the anal glands of a civet cat. I learned this fact from a former guest, the owner of a perfume company that sold so-called fragrances at four hundred dollars an ounce. Why anyone would want to dab themselves with the business end of an animal is beyond my ken. Much better to use some butter with a sprinkling of cinnamon and sugar. That's guaranteed to attract a man's attention. At any rate, I knew I had my hands full with the limo lady.

I'm sure the handsome gentleman who accompanied the polished woman was a handful as well. Under torture I might admit that his dark brown curls and matching eyes sent a forbidden thrill to my nether regions. But whether my nether could weather this temptation remains a moot point, due to his two-day beard—made popular by Yasser Arafat, by the way—and rumpled clothes. Far from finding stubble attractive, I think the only place it belongs is in a grain field after harvest. At a distance the face of the man from Grape Expectations looked like it had been splattered with mud.

The woman from Grape Expectations strode briskly up the walk. Rumpled-silt-skin followed a step behind.

"Good morning," she said. "You must be Mr. and Mrs. Gingerich."

"Not by a long shot, dear," I said. After all, I am a good fifteen years younger than Ed.

"Felicia Bacchustelli," she said, extending her hand.

"Vinny Bacchustelli," he said, extending his hand as well.

I loathe shaking hands. This antiquated custom—meant to show one is unarmed—is the number one purveyor of the common cold. But because most folks take offense if I don't participate in the ritual passing of germs, I force myself to do it.

"Magdalena Yoder," I said. "This is Mr. Gingerich."

"We met yesterday at the closing," he said.

She nodded but avoided eye contact as she glanced around. "This has even more potential than I remembered. Of course the house will have to go, but the barn has possibilities. We could build the stables off to the left. Am I correct in understanding that the prevailing winds come from the west? I mean, we wouldn't want the lodge to be on the downwind side, now, would we?"

I sniffed. "I smell horse manure already."

"The house was built by my great-great-great-grandfather," Ed said.

"Yes, I'm sure it's very nice," Felicia said.

"You said you were turning my place into an experimental fruit farm."

"We did mention grapes," Vinny said. "The varieties we'll plant have never been grown in this part of Pennsylvania. You can't get any more experimental than that."

"You tricked me."

"Maybe you should have read the fine print, Mr. Gingerich," Felicia said.

"Maybe you should not have taken advantage of an old man," I said.

"Maybe you should mind your own business, Miss Odor."

"That's Yoder!"

"Ladies, please," Vinny said with a salacious smile. I had the feeling he'd have liked nothing better than to watch his wife and me engage in a catfight. Why men find that attractive, I haven't the faintest. Ditto for that whole lesbian thing. But if push came to shove, I could see myself with two men: one to do the cleaning, the other the cooking.

"Back off, pretty boy," I said politely, remembering my Mennonite manners. "This is between your wife and me."

He chuckled. "Felicia isn't my wife—she's my sister-in-law."

"My husband, Albert, is dead now," Felicia said. "He had a lot more class than his brother. Unfortunately, they were business partners."

"Yes, unfortunately," Vinny said.

I pulled myself up to my full five feet ten, which was considerably more than either of them could manage. " 'Unfortunate' seems to be the operative word, dears. You see, the community will never allow the establishment of a den of debauchery such as the one you plan to build. We are teetotalers, every one of us—and if we aren't, we know we ought to be. Some of us even abstain from tea. So, Mrs. and Mr. Baluchistani, I advise you to save yourselves further trouble and hightail it back to from whence you came."

"It's *Bacchustelli*," Felicia snipped.

"Are you sure? I thought that was one of those post-Soviet-era countries that's always in the news."

"I like a woman with fire," Vinny said apropos of nothing but his testosterone level. "I don't suppose you'd consider having dinner with me tonight."

"You might try dating the Statue of Liberty," I said. "She has her own torch. You don't often see a woman with her own torch."

"Please," Ed begged. "Won't you please consider selling this place back to me? I've got some money put away in an IRA. You can have it all."

Felicia smiled. "The bulldozers will be here at seven tomorrow morning."

There was no time to waste. I instructed Ed to gather up his most prized possessions and carry them to the front yard. Then I hopped into my car and stomped on the accelerator. I am shamed to say that the sound of gravel pinging against the limo was music to my ears. (I confessed my sin as soon as I was on the highway.)

The wisest thing to do was to drive straight to the relay station of most of Hernia's gossip: Little Samson's blacksmith's shop—and from there to the birthplace of the gossip: Sam Yoder's Corner Market. Instead, I flagged down every passing car and buggy, informing them of the imminent arrival of Sodom and Gomorrah, urging them to make a beeline for Ed Gingerich's place.

Hernians love a good cause as much as anyone, and by noon virtually every able-bodied soul, as well as a few disabled bodies, had converged at the Gingerich place. The few exceptions were a dozen or so hard-drinking Methodists, seven Presbyterians, and one heretofore closeted, imbibing Baptist. Even our two wine-sipping Jews were there to show their support for Ed Gingerich and our way of life—although the fact the one of them was my fiancé and the other my future mother-in-law may have had something to do with their appearance. Curiously absent were Hernia's first Muslim couple, Ibrahim and Faya Rashid.

Trust me, I've had plenty of experience with the media, the tabloids in particular. Not that it took any arm-twisting to get them involved. What better photo op could there be than a line of Amish buggies miles long, wending their righteous way to aid an "English" neighbor? All three major television networks were there, plus a slew of others. Diane Sawyer looked stunning in a pale yellow blouse and white slacks, and Matt Lauer—well, let's just say, if any man could turn my head, it would be this long, lanky— I think he was wearing clothes. Yes, I'm sure he was.

The photogenic Amish men, as well as others of our community, emptied Ed's house of its contents, and those of us with trucks carted off his belongings to be stored in various homes until the situation was resolved. I fully expected the Bacchustellis to capitulate, given the immense pressure on them to do so and the assuredly negative press. But I underestimated the wine peddling pair from Grape Expectations. They showed no signs of weakening, even after Agnes Mishler handcuffed herself to the metal hitching post in front of Ed Gingerich's porch.

Agnes is an experienced grandstander. A few hours later, when the cameras stopped clicking and the footage stopped rolling, and most especially the mosquitoes started biting, out came the key, which had been hidden in her bra the whole time. I no longer watch television now that decent shows like *Green Acres* are off the air, but I heard plenty about Agnes's many appearances on TV—*after* she released herself, of course. The next several days Agnes was on every talk show, even the late-night ones, where, reportedly, she cracked the hosts up with her dry wit and droll recollections of life in backward Hernia. Just how Agnes managed to come up with even a modicum of wit in such a short time remains a marvel to me. I can only assume that a professional wrote her lines and she read them from a prompter.

As for Ed Gingerich, he stayed with me for a few days in one of my rarely vacant guest rooms. After that he rotated among a variety of homes, while a team of top-notch attorneys from Pittsburgh worked feverishly to undo the disastrous deal.

In the meantime Grape Expectations carried on with their plans. The Gingerich farmhouse was razed (I am ashamed to say that most of Hernia was there to see it happen), and the foundations for the spacious lodge were poured. The site chosen was halfway up Stickleback Ridge, affording the guests a bird's-eye view of Hernia, including the roof of my inn, which is five miles out of town in the opposite direction, nine miles in all by road but just seven as the crow flies.

I was sitting in the kitchen of my inn one eventful day, chatting with my cook, Freni Hostetler. Amish families intermarry as a matter of course, and since my family was Amish until my parents' generation, I am related by blood to ninety percent of the Amish in this country. Freni and I are cousins every which way but Tuesday (when we are aunt and niece), and I am even my own cousin. Hand me a sandwich when I'm outdoors, and I become a family picnic.

At any rate, that particular day we were discussing Freni's favorite topic—her daughter-in-law, Barbara, whom she loathes yet loves because the Good Lord commands her to. Barbara, by the way, hails from the Iowa Amish and stands six feet in her thick stockings. Her chief sin was marrying Freni's only son, Jonathan. The fact that Barbara produced three grandchildren in one fell swoop has done little to mitigate the ill will between these two otherwise pious women.

"Ach, she brushes their teeth three times a day, Magdalena. Who ever heard of such a thing."

"Teeth brushing is a good thing, Freni."

"Yah, but these are the baby teeth, the ones that will fall out. If she spends this much time on brushing the little ones' teeth, how can she have time to help my Jonathan with his chores?"

I took this to be a rhetorical question. As I sipped my second cup of coffee of the day, I watched Freni make her prizewinning cinnamon rolls. First she rolled out a rectangle of sweetened bread dough on my sturdy oak table. Then she slathered the dough with softened butter. Over the butter went liberal sprinklings of cinnamon and sugar. The dough was then rolled up and sliced with a razor-sharp knife. I was salivating into my coffee by the time she popped the first pan of rolls into my industrial-size oven.

Freni wiped her eyes with the back of her hand, pushing up her floury glasses in the process. "Yah, so now I wait for your answer."

"Excuse me?"

"The chores. A wife is supposed to help her husband, yah?"

"Yah—I mean 'yes.' "

"Ach, and the children. Such beauties they are—just like their father. But they do not help with the chores, either, Magdalena. In this, I think, they are like their mama."

"But they're only three years old, for crying out loud. They're barely out of diapers."

Freni frowned. "Now you are such an expert on raising children?"

"That's a low blow," I wailed. "The fact that I'm as barren as the Gobi desert is not my fault—unless you wanted me to do the mattress mambo without the benefit of marriage."

"Always the riddles, Magdalena." Freni reached for another ball of dough from the rising kettle.

I opened my mouth to say something—even the gist of which is forgotten now—but closed it again, the better to hear. Was that a faint tapping at the back door, or was that yet another loose piston in my brain? Forty-eight isn't old by any means, but already even some of my seldom used parts have expired warranties.

No, that wasn't my brain; that was definitely my door. Unfortunately, the only folks to knock that timidly are schoolchildren coming around to sell cookies or other treats to raise money for good causes. Invariably when I answer the door, I find them halfway down the steps. I'm beginning to think they expect me to grab them and toss them into my industrial-size oven. Of course I would never do such a thing, as they are always either too scrawny or too fat.

I was certainly surprised to see Police Chief Olivia Hornsby-Anderson standing there. At her side stood her very handsome deputy, Chris Ackerman.

4

———◆———

"Good morning, Magdalena," she said. "May we come in?"

I'd detected nervousness in Chief Hornsby-Anderson's voice, which was downright silly. My oven is not large enough to hold adults—of any size.

"By all means, come in. You know my cook, Freni, don't you?"

"I am her cousin too," Freni said, not taking her eyes off the dough ball she was kneading. "I am not just the cook."

"Unless it's Tuesday."

"Yah."

Chief Hornsby-Anderson is a mildly attractive middle-aged woman who has no reason to fear starvation anytime soon. She is a native of San Diego and a veteran of the police force there. She's also a widow with three grown children, all of them living out West. We picked her to serve our community precisely because she has no local relations and therefore is likely to be impartial.

Chris Ackerman was her choice for a deputy, and we on the council unanimously approved him for the position. He is also from California and had spent five years working under our new chief—well, not technically under, if you know what I mean. That was, and is, most unlikely to happen. A young man still in his late twenties, Chris bats for the other team, as my fiancé Gabe explained to me. How Gabe knew this is still uncertain. Suffice it to say that at the time he was hired, Chris's team affiliation was not an issue, and I am of the opinion that this should remain the case. Recently there have been rumors floating around that don't bear repeating—so I won't.

"Mmm, something smells good," the matronly chief said.

Freni beamed. "Yah, you think so?"

"Smells like my mother's kitchen," Chris said.

"Such a handsome boy," Freni said. "It is a shame you are not married."

"My mother says that too."

"Miss Yoder," the chief said, "I'm afraid I have some troubling news."

"Please call me Magdalena, but if that doesn't suit you, then call me baroness."

"I beg your pardon?"

"Just something I read in a book—ha, ha. But shoot; I'm all ears."

"Always the riddles," Freni said to her lump of dough.

"It's about a Mrs. Felicia Bacchustelli," the chief said, undeterred.

"Ah yes, the Devil's mistress—were I to use such strong language."

"Then I'm afraid she may be with her lover right now."

"That's only her brother-in-law— Excuse me, what did you say?"

"She's dead, Miss Yoder."

"Face up in one of the foundation ditches," Chris said.

"It's December," I said. "Who digs ditches in December?"

"Someone who wants to get a leg up on the competition," Chris said, and winked.

The chief groaned, while I glared.

Freni's deep sigh blew some of the flour from her glasses. "I cannot understand these riddles," she confided to her dough ball. "I think maybe these English speak a foreign language."

"Grape Expectations' construction site?" I asked.

"Yes," the chief said. "The coroner's initial estimate is that she died late yesterday afternoon."

I motioned for them to sit, which they were only too glad to do. Freni's stubby arms were cranking away like the pistons on a locomotive as she punched air bubbles from the dough ball. She really is a dear, sweet Christian woman, otherwise I would be tempted to suggest it was her daughter-in-law, Barbara, who was getting the makeover. Nevertheless, it was a sight to behold.

"I assume the crew discovered her this morning," I said.

"Actually, it was Agnes Mishler. She gave me a call a little after five a.m."

"What on earth was Agnes doing out there so early—or at any time, for that matter?"

"She said she was praying. Miss Yoder—"

"Please, I asked you to call me Magdalena."

"Miss Yoder, is it a Mennonite custom to pray at construction sites?"

"The Bible tells us to pray without ceasing. It also says that women should have their heads covered when they pray. That is why some of us wear these caps—prayer caps, we call them." I patted my own white organza cap to illustrate. "That way we can pray wherever we are. But we don't normally go around and pray at construction sites. If indeed Agnes was praying there, it wasn't part of a Mennonite ritual."

"Miss Mishler doesn't wear a cap," Chris said. "What's up with that?"

"Agnes and I belong to different churches that have their own traditions. You see, a few years ago most Mennonite groups merged into a single conference, and some of the more conservative practices were abandoned. My church, however, retains the old ways—as the Good Lord intended. But speaking of dear Agnes, I'm surprised she hasn't called me with the news."

My phone rang.

"Go ahead and get it," the chief said. "I gave this number to the coroner."

I got up and ambled to my wall phone. It's an old-fashioned, sturdy black model, the type I'm sure Jesus would use if He were here today. "Hello?"

"It's Agnes. Magdalena, you won't believe what I'm about to tell you. I was out—"

"At the Grape Expectations construction site and discovered the body of Felicia Bacchustelli facedown in a cement footer. Am I right?"

Her gasp somehow made it through the phone line and sucked the rest of the flour off Freni's glasses. This is only a slight exaggeration, mind you.

"Magdalena! How did you know?"

"Chief Hornsby-Anderson and her sergeant are sitting at my kitchen table watching Freni punch the living daylights out of my future cinnamon rolls."

"Harrumph."

"Are there any details you'd like to add, dear?"

"Details?"

"Like if she struggled when you pushed her—"

Agnes need not have slammed her receiver down quite so hard. The woman has a few rough edges, if you ask me.

"Well, there's your suspect numero uno," I said to the chief. "Would you like me to tag along while you book her? Just in case she tries to confuse you again with church-speak."

"Church-speak?"

"Actually, it's something I made up just now. Pretty clever, though, if I have to say so myself."

Handsome Chris scratched his chin. "No, I've heard the term before."

"Children should be seen but not heard, dear."

"I've definitely heard that one before."

"Shall I repeat it?" I asked patiently.

Fortunately the chief came to his rescue. "Miss Yoder, I will not be booking Miss Mishler. In fact, part of the reason I'm here is to inform you that I have another suspect, about whom I may have to make some decisions soon."

"You do? Oh, not Ed! Yes, the man's a little thick—I mean, everyone knows that the fine print is where one gets taken—but since when is deceit a crime? Most of Hollywood, and half our presidents, would have criminal records, if it were."

"Miss Yoder, I'm referring to you."

"*Moi?*"

"Ach!"

I'm not sure how it happened, but the ball of dough escaped from Freni's pudgy hands and was sent flying through the air. The four of us watched open mouthed, but otherwise immobile, as thousands of calories' worth of God-given carbs came to rest in Chris Ackerman's lap. The poor lad grunted and turned white. His irises obligingly began to slowly disappear, leaving his eyes white as well.

"Quick, he needs mouth to mouth," I shouted.

Chief Hornsby-Anderson merely leaned over and rolled the offending dough onto the floor. Apparently it had been pressing against the young man's diaphragm, because almost immediately he sputtered to life. Freni, meanwhile, sputtered with vexation.

"Why me?" I demanded, now that CPR was no longer needed PDQ.

"Miss Yoder, I have a witness who claims that you threatened the deceased."

"Rumpled-silt-skin?"

"Ach, more riddles," Freni said, this time from underneath the table, where she'd ducked to retrieve her dough. Waste not, want not.

"Mr. Bacchustelli," I hissed. "But it wasn't really a threat—more like a stern warning. I told them to give poor Ed back his property and hightail it out of here."

"And what did you tell them would happen if they didn't leave?"

"I didn't get specific. I just said that they'd save themselves a lot of trouble."

"That sounds like a warning to me, chief," Chris said.

I gave him my infamous "look," which is one step beyond a glare. My pseudo-stepdaughter, Alison, and my sister Susannah call it the evil eye. My fiancé, Gabe, goes one step further and claims I look like a constipated frog.

The chief was apparently neither amused nor intimidated by the "look." "Miss Yoder, this contended threat aside, I have another reason to speak to you."

I breathed an enormous sigh of relief, stirring clouds of flour that then settled like snow showers on my navy blue dress. Freni was still under the table, so her glasses were spared.

"Speak to me!" I cried.

"Perhaps you prefer that we speak in private."

"Whatever." I turned to Chris Ackerman. "See you later, alligator."

"Miss Yoder," the chief said with surprising sharpness, "it's Mrs. Hostetler who should leave the room."

"Ach!" Freni squawked. Then we heard a thump that could

mean that her septuagenarian head and the two-hundred-year-old planks connected. "Ach, *du lieber.*"

I spread my legs so I could bend over and peer under the table. "Are you all right, dear?"

I need not have worried. Freni and I both have guardian angels who work overtime. Freni's angel has a sense of humor as well. My kinswoman was on her hands and knees, but wedged between her head and that table was the dough ball.

"Having fun, dear?" I asked.

Her dark beady eyes bored through the bottle-thick glasses. "I will not leave the room, yah?"

"Yah." I straightened. "She stays."

"Very well," the chief said. She sighed and looked down at her hands. The fourth finger on the left hand bore a telltale band of lighter skin. Although she'd said she was single during her job interviews, rumor had it she was in the process of divorcing. The more vicious gossipmongers claimed her soon-to-be ex-husband had traded in a forty for two twenties.

"Christmas is coming, dear," I said gently.

"Excuse me?"

"There's just so long an old Amish woman can spend on her hands and knees—unless we're talking about Esther Schwartzengruber—" I slapped a hand over my wicked mouth. "My point is, time's a-wasting!"

"Yes, of course. Miss Yoder, I don't know how else to say it. You are the number one suspect."

"Ach!" The table bucked like it was assuming a life of its own. "*What* did you say?"

"You have the most at stake if Grape Expectations is a success."

"Perhaps, but do I look like a killer to you?"

"Killers come in all sizes, shapes, and colors," Chris Ackerman said.

"*Et tu*, Brutus?" I wailed.

The table bucked one last time, and Freni emerged on the far side. The dough now encased her head like a football helmet. Globs of gooey stuff hung over her glasses like the wattles of a very pale turkey.

"Riddles," she hissed. She turned her attention to the chief. "So, is Magdalena going to jail again?" Freni sounded almost hopeful.

"There was only that one time! Okay—maybe two. But that's it."

The chief actually smiled. "I'm afraid, Mrs. Hostetler, that your cousin will be staying right here." The chief turned to me. "Miss Yoder—I mean, Magdalena—I understand that you have quite a bit of experience in criminal investigation. Am I correct?"

"Our previous Chief of Police couldn't pour water out of his shoes, even if the instructions were printed on the heels. Someone had to do his job."

"And you also know the people of this community."

"Nobody knows them better—unless it's Esther Schwartzengruber."

"Ach!"

The chief smiled. "I'll have to ask you about her later. In the meantime, do you think you could spare the time to help me with investigating the death of Felicia Bacchustelli?"

"Is this a command performance?"

"I beg your pardon?"

"Do I have a choice?"

"Certainly. But then, you see, Sergeant Ackerman and I might find ourselves concentrating too much on just one suspect."

"You mean you'll grill me like a weenie and make my life a living Hades?"

"Your words, not mine."

"I capitulate!"

"Riddles," Freni hissed again.

"There's one more thing," the chief said.

"For you anything—even up to half of my kingdom."

"Excuse me?"

"Now she makes fun of the Bible." Freni tossed her head in righteous indignation, causing the dough wattles to swing around and slap her ears.

"I was merely paraphrasing King Ahasuerus."

"I see," the chief said in a tone that implied she didn't. "Magdalena, I was thinking that you might benefit from taking shooting lessons. I could help you with target practice, and—"

Every hair on my body stood on end. Fortunately the hair on my head is braided and then coiled tightly into a bun. Nonetheless, I'm sure that my prayer cap bobbled.

"Are you talking about guns?"

"Firearms," Chris Ackerman said.

I gave him a well-deserved glare for butting in. "I don't care if they're called bananas, dear. I am a Mennonite, my parents were both Mennonite, and their parents Amish. I can trace them back five hundred years to Switzerland, where they were persecuted for their Anabaptist beliefs. And do you know how they reacted when they were tortured on the stretching racks or thrown into icy lakes? Well, I'll tell you—they prayed. They didn't fight back. Not one of them. If I pick up a gun, I'll dishonor the memory of all those who came before. It would also mean betraying myself."

"You go, girl," Freni said, and punched the air with a dough encrusted finger. That is not, by the way, an Amish expression, but one my kinswoman picked up from my sister Susannah.

The chief stood. "I respect that, Miss Yoder. Will you at least agree to carry a cell phone?"

"I'm religious, not stupid. But you really don't have to worry about me; I'm pretty good about getting out of scrapes without having to scrape anyone, thanks to my sturdy Christian underwear."

Young Chris's eyes widened. "Say what?"

"You heard me, dear. And just so you know, the giantess I disabled with my bra was merely stunned, not seriously hurt."

Although she'd heard the story dozens of times, Freni covered her ears and fled into the dining room.

"Your bra?" Chris asked incredulously when the coast was clear.

"Yes, sir. But it wasn't one of those flimsy things, like the ones Victoria's Secret sells. It was a Hanes Her Way from Sears with a double hook closure and an adjustable strap. It can't be padded either, because the cup has to fold around the stone. Besides, a padded bra is the same as telling a lie, isn't it?"

Chris chuckled. "You're kidding, right?"

"I never joke about underwear, dear."

"I must say," the chief said, "you do tell some colorful tales."

"No, sir—I mean, ma'am. This isn't a tale. You can ask anyone in Hernia; it really did happen. But speaking of colorful—sturdy Christian underwear should only be white, like the Good Lord intended. You don't think Jesus paraded around Galilee in pink, do you? And you can be sure he wore boxers, not briefs."

"I doubt if he wore either," Chris said. "Underwear had yet to be invented."

I stifled an image that popped into my brain involuntarily. "Get behind me, Satan!"

"We really must be going," the chief said. I could see her give Chris the old half-roll with her eyes. It means vamoose in any language, as in "let's scram before the crazy lady whacks us over the head with her cook's rolling pin."

"You're a hoot, Miss Yoder," the boy said as his boss dragged him away by his collar.

"And a holler," I hollered after him.

I smiled as I watched them get into Hernia's only squad car and drive away. They were a good pick; just the ticket to write up a ticket for the occasional Amish man who didn't clean up after his horse. And so far they'd done a bang-up job of catching the teenagers who banged up their parents' cars drag racing through town on Saturday nights. But when it came to real crime, they came to me.

Of course I was capable of solving the mystery that surrounded Felicia Bacchustelli's death. At least I was pretty sure I could.

I shook my head vigorously, clearing it of doubt—possibly even a few wits. When I realized that might be the case, I stopped shaking immediately. I was going to need as many wits as possible to deal with the man who was walking up my drive through the settling dust.

5

Stuffed Cornish Game Hens

6 Cornish game hens, thawed if
    frozen
Salt and pepper
2 tablespoons butter or margarine
Game hen livers
2 tablespoons chopped onions
¼ teaspoon poultry seasoning
1 tablespoon brandy or sherry
¼ cup chopped onions

6 tablespoons melted butter or
    margarine
¼ cup dry white wine
¼ cup Concord grape juice
¼ cup Concord grape jelly
1½ cups canned beef gravy
2 tablespoons lemon juice
¼ teaspoon curry powder

Remove giblets and set aside game hen livers. Sprinkle game hens inside and out with salt and pepper. Heat butter and saute game hen livers until livers are cooked. Chop livers with onion. Stir in poultry seasoning, brandy, bamboo shoots. Cook wild rice mix according to package directions until tender. Stir ½ of the rice into liver mixture. Use mixture to stuff game hens. Sew or skewer opening. Place hens side by side in a foil lined baking pan. Sprinkle with chopped onions and brush with melted butter. Roast in a preheated moderate oven (350°F) for 30 minutes. Mix wine and Concord grape juice and spoon over game hens every 10 minutes. Roast another 30 to 40 minutes or until game hens are tender. Place game hens on serving platter and keep warm. Pour pan juices into a saucepan. Stir in Concord grape jelly, gravy, lemon juice and curry powder. Simmer until bubbly. Spoon over game hens and surround with remaining wild rice.

MAKES 6 SERVINGS

6

Although he doesn't wear a uniform, Gabriel Rosen really is Hernia's finest—at least in the looks department. The Babester, as I like to call him, is a doctor who retired early from his practice in Manhattan and purposely sought out the wilds of Pennsylvania as the place to begin his new career: that of a mystery novelist. Frankly, I think this is unrealistic. The man doesn't possess a shred of creativity. Once I peeked at a letter Gabe received from an editor in New York. The woman was very angry. She'd read a portion of my beloved's manuscript immediately following a luncheon and proceeded to throw up all over the copyedited pages of a very important author. Please, the poor woman begged, do all of the publishing world a favor and never submit again.

The Babester might be clueless when it comes to writing mysteries, but he's a real pro when it comes to women. He scooped me into his arms when I opened the door and carried me out onto the small porch, where he planted a big one on my kisser. That, by the way, is about as far as he'll get until our wedding night.

Incidentally, one does not have to be beautiful in order to catch a man. Consider *moi*, the case in point. I'm too tall, too skinny, and, well, let's face it—horsey. When the Good Lord made me, He forgot to slap a saddle on my back and yell, "Giddyup." I do, however, seem to attract very handsome men. Go figure.

"You all right, hon?" this very handsome man said after ending our smooch.

"Fine as frog hair split three ways," I said, quoting a friend of mine in Charleston.

"I didn't know frogs had hair."

"It's so fine you can't see it. Why did you ask if I'm all right?"

"Chief Hornsby-Anderson and that Ackerman fellow were here. Where I come from, the police don't stop by just for a piece of pie and a chat."

"There would have been cinnamon rolls, dear, but right now they're hanging from Freni's glasses."

"Always one with the jokes, hon. How long do I have to wait until you tell me what's really going on?"

I grabbed one of Gabe's hands—he currently has two—and pulled him down the steps and to the shade of a large maple. A few weeks ago my beau hung a swing from one of the ancient limbs. It was a birthday present for my pseudo-stepdaughter, Alison. Alas, the Babester might know how to treat a woman, but he doesn't know beans about junior high girls. Alison would rather be grounded for a month than have her peers see her on a "child's toy." Fortunately Babe made the swing sturdy enough, and just wide enough, for two. On second thought, maybe he does know something about teenagers.

As I knew he would, Babe put his arm around me to keep me from falling backward off the swing. As he must have known I would, I pretended to lose my balance a couple of times.

"Well," I finally said, "it seems as if Grape Expectations has met with an unexpected setback."

"Which is?"

"Felicia Bacchustelli, one of the owners, was found dead this morning—encased in a cement footer."

"Holy guacamole!"

"The chief wants me to help with the investigation."

"But Mags, hon, I thought you agreed not to play detective for a while."

"I did. But you see—well, a gal has a right to change her mind, doesn't she?"

Gabe withdrew his arm. "Wait one barn-raising minute. You're a suspect, aren't you?"

"Not just any suspect, mind you. I'm suspect numero uno."

"You're proud of that?"

"Aren't we all supposed to be the best that we can be? As long as I'm a suspect, there is no point in being second-rate."

The Babester shook his handsome head. "I guess I should be glad you aren't a gangster. Just promise me one thing, will you?"

"What?"

"Promise first."

"Sight unseen?" The last time I made a sight unseen promise, I was in for the shock of my life. I had just married Aaron Miller, my pseudo-stepdaughter's father, and the fires of passion were still burning brightly. One night we—well, never you mind. Suffice it to say, that explains the footprints on my bedroom ceiling.

"Do you love me enough to make a sight-unseen promise?" Gabe asked gently.

"Yes, but—okay, I promise. Now what is it?"

"I want you to promise that you will not knowingly put yourself into any dangerous situation."

"Is that all?"

"I mean it, Mags. Until I met you, I was a confirmed bachelor. As selfish as it may sound, there wasn't anyone with whom I wanted to share my life."

"Besides your mother."

"Now that was a low blow."

"Sorry." But I wasn't. The only drawback I can see to marrying this fine specimen of a man is Ida Rosen, the woman who endured twenty-six hours of excruciating pain to bring him into the world. They're still connected; not by apron strings but an umbilical cord as thick as the transatlantic cable. She still cuts his meat for him, for crying out loud. I might even be able to deal with this were it not for the fact that Gabe is a surgeon. Thank heavens Ida has recently begun dating Doc Shafor, who, although an octogenarian, has the libido of a high school football team. Much to Gabe's consternation, and my joy, I've been seeing less and less of her.

"You know Ma's just trying to be helpful," he said. "But enough about her. How's the search for a new reverend going?"

"Not very well," I said.

Beechy Grove Mennonite has been without a pastor for almost six months. Reverend Schrock, a wonderful man and a good friend, was murdered by our former Chief of Police—who also happens to be my brother-in-law. Because I am both a deaconess and the congregation's biggest supporter, I am on the committee to find a replacement preacher. This has been a far tougher job than finding a new law enforcement team.

Beechy Grove wants a man who is dynamic and inspiring yet traditional. So far we have interviewed a number of candidates who fit the bill. However, there is one caveat: I want a pastor who will be willing to perform a mixed marriage—namely mine and Gabe's. Reverend Schrock, may he rest in peace, was open-minded enough to agree to this, but his potential replacements have, to a man, informed me that they will perform only Christian marriages. My argument—that Jesus's parents were not married in a Christian ceremony—has so far fallen on deaf ears. Meanwhile, the rest of the search committee is losing patience with me.

"Maybe we can find a rabbi in Pittsburgh," Gabe said.

"*Excusez moi?*"

"Well, you keep saying it was good enough for Mary and Joseph."

"Yes, but I didn't say anything about a rabbi."

"On second thought, it might be hard to find a rabbi to perform a mixed marriage, seeing as how I don't belong to a synagogue there."

I recoiled in shock. "Why would a rabbi *not* want to marry us?"

"The same reason a minister wouldn't want to marry us: because you're not of the faith."

"But I am of the faith!"

"Which faith would that be?"

"The right faith, of course. I mean—it's the right faith for me."

"Are you saying that *I* don't belong to the right faith?"

"I can't help what the Bible says," I wailed. "You try to explain John 3:18!"

"I don't have to, hon. It's not in my Bible."

"That's because yours isn't complete."

"Uh-oh, I think we've just stepped over the line."

"Maybe we did—"

"I really didn't mean 'we,' hon. I meant you."

"Me?"

"Why is it that you get to say that my scriptures are incomplete—I hear that all the time from Christians, by the way—but if I were to say that your Bible has a bunch of made-up stuff tacked on the end, courtesy of some guy named Paul, aka Saul of Tarsus, I'd have holy heck to pay?"

"But the truth is the truth."

"I guess that depends on whose version we're talking about."

"There is only one truth."

Gabe slid off the swing. "Maybe it's just as well that we've had this conversation now."

I jumped off the swing too. "What are you saying? Are you trying to tell me that our engagement is off?"

"No, but I think we should do some serious thinking."

The morning was bright and sunny, and there were birds singing in the other large maple on the far side of the lawn, but the day felt anything but glorious. I felt like that wolf in nursery tales, the one that had stones sewn into his belly while he slept. It was all I could do to keep from collapsing.

I couldn't tell what Gabe was thinking—the sun was at his back—but he was breathing hard. Perhaps he was fighting back tears. Maybe he was struggling not to shout at me.

That's what I wanted to do to him: shout. I wanted to back him up against a wall and shout the truth into him. And yes, I'd even go so far as to whack him over the head with a Bible—if I thought it would do any good. But with a belly full of stones, I'd do well just to make it back inside and to the comfort of my bed.

"Yes, you think about it real hard," I said.

He turned and walked slowly back down my drive.

As I'm sure you'll understand, I was in a foul mood when I rang Agnes Mishler's doorbell a mere twenty minutes later. She lives in a renovated farmhouse, by the way, adjacent to the house her uncles own. The Mishler brothers eschew clothing and are often to be seen performing chores—such as cutting firewood—in the altogether. Of course, we have an ordinance prohibiting public nudity, but the Mishler clan lives way out at the end of Dust Devil Road. Besides, the brothers have nothing to brag about. Especially in the winter, like now. All fluff, no stuff—if you know what I mean.

Agnes answered the door instantly, as if she'd been peering out through a window, waiting for my arrival. Perhaps she had been.

"What brings you all the way out here, Magdalena?"

"Be a dear and invite me in. It's turning colder by the minute."

"It feels fine to me, Magdalena."

"That may be, but according to your uncles' brr-ometers, it's well below freezing."

"Why, Magdalena, I never!"

"This is no time to discuss your sex life, dear. Besides, it's none of my business. I was hoping you would invite me in so we could have ourselves a nice little chat. Oh, and some hot chocolate would be wonderful—piled high with those mini-marshmallows. Although, if you don't have the tiny ones, the regular ones will do. I'm not in the least bit picky. Of course some ladyfingers would be nice for dipping, once the marshmallows are gone."

Agnes stared at me with eyes the size of coffee mugs.

"Oh no," I said, and laughed reassuringly. "I don't mean *real* lady fingers. I mean the cake variety—the kind you buy at the store."

That seemed to do the trick. "I'm sorry, Magdalena, but I can't invite you in."

"Don't be silly, dear. I already know you're a terrible house-keeper. Everyone in town knows that." Come to think of it, it wasn't a good idea to drink out of Agnes Mishler's mugs unless one was midway through a course of antibiotics.

Agnes Mishler puffed up like an overinflated air mattress. "*What* did you say?"

"Uh—well, I'm sure it's perfectly normal to name your dust bunnies. Besides, who is Nora Ediger to talk, anyway? In second grade she named her lunchbox Billy."

"That was me."

"Oops. Well, I just need a few minutes of your time, dear. I suppose if you really insist, we can do it outside."

"I didn't do it. That woman was dead when I found her. I know you don't believe me—"

"I do believe you. I didn't come here to accuse you of murdering Mrs. Bacchustelli. I came here because you are a very observant woman, and I want to pick your brain for details."

A much relieved and only somewhat indignant Agnes deflated until she was her normal size. "Come on in," she said, and stood aside to let me pass.

I put one foot over the sill but then stopped short. I thought I was prepared for anything, but what I saw, just stepping halfway into her house, shocked me from the top of my bun to the tips of my stocking-clad tootsies.

7

Agnes Mishler was a pack rat. Perhaps there was even a pack of rats living within her shifting shape. Every flat surface in the front room was piled as high as she could reach with everything imaginable, *including* soup and nuts.

A cursory glance revealed, among other things (besides the two aforementioned dinner courses), clothes, dirty dishes, books, empty bottles, newspapers, a slew of presumably defunct electrical appliances, and tub after plastic storage tub of gewgaws and doodads.

A narrow winding aisle disappeared between a stack of gewgaws and carpet samples, but there was no place to sit as far as I could see. What is the use of having feet as large as mine if one can't think fast on them?

"Uh—on second thought, I don't have the time to come inside." I tried to slip past her, but she'd inflated again, blocking my exit.

"Sure you do. It doesn't take any more time to talk inside than it does out."

"Yes, but I left my dog in the car. And as you can see, it's really getting cold outside."

"You don't have a dog, Magdalena."

"I don't? I mean, of course I do. You see, I'm keeping my sister's mangy mutt—"

"Shnookums lives in Susannah's bra. Is he in your bra now, Magdalena? Because I know that poor little pooch, and he is terrified of riding in cars unless he's surrounded by a nice padded cup."

I slapped my forehead with the palm of my hand. It is a gesture learned from my pseudo-stepdaughter, Alison.

"Duh!" I said. "I totally forgot that Susannah got back from her trip last night."

"Why, Magdalena Yoder, shame on you! You just lied to me."

"I did? I mean, I did no such thing."

"There you go again. I guess that prayer cap you wear doesn't prevent your mouth from breaking one of the big ten."

"But it was for a good cause," I wailed.

"And what would that be? To spare my feelings?"

"That's ridiculous— Okay, you're right. But like I said, my intentions were good."

"Maybe so, but now they're paving stones for the road to Hell. Magdalena, if you really want to do the Christian thing, then come all the way inside. Better yet, have that cup of hot chocolate you so rudely requested."

I took a deep breath, one that might have to last me for the length of my visit. Without waiting for instructions I followed the winding aisle to the kitchen. There were several other aisles that spurred off in various directions, but I let my Yoder nose lead the way. While Agnes obviously lacked the Mennonite clean gene, she nonetheless possessed the extra cooking chromosome with which most of my people are blessed. I'd inadvertently (Agnes knows better than to label her dishes) eaten her goodies at community potlucks, and I knew she was a master of the craft.

Perhaps she was concerned that I would get lost in her amazing maze. At any rate Agnes trailed so closely that twice she stepped on my heels. It was all I could do to suppress yelps of pain, knowing as I did that I'd have to breathe afterward.

"Magdalena, you're not fooling me. You're going to have to come up for air sometime—if you expect to ask me any questions."

"I do?" I managed to say without inhaling.

"It's not as if by breathing, you're going to topple over like a miner's canary."

"Don't be silly, dear." I'd reached the kitchen, which was cleaner than I'd expected. What had begun as a sigh of relief ended as a gulp for oxygen.

Agnes chuckled happily over her victory. "Now, where were

we? Oh yes, first some nice hot chocolate, and maybe some ladyfin-gers—am I right? Or, given the cold outside, would you prefer something a little stronger?"

"How strong? I'm not opposed to you putting two pouches of instant cocoa into my cup."

"I never use the instant. But no, I meant a little wine." She picked a bottle off the counter and held it out. "I don't drink the really hard stuff; just what Jesus drank."

"That's a mistake in translation," I said.

"Is that so? Then how about the passage that says not one jot nor one tittle of the Bible will be changed before the end of time?"

"So the jots and tittles haven't changed, but maybe the word for wine did."

Agnes returned the bottle of forbidden beverage to its place on the counter. "Hot chocolate it is. You want two packets, right?"

I nodded, but my attention was captured by something moving in the far corner of the room. "Uh—Agnes, we seem to have com-pany."

She turned, seemingly not the least surprised. "Oh, that's just Mickey."

"Mickey's a field mouse."

"Yes. *Apodemus sylvaticus*. Very good, Magdalena. Not everyone can distinguish a field mouse from a house mouse."

"Field mice sometimes find their way into the PennDutch when it's really cold outside. Freni and I try to catch them alive and re-lease them in the woods. My fiancé thinks this is crazy. But then again, he calls all mice rats. If he sees one, he practically jumps on the sofa."

"You don't say. Did you know, Magdalena, that rats traveling with early Polynesian settlers often had deleterious consequences on the fauna of newly discovered islands?"

I was too busy observing a second mouse to answer. "I suppose this one is Minnie," I said.

"Right gender, wrong name. Look at her closely, Magdalena."

"Oh my gracious," I said with a start. "She looks exactly like Doreen Hershberger."

"Although Doreen's eyes are beadier."

I know it wasn't Christian of us, not to mention mature, but

Agnes Mishler and I laughed until our sides hurt. We laughed so hard we scared Mickey and Doreen away, which caused us to laugh even harder. When it got to the point I had to either stop or risk using Agnes's toilet, I closed my eyes and recalled the time Mama spanked me for dropping a forkful of rhubarb pie on her new Sunday dress. This is a little trick I learned in church. When something strikes my funny bone so hard that I am in danger of losing control in an inappropriate situation, I try to conjure up a vivid image of something sobering. Mama's "this hurts me more than it will hurt you" sessions usually do the trick. Although sometimes I have to go so far as to conjure up mashed boiled turnips. That morning, in Agnes Mishler's rodent-infected kitchen, I brought Mama, boiled turnips, *and* fried liver to life.

It took Agnes even longer to calm down. "Magdalena," she finally said, "don't take this the wrong way, but I think I like you."

"Ditto," I said.

"You're not the snobbish prig everyone says you are—oops!" She clamped her hand over her mouth.

"They say that?" Truth be told, I was feeling a mite flattered. It's when folks *stop* talking about me that I start to worry.

"Do you want the truth?"

"Nothing but."

"You're just about all everyone does talk about. 'Did you hear what Magdalena said?' 'Can you believe the nerve of that woman?' 'How on earth does she snag such handsome men?'"

"Go on," I purred.

"It would take me all day, and I promised the uncles I would take them shopping in Pittsburgh. They're hoping to find this new kind of body lotion they've seen advertised that will keep them from getting so chapped."

"Clothes aren't an option? As long as we're being honest, dear, your uncles are giving young women the wrong impression of what to expect in their connubial beds. After my wedding night—illegal, though it was—I couldn't look at a turkey neck again without blushing. Your uncles, however, bring to mind sparrows."

My new friend grinned. "Magdalena, you're so naughty. Who knew?"

As enjoyable as the conversation was, it was time to cut to the chase. "Moving right along, dear, please tell me more about what happened this morning. Were you really praying at the construction site?"

"I was. Only I wasn't praying that Ed Gingerich would get his farm back; I was praying for myself."

"Oh?"

"You may not have noticed, Magdalena, but I have a slight affliction."

These days one has to admire a woman who uses the word "affliction" in a sentence, even if said woman is sailing down Denial River in a felucca. "Are you referring to your propensity to hoard junk like an army of Depression-era retirees?"

"I try to throw away things, Magdalena. But I just can't. Lately, I've been taking long walks early in the morning, even before the cows get up. That's when I do most of my praying."

"I see. So you were praying, and then what?"

"I'd just asked the Lord to give me a sign that I would be cured, and I opened my eyes, and there was that woman staring back at me. But dead, of course. I immediately called the police."

"Details, dear. Details."

"As you know, it rained a couple days back, and the whatchamacallit—"

"I think it's called a footer, dear."

"Yeah. Anyway, there was lots of water in the ditch, and she was lying on her back with her eyes open. The water just barely covered her face, but it was cold last night so there was a thin sheet of ice over her eyes. It made them look bigger, like they belonged to someone else's face."

"Then she'd obviously been dead for a while. Of course the autopsy should tell us how long. Are there any other details you remember that stand out? In a murder investigation—and I'm not saying it's officially been ruled that—anything might be important."

"Even if it's considered gossip?"

"Of course—well, that depends. Is it really juicy?"

"No. And you've got to promise not to tell anyone. I don't want to be misunderstood."

"Okay. But make it quick, dear. I have an investigation to conduct, remember?"

"It's about that. Magdalena, I wasn't the only person at the construction site this morning."

"Oh no, not Ed! I told him—"

"It was that new couple. The Rashids."

"Get out of town! What on earth were they doing there, and at that hour?"

"Arguing."

"About what?"

"I'm not sure. It's hard to understand her, you know."

Indeed it was. Mr. Ibrahim and Dr. Faya Rashid are Hernia's newest and most exotic immigrants. Ibrahim Rashid is a second-generation American of Lebanese ancestry who, of course, speaks flawless English. He was born and raised in New Jersey. His wife, Faya, who is a distant cousin, hails from Beirut.

Faya has a medical degree from an Italian university. In addition to Arabic, she speaks fluent Italian and French, but her English is heavily accented. Dr. Rashid is in the process of getting her license to practice medicine in America but has, according to the rumor mill, run into a few accreditation problems. In the meantime, this exceptionally beautiful and gifted woman keeps house while her husband runs a very successful dry-cleaning chain, Best Clean, that stretches across the Commonwealth of Pennsylvania.

The Rashids picked lowly Hernia as the place to live because the Best Clean headquarters is in nearby Bedford and because our little town shares similar values with our first Muslim family. The Rashids are far from being fundamentalists, but they do shun alcohol and place a strong emphasis on family and what we call "just plain clean living."

At any rate, you couldn't find a nicer woman than Dr. Rashid. English, however, is not Faya's forte.

"Well, what did *he* say?" I prompted.

"He was begging her not to go home. 'Give it one more year,' he said."

"Go home? To Lebanon?"

"That's what it sounded like. Apparently her mother still lives there, and Faya's very homesick. When she was a med student in Italy, she got to go home more often, because Rome is not that far."

"Did they talk about anything else?"

"Not really. Oh, except that he wants her to cut her hair, and she doesn't want to. He says she'll look more like an American if she does."

"Well, good for her," I said. Dr. Faya Rashid wears her long hair piled high and held in place with jeweled combs, displaying to its best advantage a neck that I'm sure is the envy of swans. Although few waterfowl admire my neck, I too wear my hair long and piled high, albeit in a bun and held in place with bobby pins. So what if her hair is a luxuriant dark chestnut and mine a mousy brown? We seem to both believe that a woman's hair is her crowning glory, and not to be shown to just anyone.

Agnes Mishler has short thick hair. If you glued a Ping-Pong paddle to her head, she'd make a convincing beaver. She shook this pelt vigorously to underscore her disagreement.

"This is the twenty-first century, Magdalena. I think it's great that her husband is encouraging her to become a modern woman."

When the going gets tough, change direction. "Did the Rashids say anything about Grape Expectations?"

"Not a word—that I heard."

"Did they see you kneeling there, as you were praying in front of a dead body?"

"I don't always kneel when I pray, Magdalena. And no, they didn't see me. I had just arrived and was leaning against a cement truck, catching my breath, when they drove up in their Hummer."

"Their what?"

"It's a type of car—a sort of weaponless tank the rich and wasteful are fond of driving these days."

"Ah yes, I have seen those. Go on."

"So anyway, I heard them drive up, but I didn't know who it was, so I stayed behind the cement truck. They both got out and immediately started waving their arms and yelling—like they'd been into it for a while and just needed a place to pull over."

"But the lodge Grape Expectations is building is halfway up the mountain."

"That's what happened, Magdalena, like it or not."

I didn't, so I jotted down that detail. "Agnes, you said you were catching your breath. What was the reason for that?"

"You would too, if you'd jogged eight point two miles."

"You *jogged* all the way out there?"

"Round-trip. In case you haven't noticed, Magdalena, I'm not beanpole thin like some. I may be fat, but I'm fit, and fit is what it's all about."

"Consider the shrew," I said shrewdly.

"What?"

"The shrew is the smallest of all mammals. The elephant is the largest. They share the same number of heartbeats before their respective tickers wear out. The shrew lives only two years, the elephant as much as sixty. The moral of the story? Save your movements. Don't waste them on exercise. The second you use up all those heartbeats, that's the second you'll topple over dead."

"Magdalena, you're every bit as loony as they say."

"I'll take that as a compliment, dear. Now, where was I? Oh yes. What was the Rashids' reaction when they saw the body lying half-frozen in a ditch?"

"They didn't see it—at least not that I'm aware of. They argued for about ten minutes and then took off. I was breathing rather heavily for the first few minutes—I was scared to death they'd see me. I mean, how would I explain my presence behind that cement truck? They might think I was some sort of pervert."

"Indeed. So it wasn't until after they drove away in their Bummer that you discovered Mrs. Bacchustelli's body?"

"That's Hummer, Magdalena."

"Whatever."

"Your answer, by the way, is yes."

"Agnes, why didn't you tell Chief Hornsby-Anderson that you saw the Rashids at the scene of the crime?"

"Because it was obvious they didn't have anything to do with it."

"Obvious to whom? No offense, Agnes, but that's a matter for the police to decide."

She sighed and rubbed her eyes, creating that squeaky sound I find so distressing. "Magdalena, use that huge intellect God blessed you with. Folks are already suspicious of them just because they're Muslim and she's from overseas. Then there's the fact they're teetotalers. If I told the police, the next thing you know people would be accusing the Rashids of being hate-mongering fundamentalists who would do anything to stop the construction of a business that was based on a product that violated their religion."

I put that huge, God-given intellect—her words, not mine—through its paces. Thinking, incidentally, does not contribute to Dead Shrew syndrome.

"You're right," I said. "At the moment there's nothing to be gained by telling anyone. But just so you know, I might have to at some point."

"I understand. Like I said, Magdalena, you're okay."

"You're not as bad as I thought either—oops. I'm sure you know what I mean."

"Do you think we could be friends?"

"Stranger things have happened, dear. In the meantime, we could certainly be first-class acquaintances."

"I'd like that."

I stood. "Well, I need to hustle my bustle. Agnes, I'd appreciate it if you'd use that keen observation of yours and report—to me—anything else you see around town that you think may be relevant to this case."

Her eyes shone with pleasure. "Magdalena, do you mind if I ask *you* a question?"

"Ask away! We're burning daylight."

"If you could have just one wish come true, what would it be?"

"Hmm. Speaking of light, I guess it would be that my fiancé saw the Light."

"Perhaps there's more than one Light, Magdalena. Have you ever thought about that? Maybe there's an entire celestial chandelier."

"And you call yourself a Mennonite!"

"I try to keep an open mind, that's all."

"If you keep your mind open too wide, your brain will fall out." I started to trot back to the front door, hoping mightily that I wouldn't make a wrong turn when I got to the fork in the path.

"Don't you want to know what my wish would be?"

"Sure, but make it quick."

"I wish my uncles would keep their clothes on."

"You and half of Hernia."

"There is a second part to that wish, Magdalena."

"Oh?"

"I wish that my uncles and I got along better."

"Their nudity rubs you the wrong way—oops, that's not what I meant."

"Yes, it does irritate me, but there is nothing I can do about that, short of having them committed, and that's easier said than done. I've had them examined by two sets of psychiatrists, and they all agreed that while my uncles are eccentric, they are not pathologically disturbed. They are not a danger to themselves or anyone else. Anyway, that's not it. This is something much bigger."

"Do tell—and I won't." How clever I can be at times.

"It's this: my uncles are dead broke."

"Get out of town!"

"Their house, their land, even their car—I own it all. Before Daddy died he made me promise that I would take care of his two younger brothers, on account of they've never worked a day in their lives and wouldn't have a clue as how to provide for themselves."

I'd known of the Mishler brothers my entire life—indeed, as teenagers we used to sneak around in their woods and try to catch a glimpse—but they were already young adults when I was born. By the time it occurred to me to wonder how they supported themselves, they were already drawing Social Security.

"Go on, dear. I'm all ears."

"It used to be that I could put up with the embarrassment and the teasing, but I can't anymore. I'm not too old to live a normal life—am I, Magdalena?"

"You're never too old to try, dear."

"So anyway, about a month ago I decided to put my foot down. I told the uncles that either they covered up when they went outside, or they had to move out and find a place of their own."

"How did they take that?"

"They were pissed. May I use that word, Magdalena?"

"Most emphatically not. And you a Mennonite!"

"But that's what they were. They were furious. Uncle Big said I was a disappointment to the family, and who was I to say they were an embarrassment."

"And Uncle Little?" For as long as I can remember the Mishler brothers have gone by their nicknames, Big Goober and Little Goober. To my knowledge Agnes has never called them Goober.

"Uncle Little said Daddy was turning over in his grave, and didn't I remember my promise to take care of them?"

"How awful."

"Oh, I don't mind the anger so much as the silent treatment. Neither of them has said a word to me since. And as you can see, they haven't started wearing clothes."

"Don't they freeze their little, uh, hinnies off?"

"They've been running naked since they were toddlers. The only time they bother to get dressed is when they go into town, and that's only because they have to. Speaking of which, I used to run a lot of errands for them, which I've stopped altogether. That's another thing that's really got them boiling mad at me."

"But I thought you were taking them to Pittsburgh."

"That was a little white lie so I could stop singing your praises. Magdalena, I wish more than anything that we could be a normal family—like yours. That my uncles would grow up, and that we could have Norman Rockwell–type holidays. But things just keep getting worse and worse. I shudder to think how it all might end. Magdalena, seeing as how you're so much older and wiser than me, can you tell me what to do?"

"Never substitute the objective form for the subjective, even in dialogue, or readers with too much time on their hands will jump all over you."

"*What?*"

"Never mind! That just popped into my head; I have no idea where that came from. And I'm sorry, I don't have any advice for you—except not to waste a wish on having a family like mine. If it wasn't for dysfunction, my family wouldn't have function at all. But hang in there. What doesn't kill us, makes us extremely ill—or something like that. And remember, fifty years from now this will all be over." I reached out and patted her arm in what I hoped she took as an affectionate gesture. Nature allows me less than a dozen such maudlin expressions a year. It would be a shame to have one go unappreciated.

I need not have worried. "Magdalena, thanks for coming. I mean that. You've been a blessing to me." She patted me clumsily in return, a sure sign that there was a blood relationship somewhere back down the line.

"No problemo." It was past time for me to scoot. Ahead I could see a narrow shaft of light, a promise that the doorway lay just ahead, and beyond it a more normal world. Or not.

8

The Rashids live in the upscale part of Foxcroft, Hernia's only real suburb. My sister, Susannah, lives in the downscale portion. Although how it is that a house costing over a hundred thousand dollars could be considered downscale is beyond my ken. Whoever heard of paying so much for a place to hang your prayer cap?

If anything, the Rashids live in the upper reaches of their scale, in that zone well past the two hundred mark. Their mansion is clad in genuine white fiberglass siding, and the pillars that pretend to hold up the porch roof were milled from the finest composite wood. I know, because I gave them the tap test.

But what makes the Rashid manor the talk of the town (aside from its owners) is that it is home to Hernia's first in-ground swimming pool. For months, that's all anyone could talk about. The buzz hit a feverish level when invitations went out welcoming everyone who is anyone to a poolside barbecue on the Fourth of July. Being someone, I was, of course, invited. A postscript on the stiff, embossed paper requested guests to wear modest bathing attire.

The Rashids need not have worried. The Mishler brothers aside, we Hernians are loathe to bare our flesh. Although several in attendance dangled their feet in the water, the only person to actually show up in a suit and immerse herself was Betty-Anne Justice. The woman is a Baptist, which explains her boldness. Her claim to being anyone is the fact that her cousin's husband's first wife's nephew invented the electric rake. I hear this is supposed to be all the rage out in California, but frankly, I've seen very few of these devices hereabouts.

When the Rashids didn't answer the doorbell, I switched over to knuckle power. My raps are the envy of woodpeckers. Within a minute I heard someone thumping down the grand staircase and then the sound of a throat being cleared.

"Who is it?" Faya Rashid called. Her tone was surprisingly timorous.

"*C'est moi,* Magdalena Yoder," I said, using all that I remembered from two years of high school French.

"Who did you say?"

"Magdalena Yoder," I chirped. "Big as life, and twice as ugly."

"No thank you. I think I am not wanting to buy anything today."

"And I'm not selling. I merely want to chat."

There was a moment of silence. "I do not think I know you."

"Sure you do. Look through the peephole, dear, and tell me if this nose doesn't ring a bell." Truth be told, I have used my schnoz to press doorbells when my hands are full. I have even used it for typing, although going too fast makes me dizzy, and I can only type lowercase.

"Ah, yes." The door opened just wide enough for her head to fill the space. It was obvious she'd been sleeping, although it was the middle of the day. Although her hair was tousled and hung loose about her shoulders and there were dark circles under her eyes, she was still a beautiful woman.

"Is your husband there as well, Dr. Rashid?"

"No. He is work in one of Bedford shops. Is it him you wish to speak with?"

"You'll do for the moment. May I come in?"

She hesitated just long enough for me to get the hint that it was to be a short visit. "Please to forgive the way I am dressing."

I glanced at her clothes. Flannel nightgown, thick chenille robe . . . The woman might be a Muslim, but she was dressed like a proper Christian.

"There's nothing to forgive," I said approvingly, and sailed past her and into the formal living room.

"Please to have a seat."

"Don't mind if I do." The furniture was fit for a queen. I selected an ornately carved and gilded armchair upholstered in white silk brocade. For a few seconds I fantasized that I was sitting on a throne and that Prince William was at my feet, declaring himself my liege man.

"May I offer some drinks?"

"Some hot chocolate would be nice. I'll take a mug, not a cup, and there's no such thing as piling it too high with those little marshmallows."

"Pardon?"

"Of course, if you don't have the little ones, two big ones— Uh, I've lost you, haven't I?"

"My English is not so good."

"You're not alone, dear. Most native-born Americans speak English that is not so good—myself included, I'm afraid. Why, just the other day I used the nominative case in place of the objective— Uh, ix-nay on the hot chocolate. Please sit as well. I want to speak to you about your whereabouts this morning."

She perched on the edge of a matching chair, looking as if at any moment she would flap her chenille wings and fly back upstairs. "I do not understand, Mrs. Odor."

"That's Yoder, dear. And I'm a Miss, not a Mrs. What I am asking is, where were you this morning?"

"I was—I was asleep."

"I'm sure you were. But where were you between the hours of four and five o'clock this morning?"

She glanced at the telephone on an end table situated between our two thrones. "Miss Yoder, why do you ask this question?"

"Silly me, I guess you haven't heard that I am an amateur sleuth—uh, like a detective. Just not official. Because I grew up in Hernia and know most of the people, I sometimes help the police solve crimes."

Dark eyes that had been merely alert now broadcast terror. "Crimes?"

"Murders usually. For a small town, we seem to have more than our share."

"But I did not kill anyone, Miss Yoder. And my husband did not kill anyone. Please to believe me."

"Oh, I'm not accusing you. But someone was killed last night, and I need to ask questions."

"I am afraid I cannot help you, Miss Yoder. I do not know this man who was killed."

"Who said anything about a man?"

She blinked rapidly, her eyes still on the phone. "Is it not usually a man who gets killed?"

"I suppose that depends where the murder takes place. In Hernia it seems that more women than men are the victims of violent crime. But back to my question, dear. Where were you early this morning?"

"In the car—yes, we were making the journey home from Pittsburgh?" She pronounced it "Pete's-burgh." An improvement, if you ask me.

"At that hour?"

"We were visiting friends. From Lebanon. We stay very late, and then we must drive home because my husband has to be at the store at seven o'clock."

"Did you make any stops on the way back from Pittsburgh?"

She stared so hard at the phone that I thought it might levitate. "Pete's-burgh?"

"It's a simple yes or no question. Did you stop on the way home?"

"Miss Yoder, my husband and I do not have much disagreement. But this one thing—we have much discussion about it."

"About you going home to Lebanon?"

She didn't seem surprised by my guess. "It is very difficult for me here. I do not make friends, and I cannot yet receive work as a doctor. In Beirut there is much I could do."

"So you did stop on the way back. At the future site of Grape Expectations to be exact."

She appeared to give up on whatever help the phone might have brought. "In America are there many spies?"

"Dr. Rashid, you were not being spied on last night—technically, early this morning. As it so happened a woman was out jogging—that means running—and she stopped to rest beside the cement truck. She was there when you and your husband arrived, and she overheard your conversation."

"Why does a woman run alone when it is yet dark?"

"That's a good question. But she did. And after you left she discovered a dead body in the foundation ditch."

Doctor or not, she recoiled when I mentioned the corpse. "A dead person, yes?"

"Yes. A woman."

Her eyes, the window to her soul, now registered anger. "And you think my husband and I had something to do with this?"

"No. I'm just gathering information. Impressions, if you will." I had no intention of letting her know that I adhered to the old adage that killers invariably return to the scene of the crime. Of course, innocent people also find their way to crime sites. Folks like poor Agnes Mishler.

"I assure you that we are not killers."

"I haven't accused you of anything. I'm here only to ask you what you saw and heard at the construction site."

The fire left her eyes. "I remember very little, Miss Yoder, except for this argument. It was very cold—I was having the shivers, yes? And I heard the bark of a dog. But I did not see the woman who runs, or the one who is dead."

"Did the argument occur inside or outside your car?"

"We were on the outside. Ibrahim smokes cigarettes—Egyptian cigarettes without the filtration, yes? But he does not do this in the car for my sake."

"Dr. Rashid, what were you and your husband doing on Hungry Neck Road in the first place? It's a dead end, for crying out loud. And it certainly isn't on your way home from Pittsburgh."

"It was to shorten the trip, but we got lost."

That was a reasonable answer. Our terrain consists of steep parallel ridges we call mountains—much to the amusement of Westerners. By and large we live and farm in the valleys that lie in between. I have myself been on a ridgetop and spotted my destination on a second ridge, but with no clear idea of how to get there.

"One last question," I said, and her eyes brightened. "Why weren't you and your husband at the demonstration against Grape Expectations? After all, its whole purpose is to sell wine, something which I happen to know is forbidden by your religion."

She fingered the belt of her chenille robe as if it were a string of worry beads. "My husband travels much for his job. He was in Harrisburg on that day. We have two stores there, Miss Yoder."

"What about you, dear?"

"I do not have the driving license."

"Oh."

"But I am wanting one, yes?"

"Yes—I mean, I guess so."

She planted both feet firmly on the floor and leaned forward, her eyes blazing with passion. "Ibrahim will not allow this. Miss Yoder, this is another reason for which we disagree. You see, back home, in Beirut, I am driving, but here—"

"Dr. Rashid, I really don't want to get into a religious discussion just now. I mean, if you want to see the Light, I am always available. But you need to call me at home for that. For the moment, I would like to restrict this conversation to police work."

"But this is not about religion, Miss Yoder. In Lebanon many Muslim women drive—just as they do here in America. This is about my husband, Ibrahim."

"Oh?" On second thought, in a thorough investigation, just about anything can be relevant.

"Do you think I am beautiful, Miss Yoder?"

"Excuse me? I don't understand what this has to do with the case at hand."

"Ibrahim says I am very beautiful. Do you agree?"

"Yes, but—"

"That is my main problem. Because Ibrahim thinks I am beautiful, he will not agree to the driving. I am not permitted even to take the lessons. And because I cannot drive in America, I cannot take the course of study I need to pass the exam for American doctors. Miss Yoder, I cannot even go to the little food store in town by myself."

"What about the juicy marital tidbits?" I wailed.

"Now it is I who do not understand."

"When you said this was about your husband, for a moment there I thought—just forget it. And you may as well forget about shopping at Yoder's Corner Market too. Sam's prices are outrageous, and none of his produce is fresh. Every summer I gouge my initials into a beet or a head of cabbage, and the dang thing is still there a year later."

"There are more stores in Bedford," she said, her gaze unwavering. "I would very much like to shop at those alone."

"Well, dear, we can't have everything we— Just one corn-shucking minute. Yes, we can! At least *you* can. Dr. Rashid, how would you like me to teach you how to drive?"

Her face shone, lit on the inside by a spark of hope. "You would do this for a stranger?"

"Believe me, by the time we are through, you won't be a stranger. I taught my sister to drive in these mountains. I wore a hole through the floorboards on the passenger side of the car."

She bit her lip. "Ibrahim will be very angry when he learns that I have disobeyed."

"Leave it to me, dear. I'll point out how much money he's saved on driving lessons. Not to mention how much more money you will make as a doctor instead of a housewife."

"But my beauty—I am afraid the jealousy will not change."

"Hmm. Do you have scissors?"

"*What?*"

"Snip, snip. It will only take a second, I promise."

She looked at me with horror. "Miss Yoder!"

9

"Oh no, dear, I didn't mean your hair. There's a humongous thread hanging from the sleeve of your robe."

"Please, Miss Yoder, my heart is pounding. I have not been so setup since I see this house."

"Setup? Trust me, no one has set you—ah, upset!"

"Yes, upset. Ibrahim, I say, for what do we need five thousand square feets, when we have no children? 'They will come,' he says. Be patient. In the meantime, I should be glad we are not living in a small house like we did in New Jersey."

"Five thousand square feets—I mean, feet?"

"A shame, yes?"

"An infraction of the rules, dear. Hernia has an ordinance limiting residences to thirty-five hundred square feet. The intent is to—Never mind the intent. The fact remains that your husband broke the law. Technically, the town council—and that includes yours truly—can require that he tear down fifteen hundred of those square feet to comply with the ordinance."

Dr. Faya Rashid's olive skin turned polar bear pale. "This infarction you speak of, this means to break a law?"

"That's infraction, dear. Infarction is a medical term. But yes, that's what it means."

"My husband will be most—uh—upset. This house means a great deal to him. It is his house of dreams."

"Let's make a deal," I said.

"Like in the television program? I choose door number two!" She giggled nervously.

Of course I have never seen the show, but the phrase it made popular is now part of the American lexicon. "Then you're a very lucky woman, Dr. Rashid. Behind door number two are free driving lessons along with a promise that your husband will not object too strenuously. If so—well, he'll have less property taxes to pay next year. So you see, it's sort of a win-win situation."

Perfectly arched eyebrows came together for a second or two. "I do not understand everything you say, Miss Yoder, but I like you." She smiled unexpectedly. "When do the driving lessons begin?"

"Soon, dear. Right now I'm hot on the heels of a cold-blooded killer."

There are two Best Cleans in Bedford, at opposite ends of the city. Fortunately Highway 92 from Hernia passes directly in front of the southwestern store. I pressed the pedal to the metal and drove the twelve miles in record time.

The thing that has made the Best Clean chain such a success is that it lives up to its name. I personally believe in a good washing machine, but friends and guests who've used Best Clean rave about it. They all say that hands down, Best Clean is head and shoulders above its competition when it comes to removing stains and underarm odors. I am inclined to believe them, because once this company got a foot in the door, its competitors found themselves scrambling like one-legged soccer players. Of course there were a few people across the state who complained about the "foreigner" with a stranglehold around their necks, so to speak, but I'm proud to say that most folks living in Bedford County don't have the stomach for bigotry.

As a faithful Christian I don't believe in luck, but if I did, I'd have to say that so far that day, it was with me. Ibrahim Rashid was not only on the premises of the nearest Best Clean, he was standing behind the counter, entirely accessible.

"Can I help you?" he asked.

"My name is Magdalena Yoder. I am—"

"I know who you are. Do you have your ticket?"

"Ticket?"

"You're picking up, right?"

"Not exactly. Mr. Rashid, do you have a minute?"

"Sure." He called a middle-aged woman named Beth from behind the revolving racks of clothes and asked her to man the register. Then he led me into the cubicle that served as his office. I could see that low overhead was yet another way he made his business profitable. In fact, his desk was one of those put-together jobs from Home Depot. "Please, have a seat," he said, offering me the only chair.

"Thanks, don't mind if I do."

"Would you care for something to drink?"

"A cup of hot chocolate would be nice. And some ladyfingers, if you happen to have some handy."

He flashed me an abbreviated smile. "I'm afraid your choices are limited to water and diet cola."

"In that case I'll pass. Mr. Rashid, how did you know who I am?"

"Everyone in Hernia knows who you are, Miss Yoder. You're practically an institution."

That was the kindest thing anyone has ever said to me, using the word "institution." Already the man was piling up points in the credit column. And I suppose I should mention the fact that he started out with a bunch because next to the Babester, the founder of Best Clean was the most handsome man I'd ever seen.

"You're something of a phenomenon yourself," I said.

"Miss Yoder, I don't mean to be rude, but Beth is still being trained. Besides, as I'm sure you well know, time is money."

"So much money, so little time to spend it."

"Miss Yoder—"

"I know, hurry it along, right? Okay. I'm here because this morning a corpse was discovered in one of the foundation ditches of the forthcoming Grape Expectations complex."

Other than the flicker of incredibly long, dark eyelashes, he offered no physical cues about his mental state. "I fail to see how this concerns me—or you, for that matter."

"Well, dear, it concerns me because I'm working with Chief Hornsby-Anderson on the case, and it concerns you because you and your charming wife were observed just steps away from the scene of the crime."

This time a vein at his temple twitched. "It is true, Miss Yoder, that my wife and I were out there in the wee hours this morning, but neither of us had a clue that there was a corpse nearby."

"What were you doing there, Mr. Rashid?"

He didn't pause a beat. "What was your witness doing there, Miss Yoder?"

"Praying."

Now *that* got his attention. "Did you say 'praying'?"

"Indeed. Now it's your turn, Mr. Rashid."

"Uh, my wife and I have been married for only two years. It was a beautiful, moonlit night and—uh, I'm sure you know what I mean."

"Whether I do or don't is none of your business. But I'm afraid your explanation won't suffice. At the time my witness observed you, it was teeth-chattering cold, and you and your lovely spouse were doing anything but the horizontal hootchy-kootchy."

"Excuse me?"

"The mattress mambo. The Sealy Posturepedic polka. The bedspread bossa nova. The sleeping bag—"

"I get the picture," he said, fighting back a grin. "Okay, you win. There are two things my wife and I argue about almost constantly: her desire to return home to Lebanon, and her desire to get a Pennsylvania driver's license. Frankly, I can't remember which of those we got into last night, but since your spy appears to be on top of things, I'll confess to both of them."

"Confess?"

"A poor choice of words. You know what I mean."

"Mr. Rashid—"

"Please, call me Ibrahim. Or Abe, if you prefer."

"Ibrahim," I said, attempting to roll the *r*, "what were you doing way out there on Hungry Neck Road?"

"We were coming back from Pittsburgh, and I was tired of driving, so I thought I would take a shortcut. If you must know, we stopped because I had a nicotine craving. In a serious way. The smoke bothers Faya more than it does most people."

"Ever think of giving it up?"

"They say that nicotine is even more addictive than heroin. Of course I've tried giving it up."

So far his story jibed with hers. "Ibrahim, why didn't you and your wife attend the community protest against Grape Expectations?"

"Believe me, Miss Yoder, I would have liked nothing better. I was in Harrisburg that day—the next day as well. But I saw it on TV that evening on the news, and the same thing the next morning. I even saw you."

"You *did*? How did you know it was me?"

So help me, if he said it was my nose or the fact that I am vertically enhanced, or made some comment about me weighing less than my shadow . . .

"Miss Yoder, you are an uncommonly attractive woman. A man would have to be blind not to notice you."

"I am? He would?" I brushed a wisp of hair from my cheek and tucked it into the beginnings of a braid.

"Please don't misconstrue what I said, Miss Yoder. I am a Muslim—albeit a rather liberal one—and a married man. But that doesn't mean I can't appreciate a thing of beauty. And I must say that in your case the veil would be indicated."

"It would?" It would certainly hide my probing proboscis, not to mention my uncommon attractiveness—his comment could mean just about anything. "Wait just one Mennonite minute! I'm not sure that was a compliment!"

Ibrahim Rashid smiled broadly and shook his handsome head. "Miss Yoder, you certainly are everything they say you are."

"And more," I said modestly. "By the way, Abe, are you aware that your house exceeds Hernia's zoning limitations?"

"I beg your pardon?"

"It's too big."

"Who told you that?"

"Well, it's obvious, isn't it? I mean, do you see any other houses that large around town?"

His eyes flashed. "No."

"Why do you suppose that is?"

"I doubt if anyone else in this multi-horse town can afford one as large as mine."

"That's beside the point, dear. The code prohibits single-family dwellings from exceeding thirty-five hundred feet. How big is yours? Six thousand feet?"

"It's five," he said through clenched teeth.

You see how easy it is to get an admission? "Oh, dear. Which fifteen hundred are you prepared to lose?"

"I'm prepared to fight the town council. I can afford the best lawyer in Pennsylvania. Those fossilized old goats won't know what hit them."

"Baaaaa."

To his credit, he barely blinked. "We're both businesspeople, Miss Yoder."

"What's that supposed to mean? Are you offering me a bribe?"

He swallowed my bait—hook, line, and sinker. "No, of course not. But I am willing to negotiate. Isn't that what businesspeople do?"

"Well, in that case . . . sure, I'll negotiate. But it's sight unseen."

"Excuse me?"

"I won't mention your building infraction to the other council members—in fact, I'll defend you if the subject ever comes up—and you, my dear, make me a promise."

"A promise to do what?"

"I can't tell you in advance. That's what makes it sight unseen."

"Does it involve religion, politics, or my finances?"

"It does not. It's really a very minor issue. You have my word."

He shook his head. "They should have warned me about you in business school."

"Then you attended the wrong one, dear. I'm told there are several schools out there now with a course titled Magdalena Yoder 101."

"You're kidding, aren't you?"

"Yes, but a gal has a right to hope, doesn't she? Look, Abe, what I want from you is a good thing. And it will enable you to keep your oversized house intact. Conspicuous consumption—isn't that the American Dream?"

He sighed. "Okay, I promise—although I know I'm going to regret this. Now what is it?"

"That you won't get mad at your wife."

"My wife? Why would I get mad at her— Wait one boring Hernia minute. This is about her driving, isn't it?"

"Eventually. In the meantime, it's about me giving her lessons."

Abe glared at me. "How dare you," he said, spitting each word out as if it were a nail shot from a carpenter's electric gun. "My family life is none of your business."

"Ah, but your house size is. And this old goat can be mighty cantankerous at times."

He continued to glare, but I focused on the tip of his nose. That way I appeared to be returning the look yet didn't have to make quite the same emotional investment. Of course I didn't say anything. A wise woman once said that a tongue held is worth two in the bush—or something like that. Her point was that silence is a powerful although often elusive weapon.

"Someday, Miss Yoder, I'm going to be elected to town council. When I am, two-bit motel owners are going to find themselves under the gun."

That hiked my hackles so high they scratched my armpits. "The PennDutch is neither two-bit nor a motel. You will rue the day— Uh, does this mean you'll permit your wife to take driving lessons? Without immediate recrimination, that is."

"Bingo. Now, if you'll excuse me, I'm sure Beth needs my help. This is only her second week on the job. New employees—you know how that is."

"Actually, I don't. Freni Hostetler has been with me from the beginning. Look, dear, just one more question, and I'll go on my merry way."

"The interview is over."

"Just one more," I pleaded. "Honest, Abe."

But I was speaking to his back.

A gal can get plenty hungry trying to sort out the truth, and I had yet to connect with a cup of hot chocolate—piled high with marshmallows, of course—since leaving the inn. Fortunately, the Sausage Barn is only a stale biscuit toss from Best Clean. Unfortunately, this greasy spoon eatery is owned and run by Wanda Hemphopple.

Wanda is a liberal Mennonite, and although she does not wear the traditional prayer cap, she does wear her long hair piled high in a beehive. In fact, it was she who invented the beehive hairdo back when the Good Lord Himself was just a boy, and I don't think she's washed it since. Like the Tower of Babel, Wanda's do strives to reach the heavens. Should Hemphopple's tower topple, Hernia could be obliterated by an avalanche of dandruff and assorted vermin. Rumor even has it that the U.S. military has been begging Wanda to travel to various hot spots in the world and let down her hair. I did not start that particular rumor, by the way. I merely passed it on.

But I digress. For some reason I get under Wanda's dandruff-flecked skin. The Good Lord knows I try to love the woman, despite her feelings toward me, but I'm not always successful. My point is that a visit to the Sausage Barn is, for me, a double-edged sword: I must fight to keep my tongue under control, as well as stave off the sin of gluttony. Wanda's Mennonite roots manifest themselves in her attitude toward the food she serves—fat is where it's at.

"Good morning, dear," I said with a pleasing smile as I breezed past the front counter.

"Come back here, Magdalena! You're not allowed to seat yourself."

"But the place is half empty."

"For all you know those tables are reserved."

"You don't take reservations," I said, still smiling pleasantly.

"Quit sneering at me, Magdalena."

"I wasn't."

"Now, where do you want to sit? Tables six and eight are open, and so is thirteen."

"My usual would be fine, dear." Not only is this table close to the kitchen, ensuring that at least some of the fat served will still be molten, but it is curtained off by a wall of plastic plants. Hot fat and privacy—can it get any better?

"Your *usual* is occupied," she said triumphantly.

"It is?"

"That young police officer from California. The one who everyone thinks is—well, what about you, Magdalena? Do you think he's gay?"

"I'm sure it's none of my business, dear. But speaking of him, I believe I'll join him." I trotted down the aisle, between tables, with Wanda nipping at my heels.

"You can't do that! You can't seat yourself, and you certainly can't disturb one of my customers."

But I did. I swooped into the booth and plopped my patooty on the faux-leather bench. Sergeant Chris Ackerman dropped his fork with a loud clatter but otherwise retained his composure.

"Do you mind if I join you?"

"He certainly does." Wanda's beehive had taken a second to catch up with her, and it was wobbling precariously.

"Actually, I don't," Chris said.

"There, you see? He doesn't— Officer, are you sure?"

"Positive."

I pretended I was sucking on a stalk of rhubarb so that Wanda wouldn't think I was gloating. I may have gotten the seat I desired, but it was within Wanda's power to sabotage my order.

"Harrumph," Wanda said. "So, Magdalena, what is it you want?"

"Some privacy would be nice, dear."

"You have to place your order first, because I'm doing double duty today. Caitlyn threw up all over table fourteen so I sent her home, and Opal doesn't start until two."

"Eggs poached hard—but not to the point that the yolks are dry; bacon—crisp, but with a little play both ends; and raisin cinnamon toast—pale, of course. I don't ingest charcoal. Oh, and a tall orange juice—not from concentrate, pulp preferable; coffee—freshly ground, not from a can; and so much cream that Bessie begged for mercy."

Wanda rolled her eyes like a teenager. "Will that be all, Your Royal Highness?"

"No. I'd like a glass of sky juice as well."

"All we have is orange, grapefruit, and tomato. Although I suppose I could round up some prune juice. Have you reached that age yet, Magdalena?" She twittered as the tower on her head teetered.

Chris snickered. "Oh, I get it."

"What is this?" she demanded. "Some kind of inside joke?"

"Sky juice is water," I said, "because it comes from clouds."

"That's just stupid. People don't call milk cow juice, do they?"

"Susannah does."

"No offense, Magdalena, but your sister is nuttier than a Pay-Day."

"Make up your mind, dear. Last time you said it was a Snickers. And another thing, I wouldn't be bringing up prune juice to someone who is younger than you."

"Younger? Are you sure?"

"Positive," I said. I was referring to Chris, so it was clearly not a lie, merely a misrepresentation of the truth. Presidents do it all the time.

"I know you're not allowed to swear, Magdalena, on account of you attend Beechy Grove Mennonite, but would you still say 'positive' if I put your hand on a stack of Bibles?"

"Affirmative."

For the first time since I've known her—which is my entire life—Wanda seemed on the verge of tears. "Magdalena, you're not going to spread this around, are you? I mean about me being older. I wouldn't care so much, but since you look so much older than I— well, folks will start to say that I've had a face-lift. Then someone will tell Hebert. And you know my husband: he jumps to conclusions easier than you do. He'll discover that I cashed in those bonds my daddy left us, which I did, but it wasn't for a face-lift."

Sometimes gossip is as good as caffeine. "Why did you cash in those bonds?"

"I was trying to be helpful—and invest in our future. That letter from the man in Nigeria sounded so convincing. If I loaned him just ten thousand dollars, he could redeem an account that was frozen during their civil war. He said it was worth millions, and I would get half."

I'd received similar e-mails. "Don't worry, dear. They say that dates are one of the first things we forget. I'm sure you'll help me forget your birth date as well."

"I beg your pardon?"

"Free breakfast for both of us will go a long way toward amnesia. You know what they say about bacon fat clogging the arteries that lead to the brain."

"Wait just one fat-congealing minute! You're blackmailing me for a free breakfast."

"Righto."

"Magdalena, you're despicable. Did you want butter on that cinnamon toast?"

"Yes, and remember, I tip generously," I said to ensure she did not spit on my eggs.

"That will be a first," she snorted before retreating to the counter. The beehive bobbled along behind her.

I turned my attention to Chris. "What's the matter? Did Dunkin' Donuts close?"

"No. It's just that I was hungry for— Hey, that was a dig, wasn't it?" He laughed agreeably. "Like I said, you're a hoot, Miss Yoder. But the truth is, I really do like doughnuts. I especially like doughnut holes."

"I'm an old-fashioned girl myself."

"Miss Yoder, I'm glad you're here. I just got off the phone with the chief. She says I'm to be at your disposal twenty-four/seven."

"Sounds like a husband, but without any of the bother."

"Excuse me?"

"Never mind me. I'm just babbling as usual. Tell me, how do you feel about this assignment?"

He popped a piece of crisp bacon into his mouth before answering. "I think it's great. Miss Yoder, I'm not a sexist, or I wouldn't be working for the chief."

"Touché."

"And from what I hear there's a lot you could teach me."

I patted my prayer cap, lest there were any stray hairs protruding from my bun. "Flattery will get you everywhere with me—well, almost everywhere. But just to bring you up to speed, so far I've interviewed Agnes Mishler, the woman who discovered the corpse; Dr. Faya Rashid, who is Muslim and therefore theoretically opposed to alcohol consumption; and her husband, Ibrahim Rashid. I have a gut feeling Agnes is telling the truth, and the Rashids' stories jibe."

"Who are you putting the screws to next?"

"I beg your pardon! Is that official police talk?"

"No, ma'am, I saw that in a movie once. What I meant was, who are you going to question next?"

"Well, I need to give that some thought— The man who just walked in!"

10

Grape Glazed Carrots

2 bunches young carrots
1 tablespoon butter or margarine
½ cup Concord grape jam
2 tablespoons lemon juice

½ teaspoon grated lemon peel
¼ teaspoon ground ginger
2 tablespoons toasted chopped
  pecans

Pare carrots and cut into 2-inch pieces by slicing diagonally. Cook until tender in lightly salted water. Drain. Combine butter, Concord grape jam, lemon juice, lemon peel and ginger in a saucepan. Add carrots. Cook for 10 minutes over moderate heat, turning often to thoroughly glaze carrots. Garnish with pecans.

MAKES 4–6 SERVINGS

11

"Who?" He started to turn his head.

"Don't look now!"

He looked anyway. "Looks a little bit like Mel Gibson, but with sad eyes. Neck may be thicker as well."

"That's him. The thick neck comes from being a farmer—all that hard work."

" 'Tote that barge, lift that bale.' "

"We don't have barges here," I said kindly. The poor lad still had California neurons firing in his brain.

"So, what's this guy's name, and why is he on your list?"

"His name is Hiram Stutzman. Two years ago come Easter, his wife and seven children were killed by a drunk driver. Easter! Can you imagine? I can see why someone might want a drink at Christmas—not that *I* would, mind you—because it can be depressing if you have no family to speak of, and the days being dark and all, not to mention the tremendous pressures put on you by merchants. But Easter is all about hope, and life, and crocuses blooming, and longer days. I mean, you're hardly even expected to send Easter cards anymore. Uh—where was I?"

"His family was killed by a drunk."

"Right. It was perhaps the worst tragedy in Hernia's history. Hiram stayed home from church that day because one of his dairy cows was having a difficult labor. His wife, Marie, and the kids were driving home from church, and when they got to Dead Man's Curve, they were hit head-on by another car. The poor man has got to be outraged about Grape Expectations. I'm sure that on some level he blames the Bacchustellis because they plan to sell alcohol."

"Dead Man's Curve? Isn't that out there on Hershberger Road, just after you cross Slave Creek?"

"Yes. There have been tons of accidents there in the past, and a number of deaths, but not for several years. And never eight people at one time. There are plenty of signs up now, and the shoulder is wider, so it's not nearly as bad as it used to be. Besides, Maria was an exceptionally careful driver, and the sheriff's investigation showed that she was in her lane when it happened. The other driver, however, was not."

"Was he or she killed as well?"

"*He* is an Amish boy. Luke Hostetler—a distant cousin of Freni and of course myself. Luke was sixteen at the time. His car had an air bag, and he didn't even get a scratch. Marie's car didn't have air bags. She and the two oldest went through the windshield. Trust me, you don't want to know the details."

"I thought the Amish weren't allowed to drive cars. Or to drink, for that matter."

"You're right. But Luke was in *rumschpringe*. This is a period during adolescence during which Amish children are given free rein to sow their wild oats in the hope that they'll get it out of their system and settle down as obedient Amish."

"I guess most do."

"Most. But about twenty percent still leave the fold. Some, of course, kill themselves."

"Did I hear correctly? Did you say *kill* themselves?"

"If you think it's hard being gay out in the world—not that you would have personal experience or anything—think how hard it must be for an Amish teenager. If they come out, as everyone calls it these days, they have no choice but to leave home or totally repress it. There can be no middle ground. *None*. Conformity is everything."

"That's sobering."

"At any rate, when Carolyn Augsberger arrived on the scene— she was the one who reported it—Luke was staggering around in the middle of the highway chanting the lyrics to a rap song. He didn't even realize there had been an accident."

"Shoot," Chris said (he actually used a much stronger word), "I wouldn't blame Mr. Stutzman for going off the deep end."

"Who told you?"

"Excuse me?"

"Because that's exactly what Hiram did. He didn't say a word for weeks. Just sat like a stone—wouldn't eat or anything. His brother put him in a hospital in Pittsburgh until he came out of it. He was there a month or so. In the meantime, everyone in the community pitched in to do his chores. Especially the Amish. They felt terrible that one of their own was responsible for what happened. I don't mean to be flip, but when Hiram finally snapped out of it, his farm never looked better."

"So he talks now?"

"Only when spoken to."

"What happened to the Amish boy?"

"Ah, that. Well, a few days after the accident young Luke hung himself with his suspenders in his jail cell. Of course he wasn't supposed to have them, but he claimed his religious rights were being trampled when they tried to take them away from him. I know this sounds awful, but you could almost feel the sigh of relief that swept over the community as the news spread."

"I can imagine."

"Luke's parents moved to Indiana shortly after that. Freni heard from another cousin there that they still feel a lot of shame."

"Miss Yoder, how are you going to interview Mr. Stutzman? I mean, it doesn't feel right somehow. The poor guy has been through enough."

I chose my words carefully. It was hard work with that undeveloped part of my brain.

"Sergeant, I'm sure you'll agree that although Felicia Bacchustelli was an underhanded businesswoman, she didn't deserve to die. And she was right about one thing: Ed should have read the fine print. In fact there were steps we all could have taken to prevent Grape Expectations from getting a foothold in our community. Yes, Hiram Stutzman has suffered a loss neither of us can comprehend. But if he killed Mrs. Bacchustelli, he still has to be made accountable. It wasn't she who destroyed his family."

He took a slow sip of coffee. "But you'll go easy on him, won't you?"

"Watch and see."

I am a woman of my many words, so yes, I did leave Wanda a big fat tip. She acknowledged it by snorting and then demanding that I pay for the two chocolate mint patties I had palmed from one end of the counter. And yes, there was a small sign saying they cost two bits each, but believe me, the tip I left Wanda would pay for a small cocoa plantation on the west coast of Africa.

"Toodle-loo," I said cheerily, despite my soured mood, and traipsed out the door, head held high, with pretty boy Chris at my heels.

"But Miss Yoder," he protested, "Mr. Stutzman is still in there."

"Of course, dear. Now you go back in and tell Wanda that you've lost something very important in the crack between the bench and backrest of the booth we were just in."

"Something important?"

"Car keys, driver's license, photograph of your significant other—you get the picture—no pun intended. Pour on that California charm. Get her to help you look for it. Tear apart the booth if you have to. Meanwhile I'll slip back in and pay Hiram a nice little visit."

"But I didn't lose anything. I would have to lie."

"You're a police officer, for crying out loud!"

"I don't lie, Miss Yoder."

"Not even for a good cause?"

"I don't know where you got your information about police officers, Miss Yoder, but most of us are straight. Well, you know what I mean."

I sighed and took a fifty-dollar bill from my wallet. Sergeant Chris Ackerman was still a boy. After he'd lived awhile he'd come to appreciate that not everything is black or white. Indeed, if that's how the Good Lord expected us to see things, he wouldn't have created gray.

"Here," I said, "take this and drop it down the crack. Then tell her you dropped it. That way you won't be lying. If you manage to recover it, there will be no need to act happy, because it's yours to keep."

"The chief said I'd learn a lot from you." It sounded more like an accusation than a compliment.

"You'll do it?"

"I guess."

I gave him a gentle push toward the door and then waited until I saw Wanda trot after him in the direction of the booth. I'm tall but thin, so I offer little wind resistance and not much of a shadow. I was able to slip past the cashier station without being noticed by the woman with a deadly do, although it took me longer than I'd expected to locate Hiram. At last I spotted him sitting between a pair of hefty tourists from Ohio (one can tell by their accents) and the bathroom.

His back was toward me so he didn't know that I was there until I slid into the booth beside him. I would have jumped and screamed if someone had done that to me, possibly even caught my bun in the ceiling vent, but Hiram merely turned his head slowly in my direction, as if highly sedated.

"Magdalena," he mumbled.

"As big as life, and twice as ugly. May I join you?"

"I'm not up to talking these days."

"No need, dear; I'll do the talking. All you have to do is nod or shake your head. Although feel free to grunt, if the spirit moves you. But please, don't express yourself the way Glenn Gerber does." Glenn lost his larynx in a tragic hunting accident and now communicates with the help of beans and cabbage. Use your imagination to connect the dots.

Hiram grunted and turned his attention back to a stack of hotcakes.

"Did you hear about the murder out on Hungry Neck Road last night?" I asked in as neutral a tone as I could muster.

"No."

"A young reporter from New York, they say. Funny, but we don't get many African-Americans out here, and then one shows up, and wham, the next day she's dead."

He'd put his fork down and was staring at me. "You sure?"

"Sure about what, dear?"

"That she was black?"

"Pretty sure. Of course, from what I've read the whole concept of race is being questioned these days, on account of historically ad-jacent populations have intermarried with each other and blurred the racial lines. But a missing person's report listed her as African-American." Lest I be judged for lying, I feel obligated to point out that the trap I was laying was for a good cause.

Hiram picked up his fork, licked the syrup off, and set it down again. "Bacchustelli sounds Italian to me."

"It is. Who said I was speaking about her?"

There was nothing nebulous about the sound I was treated to next. "Hells bells, Magdalena," Hiram roared. "What the heck is it you want?"

"Tsk-tsk for the language, dear. All I want is the truth. Where were you last night?"

"What time last night?"

"Say between the hours of seven and five this morning."

"Are you asking this in your pseudo-official position as a crimi-nal investigator or as Magdalena Busybody Yoder?"

"Why, I never! Hiram Stutzman, shame on you—you big kidder, you." I was suddenly acutely aware of the fact that ears all over the restaurant were turned our way, like miniature, ill-shapen satellite dishes. "I'm asking on behalf of the Chief of Police, of course."

"If you must know, Magdalena, I was in Bedford relieving ten-sion."

"What about the other nine hours and fifty-seven minutes, dear?"

"Excuse me?"

Occasionally my hunches are wrong. "Uh—exactly how were you relieving your tensions?"

"I've taken up racquetball. My therapist recommended it. He said the exercise would help with the depression."

"Has it?"

12

"Some. Look, Magdalena, I know that you and just about everyone in Hernia thinks I'm a walking time bomb. Maybe I am. But for the moment, I'm a broken man, not an angry one. I haven't reached that stage yet. Believe me, when I do, I'm not going to kill the snobbish owner of an upscale vineyard and winery. I'm going to lie in the tuley weeds next to my driveway and shoot one of those son-of-a-beach Amish kids when they come roaring by drunk out of their skulls on a Saturday night. Then I'm going to haul his bag-of-manure body over to the family farm and dump him on the front porch. I'll get away with it too, Magdalena, because no one's going to believe I had it in me. I'm the broken man who can hardly speak, remember?" Of course that wasn't precisely what Hiram said, but you get the gist.

"You're forgetting one thing, dear. I'll tell them about this conversation. Some folks think you're awfully cute, Hiram. How would you feel about a girlfriend named Bill?"

He turned to me with that sweet, sad look of his, the one that fooled every Hernian except *moi*. "No one believes a dead woman, Magdalena."

"Why, you murderous little maniac—"

"There she is!" Wanda bellowed. "Arrest her, Officer!"

Chris grinned sheepishly at me and then mumbled something to the raving restaurateur.

"I don't care what she says she's doing," Wanda shrieked. "You can see that she's harassing my customer!"

Hiram turned slowly, Wanda's bellows and shrieks finally impinging on his grief-stricken thoughts. His eyes were sadder than a basset hound's and he had to move his lips several times before the words came out.

"She isn't harassing me, Wanda. She's giving me comfort." He slowly turned to me. "Thank you, Miss Yoder."

"Ha," I said through clenched teeth. Oh, to be a skilled ventriloquist. I would have said a whole lot more to Hiram, maybe even used some of his own vocabulary on him. I had plenty of soap at home with which to wash my mouth out later.

Wanda Hemphopple did not become a successful businesswoman by backing down. "She's not eating anything. If she's not eating, she's not a customer, so she's got to go."

I snatched a strip of bacon from Hiram's plate and popped half of it into my mouth. "I'm eating now."

"You know what I mean, Magdalena. I want you out immediately."

There are many ways in which to become the center of attention, but this was not among the preferred. After all, I have my position in the community to consider.

"I was just leaving, dear," I said, and slid my bony butt off the genuine imitation leather and stretched my frame to its full four feet twenty-two inches.

"Good riddance," Wanda muttered.

"Look, a quarter," I said as I passed her.

As she looked down at her grease-smudged floor, I dropped the remaining half of my bacon into the gaping crater that presented itself. I'm ashamed to say it wasn't the first time I'd stooped so low.

"I can't believe you did that," Chris said once we were safely inside my car. He was not as amused as I'd hoped he'd be.

"I'm not the only one," I wailed. "Virginia Dorfman stuck a French fry in there once, and last year Albert Rickenbach dropped a miniature flashlight in there two days before Christmas. Wanda's head glowed until January second. Folks who didn't know any better thought she'd had a religious experience. And oh, did I mention the time Susannah lost her dog in that dangerous do?"

"Shnookums?"

"You know the mangy mutt?"

"I had the unfortunate experience of giving your sister a speeding ticket. It seemed to leap out of nowhere and attach itself to my hand. You can still see the marks here." He held out his right hand. "Were you aware that thing lives in her bra?"

"Nature abhors a vacuum," I said. I sighed wistfully. "All the talk of empty spaces makes me miss my pussy. You see, Little Freni was a Siamese kitten I carried around in my Maidenform for some of the happiest weeks of my life. Then Alison came to live with me. Alas, the poor child is highly allergic to cats, and I had to give my pussycat away. Don't get me wrong: the joy of raising a real child is greater than that of stroking one's pussy—well, it ought to be, at any rate."

"Miss Yoder, I hope you don't mind me saying this, but—"

"Yes, dear, I know. I shouldn't mention titillating words like 'Maidenform' in front of a man, and for that I apologize."

"Apology accepted, but—"

"Well, shall we get cracking?"

"Yes, but—"

"Either we crack, or we don't. Which is it?"

"Crack, I guess," he sighed. "Where to?"

"It's time to grill our most likely suspect."

"Mr. Bacchustelli?"

I felt a rush of disappointment. "How did you guess?"

"That's what they taught us in police academy. Start with the family—that's sort of like the Golden Rule of crime solving, right?"

"It is? I mean, forget the rules, dear. This is Hernia, not California."

"Whatever you say, Miss Yoder." From the corner of my eye I could see that he was biting his lip.

"Okay, out with it. You think I'm a silly old woman who doesn't know the first thing about law enforcement, don't you?"

"No, but—"

"Come on, spill it. You've been dying to say something. Now's your chance. Don't worry. I can take it."

"It's just that I don't have your fifty bucks."

"*Excuse* me?"

"That fifty bucks I stuffed down behind the seat, she wouldn't give it back. Said possession was nine tenths of the law, and because the booth was hers, so was the cash."

"Wanda, you wily weasel," I hissed into the rearview mirror.

The Sausage Barn disappeared as I drove around the first curve, but my indignation was going to take a long time to dissipate. Wanda Mae Hemphopple was going to yearn for the days when plastic puke from Juvenile Jokesters in Pittsburgh was the worst trick this Yoder could conjure up.

Steaming from one ear—my right ear had a slight buildup of wax—I drove in silence the rest of the way to the Bacchustellis' condominium in downtown Bedford. By the way, the very fact that the pair had chosen to live in this bustling county seat of 5,385 instead of bucolic Hernia was indicative of how they saw their place in the community. As far as I knew, they weren't even planning to live in the lodge once it was built.

As I pulled into a parking space opposite the condos, Chris's cell phone rang. "Yes, Chief," he said before the second ring.

Silence reigned as I studied my nails. I am proud to say they have never been painted. In recent years, however, they have gone from being as smooth as pearls to as rutted as washboards. Perhaps I wasn't eating enough Jell-O.

"We're just about to pay a visit to Mr. Bacchustelli," Chris said. "That is, if he's home."

I looked at my laugh lines in the rearview mirror. Not bad for my age, but not as good as Evelyn Blough's skin. Of course she was a redhead who never went anywhere without slathering sunscreen on first. Once, when in a hurry, she smeared toothpaste on her face by accident, which turned it bright pink.

"I'll certainly do my best, Chief."

I softly tapped my foot on the floorboard as I sang "Bringing in the Sheaves" in my head. When I was a little girl, I used to think the word was "sheep," instead of "sheaves."

"Yes, Chief, I'll tell her," Chris said after an annoyingly long period of silence on his end.

"Tell me what?"

"No, Chief, I won't. You have my word."

During the ensuing silence I sang all the verses to "Rock of Ages" *and* "Onward, Christian Soldiers," my least favorite hymn.

"I understand, Chief. Believe me, I do. My lips are sealed."

"But mine aren't," I wailed. "If you don't get off soon, I'll start singing out loud."

"Got to go, Chief."

The young sergeant must have heard rumors of my spectacularly bad voice. For a long time I was in denial, under the illusion that it was actually better than most folks', and that's why it sounded so—uh—different. Then one warm day last spring, as I was sitting on the banks of Miller's Pond, I raised my voice in praise of the Lord. Within minutes dead fish began bobbing to the surface, belly up.

Of course I was devastated. But after much prayer I came to the conclusion that the Good Lord doesn't make mistakes, hence my exceptionally bad voice had to be a blessing of some sort. Perhaps the armed forces could use me to sing enemy troops into surrendering. At the very least I could always feed the poor—and myself—by giving concerts along the shores of lakes and rivers.

"What was that all about?" I demanded. "You took forever."

"The chief just wanted to know where we were."

"That's not all. She told you to tell me something, and then later she told you not to tell me something. What did she say?"

He started to open his door, but I have arms that are the envy of orangutans. I grabbed the handle from him and slammed the door shut.

"I wasn't kidding. I'll sing if I have to."

Chris chuckled. "I was going to tell you as soon as we got out—but here goes. She told me to tell you that a preliminary report was just faxed to her from the coroner's office. Mrs. Bacchustelli was killed by a deer rifle. A bullet to the heart. The shot came from a long way away and had slowed considerably, so it was still in her. Also, she was already dead when she entered the water. That's all the coroner can say at the moment. It will take about three days for a more thorough exam."

"You said something about you doing your best—what's that about?"

"The chief wants me to protect you. She said she'd tan my hide and tack it up on her office wall if anything happened to you."

"And what is it you *aren't* allowed to tell me?"

"Just that she— Hey, I'm not falling for that. A promise is a promise."

"But they're made to be broken."

"Not where I come from."

"You're from California, for crying out loud. Half the people there promised to love and cherish their spouse until death did them part, but have since gotten divorced. What about that?"

"Like I told the chief, Miss Yoder, my lips are sealed."

"Oh, come on. Please, pretty please?"

"The chief said you would do that. She said you had a reputation for being pushy and that under no circumstances was I to give in."

I treated the young man to one of my infamous withering glares.

"Are you all right, Miss Yoder?"

"Yes, why wouldn't I be?"

"I'm sure we can find a bathroom for you somewhere close. Maybe in the courthouse over there."

"For your information— There he goes now," I said, and hopped out of my car, a woman on a mission.

I practically had to throw myself in front of the Grape Expectations limo to get the driver to stop. To be fair, due to the angle of the winter sun and the subsequent shadows it cast, he probably thought I was a telephone line. When he did see me, the driver, a thick-necked man from the Garden State, first leaned on the horn and then rolled down his window and let loose with a string of invectives worthy of Lucifer.

"I need to speak to Mr. Bacchustelli," I said, still struggling to remain vertical.

"He ain't here."

"Mind if I take a peek myself?"

"Look, lady, ya better scram if ya want to keep that skinny body of yours all in one piece."

"Is that a threat? Because if it is, you undoubtedly just broke the law, seeing as how I'm subbing for the Chief of Police."

"Oh yeah? I don't see no badge."

"He has one!" I pointed to Chris who, curiously, was no longer there. "Well, he does! Just give me a minute, and I'll find him."

"Lady, if you're not outta my way in a minute, someone's going to have to peel you off of my treads."

"Really? Who would that be? My backup team, which is on its way right now?"

"Yeah, right. I'm counting to three, lady. Then the pleasure of running you over is all mine."

"Go ahead and count. But just so you know, you won't look good in stripes—not if your neck size is indicative of anything."

Mr. Thick Neck put the limo in park and raced the engine. I will admit that my heart beat faster and that I was just a hair away from losing my morning's coffee, but I did not budge. Then much to my astonishment the jerk from Jersey actually allowed the limo to creep forward.

"Help!" I screamed. "He's trying to kill me."

As the car inched forward I grabbed the hood ornament and hung on for dear life. I tried walking backward, but was soon unable to keep up the pace. It was only when I felt the engine's hot breath against my diaphragm that I panicked.

"Help! Help! This time I'm really serious. Oh Lord, take me now. Please don't let me get squished like my parents."

13

They say that in life-threatening circumstances one's life flashes before one's eyes. Mercifully, the only vision that I saw was a plate piled high with ladyfingers and a mug of hot chocolate from which cascaded an avalanche of miniature marshmallows.

The people of Bedford are kind and generous souls. Therefore I must conclude that every single resident of this benevolent berg was away for the day. Well, not counting Mr. Bacchustelli. And that's exactly who saved my life. The rear door of the limo opened and out stepped Vinny Bacchustelli, looking as dapper as any man on the cover of the *GQ* magazines I'd seen for sale at Pat's I.G.A.

"Good morning, Miss Yoder," he said, just as calmly as if we'd met in the lobby of the Bank of America across the street.

"I'm having you arrested," I said between gasps.

"Miss Yoder, I'm very sorry for what just happened. Please accept my apologies."

"You tried to kill me."

"I assure you I didn't. I'm afraid there's been a misunderstanding."

"You've got that right, buster. Assaulting an officer of the law—perhaps even a pseudo-officer—is a felony. An apology is not going to cut it."

"Otto here thought you were a reporter."

"Well, I most certainly— He did?" The Bible admonishes us not to hate anyone. In fact, it exhorts us to love all of God's children, including reporters. But reporters have behaved grievously to me in the past, slandering me, my loved ones, and even my inn with their lies. One tabloid reporter went so far as to say that I was Bigfoot *and* pregnant by Hernia's ex–Chief of Police, the diabolical Melvin Stoltzfus. Had I been in a vehicle when I read that article, with that reporter right in front of me, I would still be eating my meals off a tin plate slipped under the bars of my one-room digs.

"Miss Yoder, I am so sorry I didn't recognize you earlier. I heard Otto yelling, but he's from Hoboken. Need I say more?"

"I'm sure there are some lovely people in Hoboken, just like there are in Maryland. And why is that man named Otto, anyway? I thought that was a dog's name."

Vinny Bacchustelli smiled, despite the grief he must have been feeling. In doing so he displayed teeth so bright I'm sure the flashes they emitted could be seen in outer space. By the way, it is a myth that the Great Wall of China can be seen by astronauts—not unless they visit China. Yes, it is the longest fortified structure built by man, but it isn't any wider than a four-lane highway, and highways can't be seen from up there.

"Otto is certainly built like a bulldog," the vineyardist said, "but his mother named him Otto. You'd have to ask her about the name."

"You talking about my mama?" the chauffeur growled. Just as my luck would have it, he was looking at me instead of his boss.

"Absolutely not, dear." I glanced at my car. Sergeant Ackerman was nowhere to be seen. "Uh—Mr. Bacchustelli, I was wondering if you could spare me a few minutes. I have some questions I need to ask. I promise to make this brief."

"Miss Yoder, perhaps you weren't aware of the fact that my sister-in-law died."

"Yes, I am. That's why I am here."

"I appreciate your condolences, Miss Yoder." He started to climb back into the maw of a limo that seemed to stretch on for blocks. Fortunately, I was on full Yoder mode and lunged after him, grabbing the sleeve of his merino suit jacket.

"Wait! I have to speak to you—about how she died."

He stepped down again. We stood eye to eye; mine were both blue, and his were both brown. His hair, unlike mine, had made up its mind as to which color it would be: black, and so thick and curly I wanted to rub my fingers through it. Maybe even my toes. His nose had elected for a classical shape, unlike that of *moi*, which could, if I lied a little more, be used to pick litter up along the highway. The only thing above his waist for which I had no counterpart was that three-day growth of beard, which has been perpetuated by the Hollywood crowd for far too long. Since stubble stings (so I've been told), I am forced to conclude that the significant others in the lives of these unkempt individuals are either masochists or in need of dermabrasion.

"My sister-in-law drowned," he said empathically. "She stumbled in the dark and fell into one of the foundation troughs. Once we dug them, it got too cold to pour concrete. I told her that we ought to wait until spring, but there is—was—no arguing with Felicia. Although what the hell she was doing out there in the middle of the night, I'll never know. But it's my own damn fault; I should have insisted we wait."

"She didn't drown, Mr. Bacchustelli. Maybe it's not my place to tell you this, but she was shot."

The poor man recoiled. "Are you saying she was murdered?"

"I'm afraid that's the most likely scenario. Though I suppose it's possible she was hit by a hunter's stray bullet, or maybe someone target practicing."

"Miss Yoder, may I ask why it is you who is talking to me, and not the police?"

"Certainly. You see, Hernia is a small, tightly knit town, with a large Mennonite population and surrounded by Amish farms. Because I know virtually everyone in town, the chief thought I would make more headway in the investigation than either she or her sergeant, both of whom are from the land of fruit and nuts."

"Excuse me?"

"Oops, I meant to say the land of milk and honey."

"They're Israeli?"

"Californians. Isn't that America's promised land?"

His dark eyes sparkled briefly. Perhaps I'd amused him. In that case my sometimes lacerating lingua had inadvertently performed a good deed—a matzo, as my Jewish fiancé would say.

"I see what's in this for the police, Miss Yoder, but what's in it for you?"

"Well, I—uh—I get to perform matzos for my community."

"Excuse me?"

"Good deeds. I get to help out people by giving them the bene-fit of both my shrewd observations and my rapier wit. Surely help-ing one's neighbors is not a foreign concept to you—is it?"

"Ah, mitzvoth. Miss Yoder, matzos are squares of unleavened bread. Kind of like big unsalted crackers."

"Are you sure?" I know I hadn't heard Gabe wrong.

He'd stopped listening. "Why would anyone kill Felicia?"

I cleared my throat. "You are aware that Grape Expectations was viewed by almost everyone as being a huge threat to the morals of Bedford County. The next Sodom and Gomorrah—that's what some are calling it."

"But it's just a vineyard and winery. Plus a spa and hotel. What's objectionable about that?"

I shook my head in disbelief. "Didn't you do any homework, dear? We don't drink down here. Even our Baptists feel compelled to drink in their closets. You should see Craig Bachman's closet. Uh, anyway, I thought we made that clear from the beginning."

"We thought it was mostly just posturing. You know, resisting change just for the sake of doing so. Rural towns often do that. They won't let Wal-Mart in but are happy to drive to the nearest town that does. And besides, our business plan didn't even include locals in our profit forecast. We were looking to the sophisticated urban who wanted a change of scenery."

"Unfortunately, we rural rubes enjoy our scenery just like it is. Sorry if that came off harsh."

"Miss Yoder, when I spoke to your chief early this morning, be-fore I was told anything about it being murder, she asked if I needed help making the necessary arrangements. I told her I didn't, but now I think I do."

"I'd be glad to help," I said.

"And I'd be honored to accept it."

I told him to wait and trotted back to my car to look for Chris. I found him lying on the backseat, his knees in the air and one arm flung over his eyes. His face, from the little bit I could see, was as pale as a hen's egg—the white ones, of course, like the Good Lord intended.

"Are you all right?"

"I'm feeling kind of queasy."

"I've volunteered to escort Mr. Bacchustelli to a funeral home. Just say no and I'll—"

"I'll be fine, Miss Yoder. It's probably just something I ate. You go on ahead and do what you need to do."

"Are you sure?"

"Positive."

I fumbled around under the front seat until I found a plastic grocery bag. "Be a dear and use this should the need arise."

"Gotcha," he said.

"Toodle-loo."

"Miss Yoder?"

"What?" I didn't mean to sound quite that sharp. In my defense I'd just been invited to share a limo ride with an extraordinarily handsome bachelor. The alternative was to play nursemaid to a boy who, at any moment, could hurl a Sausage Barn breakfast at me. While Wanda's food is tolerable going down, it doesn't fare so well on the return trip. This I know from experience.

"Miss Yoder, I'd be real careful if I were you. Mr. Bacchustelli might be connected."

"Connected to what?"

"The Mob."

"Now is no time to be joking, dear."

"I'm not supposed to be telling you this, Miss Yoder, but the chief is having him checked out. And the chief doesn't do things like that unless she's got a pretty good reason."

"What is her reason?"

"I can't say."

"Yes, you can."

"No, I can't."

"In for a penny, in for a pound, dear. And if you don't tell me, you're in for a ton of trouble."

He uncovered his eyes and sat up. "Okay, so I lied. But I've got a bad feeling about this guy. Did you watch *The Sopranos*?"

"They came to my church a couple of years ago on a gospel tour. They were all right, but frankly, I prefer a good tenor."

"I mean the TV show."

"I don't watch television."

"Well, there's this Mob family, you see—"

"Italian?"

"Yes. Anyway—"

"Isn't that stereotyping, dear?"

"Maybe. But still, I've got a hunch this guy's bad news."

"Haven't you heard, dear? A hunch from a woman is worth two facts from a man. A hunch from a man, on the other hand, is absolutely worthless."

I smiled sweetly before closing the door. The ability to impart insincere saccharinity is one of my greatest gifts. Unfortunately, I too had a hunch I was about to get in over my head.

14

Vinny Bacchustelli's limo was a disappointment. For starters, the upholstery was calfskin. The really expensive limousines (this I also know from personal experience) use the foreskins of whales, reputedly the softest of all leathers. The vineyardist had only one TV—a small one at that—in his car, the seats did not recline all the way, and there was no sign of a hot tub. It was definitely not top-of-the-line.

"Which funeral home were you headed to?" I asked pleasantly, pretending not to notice the banal trappings of this supposedly luxury conveyance.

"Wilhelm I. Hinkledorf and Sons. I picked it from the yellow pages. It sounded—well, sort of upscale. Felicia was a classy lady. She would have liked that."

I bit my tongue, lightly placing my teeth inside the familiar grooves. I'm of the mind that a corpse no longer has a mind, and therefore shouldn't mind what happens to it. My loved ones can toss me out on a compost heap for all I care. But to each his own.

If I must say so myself, I exercised considerable restraint when Wilhelm I. Hinkledorf Sr. gave me his dead fish handshake before leading us on the grand tour. Although I squeezed his mitt so hard that even Arnold Schwarzenegger would have winced, I said nothing about the dandruff on his collar or the fact that one of the lenses in his glasses was so smudged that there was a hair embedded in the gunk. For the record, Wilhelm I. Hinkledorf Sr. and I go back a long way—all the way back to high school, where Billy, as he was known then, was the first of my classmates to dub me "Yoder with the Odor."

"I want to see your most expensive casket," Vinny Bacchustelli said.

Those were words to warm the cockles of my heart—well, all of them except for the word "casket." They certainly warmed Wilhelm's heart. He made a beeline for a behemoth of a coffin, displayed in its own little room on a marble base. Lights embedded in the ceiling illuminated every detail.

"Behold the Slumber-berth 600. This baby is handcrafted from the finest Brazilian hickory—farm-grown trees, of course, not rain forest. Observe the sheen. What you're looking at is seventeen coats of optimum carnauba wax—again, from farm-grown trees. The brass mounts were forged to order from Welsh artisans and then chased for that Old World look."

I raised a hand politely. "Who chased them?"

"The Welsh artisans. Magdalena, are you mocking me?"

"Absolutely. Please, proceed."

He snorted. "Most caskets have several inches of padding to absorb leakage. The Slumber-berth 600 has twelve inches of all-natural kapok filling, *but*"—he reverently lifted the pillow at the head of the coffin and pulled back a corner of the lining—"see this tubing? Both air-conditioning and heating! Depending on destination—ha, ha."

"Heaven isn't cold, dear."

Wilhelm glared at me with his left eye, the one not obscured by gunk. "Are you speaking from personal experience, Magdalena?"

"I read my Bible. It mentions gold and giant pearls, but nothing about fireplaces."

He snorted again and turned to Vinny. "Please observe the lining. It is sewn from the finest Sri Lankan silk and hand-smocked by Vietnamese virgins in the city of Vung Tau."

"How do you know they were virgins?" It was a reasonable question, was it not?

"Yes, how?" Vinny said. His eyes sparkled briefly.

"Well, sir, I can only assume they are. These gifted craftswomen are novices in the Catholic convent there."

"Please, continue."

"Note the fabric on the inside of the lids—both upper and lower. It is Turkish taffeta and hand-smocked by Swedish sluts in Stockholm."

Vinny paid particularly close attention to the harlots' handi-work. I felt obliged to deliver a kick to his shins so that we could move the show along.

"Now this," Wilhelm said and, using both arms, struggled to push the lower half of the coffin lid into an upright position, "is the pièce de résistance."

Two of us gaped, while the third grinned ghoulishly. We were star-ing at a color television and a panel of buttons worthy of a cockpit.

"What the Devil!" Vinny said. (The word he actually used was the Devil's home address.)

"Local channels are included in the standard package, but we can upgrade to cable or satellite upon request. We call them the Cloud Nine options."

"Why on earth would a dead person need television?"

"Miss Yoder, I know you think you're an expert on religious matters, but the truth is no one knows for sure what happens when we die. For all we know the dead have to wait a long time before being assigned their final destination. In that event, a little distrac-tion is surely in order." My longtime nemesis flipped a switch and the television screen lit up. "The entire system can operate for six hours on our special supercharged batteries, or we can install solar power, or even hook your loved one up to public utilities. If you pay us enough we can arrange for eight dancing trolls and a French-speaking elephant. . . ."

To be honest, I'm not sure about those last words. I was—and I am deeply ashamed to admit this—mesmerized by a man with glasses and curly hair. He was the host of a show. A fighting show, I believe. Two women and a man (then again, it might have been two men and a woman) were on a stage, trading verbal insults. Every now and then they lunged at each other, but at the last second the riled parties were restrained by muscled men with necks as thick as one-hundred-year-old oaks. The dialogue was hard to follow, seeing as how the audio quality was very poor. "Jerry, Jerry . . . beep, beep, beep . . . Jerry . . . beep, beep!"

"How much is the Slumber-berth 600?" Vinny asked, just as ca-sually as if he were shopping at Sears.

That's when I snapped out of my media-induced reverie. "Good question, dear."

Wilhelm forced the corners of his mouth upward for a nanosecond. "Fully loaded, I can let this baby go for twenty."

Even I was astounded. "Twenty *dollars*?"

"I think he means twenty thousand," Vinny whispered.

Wilhelm always did have exceptional hearing. "Indeed I do. The Slumber-berth 600 takes nine Nepalese craftsmen nine months to assemble. The final product is then shipped to the United States wrapped in albino yak skins. All that takes money."

"Someone is being grossly underpaid, dear, and it isn't you."

Wilhelm recoiled indignantly. "Magdalena, I will thank you to stay out of this."

"Sorry, no can do. This entire thing is a travesty. Not only are you ripping off nuns, sluts, and mountaineers—not to mention the bereaved—but you are making a mockery of death. A person has a right to be buried with dignity, not forty-six channels of cable TV. It's a sad, sad world that allows hedonistic heathens to squander their money on junk like this."

"One hundred and thirty-six channels," he said through clenched teeth. "Double that for satellite. Besides, it isn't just hedonistic heathens who buy the Slumber-berth 600. Mennonites do as well."

"Liar. Uh, who?" One can't blame a gal for wanting to be informed.

"Silas Pearlmutter buried his wife in a Slumber-berth 600. He even requested the extra-virgin silk smocking."

"Extra-virgin?"

"The convent usually has six virgins working at one time—for this they assigned a seventh."

"I was at the Pearlmutter funeral. I didn't see anything like this."

"That's because he was afraid of people like you passing judgment. Silas paid another two grand to have the modest Humble Haven exterior fitted over this baby. Didn't you notice how large Cynthia Pearlmutter's casket was?"

"Cynthia was a large woman. And then there was the matter of her extra leg."

Wilhelm smirked openly at me before turning his attention back to Vinny. "Do you own a plot?"

"No. Not yet."

"May I suggest Heaven's Gate Memorial Gardens off U.S. Route 220? The gardens are more than halfway up Kinton's Knob and the views are spectacular." He pulled a PDA from the breast pocket of his jacket. "Plots 368 and 453 are still available."

"How much?"

"Plot 368 is one hundred thousand dollars, and plot 453 is one-fifty. I swear it's possible to see from that plot all the way to Harrisburg."

"For crying out loud," I said, unable to take any more of this blatant exploitation of the newly bereaved, "Mrs. Bacchustelli is dead. She's not going to be looking at the view, and even if she could, she'd be watching cable TV instead. Oops—no disrespect intended, Mr. Bacchustelli."

Vinny smiled wanly at me. "Miss Yoder, I appreciate your concern, but I am a grown man and of sound mind. I can make my own decisions."

"I'm sure you can, dear, but—"

"Mr. Hinkledorf, I'll take the Slumber-berth 600, extra-virgin, and plot 453 in Heaven's Gate Memorial Gardens. Which credit cards do you accept?"

Wilhelm I. Hinkledorf Sr. smiled seductively. "We accept all credit cards."

"You would," I muttered.

"I only carry Visa," Vinny said, after we'd been led to the office and settled into some swank leather chairs. "I have the others, of course, but why lug them around? And that way, if someone should steal my wallet, I only worry about having to cancel one."

As it turned out, he should have worried about paying off that one. Wilhelm I-never-met-a-credit-card-I-didn't-like Hinkledorf Sr. tried three times to get the card accepted but to no avail. The embarrassment in that room was so thick you could have spread it on a bagel.

Vinny touched my arm lightly. "Miss Yoder—I—uh—I don't suppose you have your checkbook with you."

"Forsooth, 'tis something not to be supposed."

"Excuse me?"

"I don't always carry it. But it just so happens that today I have it. You see, yesterday I had to dash out to Miller's Feed Store to buy some mash for the chickens, but I was out of cash— Oh, I get it. You want to borrow some money for the down payment." I flashed my incisors—perhaps a couple of canines too—at Wilhelm. "Will fifty dollars do?"

Frankly, I was taken aback by his guffaws. "I never knew you had a sense of humor, Magdalena."

"I most certainly don't!"

"Hmm." He glanced from me to Vinny and back again. "Well, I'm afraid I'm going to require ten percent down and payment in full within thirty days."

I may slouch from time to time, but I'm no slouch when it comes to business. "That comes to seventeen thousand dollars! You want me to write a check for seventeen thousand dollars as a down payment on something I think is morally wrong?"

"You're forgetting tax, Magdalena. I need a down payment on that too."

I huffed, and I puffed, and I tried to blow the funeral home down, but I couldn't. In the meantime, Vinny had his eyes closed, his folded hands held up to his face, the thumbs against his mouth. He looked like he was praying.

"She doesn't have the money," Wilhelm finally said. "The rumors of her wealth are unfounded. Go figure."

"I do so have the money!"

"Hmm."

Vinny opened one eye. "You won't regret this, Miss Yoder. I'm good for it. Trust me."

"It seems that legend of her brilliant financial mind is just that," Wilhelm said.

That did it. That really hiked my hackles. I tore into my purse like a hog into fresh slop. It took me a while to flail through the church bulletins, coupons, stale mints, and less-than-fresh tissues, but I found my checkbook and waved it aloft like a winning door prize ticket.

"Ha! Do you want to see what my balance is?"

Vinny opened his other eye. "Trust me," he hissed.

Perhaps he didn't hiss, but there was something about the way he said it that reminded me of the serpent in the Garden of Eden. Not that I ever met that serpent, mind you—at least not in the guise of a snake, and not in that original garden. Vinny Bacchustelli was handsome, suave, and had a silver tongue. If he could talk Ed Gingerich into selling his land for a winery, he could persuade anyone into doing anything.

"Get behind me, Satan!" I cried.

"Excuse me?"

I closed my eyes tightly. "I will not loan you one red cent for this foolishness. Living people are starving all over the world, and you want cable TV for your sister-in-law?"

"I'm choosing satellite."

"In a pig's ear, dear." With eyes still closed as tight as clams at low tide, I felt my way to the doorway of the Slumber-birth 600 room. Then I opened my peepers and ran like Eve should have run.

Unfortunately, I ran straight into the arms of trouble.

15

Concord Grape Trifle

4 egg yolks
½ cup sugar
2 teaspoons vanilla extract
1 cup milk
1 cup light cream
2 sponge cake layers, baked and
 cooled

½ cup sherry
½ cup Concord grape jam
⅓ cup shelled almonds
1 cup heavy cream
1 tablespoon sugar
Frosted grapes
Shelled almonds

In the top of a double boiler, beat egg yolks with ½ cup sugar until well blended. Add vanilla. Stir in milk and light cream. Place over boiling water and cook, stirring constantly, until custard is thick enough to coat a wooden spoon (about 15 minutes). Chill several hours.

Meanwhile, place a layer of sponge cake in a large crystal bowl. Pour ½ the sherry over the cake; spread with ½ cup Concord grape jam. Stud cake layer with ½ the almonds. Repeat with remaining layer. Refrigerate until ready to serve.

Combine heavy cream and remaining 1 tablespoon sugar; beat until stiff. Just before serving, pour custard over cake layers. Top with whipped cream. Garnish with frosted grapes and additional almonds.

MAKES 8–10 SERVINGS

16

What is more trouble than a girl who has just turned fourteen? Two of them? I suppose I gave my parents some lip in my day, but if I did, you can bet they didn't take it. Mama was so fond of the hickory stick, it's no wonder I ended up built like a twig. Papa didn't believe in corporal punishment—he didn't have to. When Papa gave you one of his sad, "I'm so disappointed in you" looks, you wanted to grab the switch from Mama and give yourself a good thrashing.

I don't hit Alison, and since my looks of disapproval are not only ineffective but often met with mockery, I am usually at a loss when she and I hit a bumpy patch in our relationship. (Yes, I've tried reasoning, but some experts believe the ability to reason isn't even present in the early teens.) Even grounding doesn't work with Alison. Tell her she's grounded for a week, and before she slams her door she'll tell you she's grounding herself for a month. What's a pseudomother to do?

Imagine, then, my state of mind when, after leaving Satan inside Wilhelm I. Hinkledorf and Sons funeral home, I found my young charge leaning against the hood of Vinny's limousine and smoking a cigarette. I did a double take, and then a triple take. It is said that we each have a twin out there—may the Good Lord have mercy on mine—and I was hoping against hope that Alison Miller, born in Minnesota, had a Pennsylvania twin. After all, her father was from these parts and every bit as inbred as I am. But alas, the smoke-puffing teenybopper I'd spotted was the real McCoy.

By the time I'd done the triple take, Alison's face had gone from winter pale to ghostly white. The cigarette now lay on the asphalt, partly covered by her shoe. Wisps of smoke escaped from the corners of her tightly drawn mouth.

"Alison!"

"M-Mom?" she sputtered, the smoke pouring from her mouth in a wave of carcinogenic fog.

"As big as life, and twice as ugly, dear."

"It isn't what you think."

"I think you're not in school."

She glanced around, as if looking for someone else I might be addressing. "Uh—it's a holiday, Mom."

I prayed for wisdom. "Which one?"

"Uh—some dead president's birthday I think. Yeah, that's it."

"Which president?"

"Grants Tomb. Something like that."

"Ah, President Tomb. I remember her well."

"He was a *she*?"

That was the first time I'd seen Alison stimulated by anything academic. I hated to derail that locomotive to nowhere.

"Grant's Tomb is where President Grant is buried—in case someone should ask. Unfortunately, we have yet to elect a woman president, even though more than half the country is female. Also, unfortunately, you're busted."

She glanced down at her chest, which had been on a growth rampage ever since she'd come to live with me. Believe me, it wasn't something in Hernia's water supply.

"Yeah. Ya think I'm bigger than you are now, Mom?"

"Don't rub it in, dear. Now, you have exactly five seconds to tell me what you're doing in downtown Bedford in the middle of a school day."

"What happens if I don't tell? Ya gonna ground me like usual?"

"No. I'm going to call the police and tell them you've run away."

Her brown Miller eyes widened. "Ya can't do that! They'll send me back to Minnesota to live with my dad and what's-her-name."

"Won't that be fun. What is it she does that you enjoy so much? Oh yes, she makes you chew each bite thirty-six times. I wouldn't worry too much about that seven thirty bedtime, though. Now that you're fourteen, she might let you stay up until eight."

Alison stamped her foot, which was a good thing, because the cigarette under it had begun to glow again. "Man, that's no fair!"

"Life isn't fair. If it was, do you think I'd look like I should have a saddle slapped on my back—"

"Stop it, Mom. You're beautiful."

"I am?"

"Way more beautiful than my friends' moms."

"I *am*?"

"Tons more beautiful. You're the most beautiful—"

"You may continue later, dear. But now I want you to tell me what you're doing here."

She sighed and rolled her eyes. "I know, it was stupid of me, but I wanted to see where Jason Dunbar lives."

"Who is Jason Dunbar?"

"Some guy I met at the basketball game Saturday. He said he was rich and lived in this big house and had an awesome sound system. Yeah, like right. He lives in this dump with plastic all over the windows, and he isn't even home. His mom said he was in school, and that's where I should be too, and that if I didn't take a hike, she was calling the cops."

"Alison, how did you get to Bedford? It's twelve miles, for crying out loud. Fourteen from our house."

"Otto."

The short hairs on my neck saluted the long hairs on my arms. "*Otto*? Which Otto?"

She kicked the closest tire. "This one. Ya know, the one who works for them wine people."

"Explain, dear," I said, my dander rising to keep my hair company.

"Well, I was hitchhiking, see, but nobody would stop, on account it was still real early and they was all Amish, and they don't stop unless you're one of them. Then Otto comes along in this awesome limo and asks me if I need a ride. And I'm, like, 'Are you crazy? Of course I want a ride.' And he's, like, 'Hop in.' Only he's got that funny accent. So anyway, I tell him to drop me off downtown—I didn't want ta know where I was going, so he wouldn't tell nobody—and then I walked to Jason's house. But it took me forever, and then he wasn't home, like I said. So then I walk back here, 'cause I don't know what else ta do, and then I see the limo, and then along you come. So what are you doing here, Mom?"

"*Moi?* Well, I thought I was doing a good deed, helping a veritable stranger, but it turns out—hey, never you mind. This is about you. And where did you get that cigarette?"

"What cigarette?"

"The one that's burning a hole in your left shoe."

I'd encourage Alison to be an actress were it not for the fact that Hollywood is filled with harlots and Democrats. "Dang! You're right, Mom. There is a cigarette." She made a great show of shaking her foot and examining the sole of her shoe for damage. Fortunately for her, there was none.

"Save the theatrics, dear. Where did you get it?"

"Ah, man, no fair! Ya always figure me out. I got it from Otto. And it's not like I asked for it, Mom. He offered."

"You expect me to believe that a grown man offered you a—"

"Ask him yourself, Mom. He's right behind you."

I whirled. Being vertically enhanced, I'm always surprised when I encounter someone who looms over me. And that's precisely what Otto did. At such close range I had to throw my head back at an uncomfortable angle to see his face. But I will have it known that I was not intimidated by such unnatural height.

"Did you give my daughter cigarettes?"

"Uh—hey, I don't have ta answer ya, lady."

"Oh yes, you do."

"Says who?"

"How about your boss, Vinny Bacchustelli?" Technically, all I did was ask a question. Therefore it was not a lie.

"He said that? No way, lady."

"Hey," Alison said, "my mom doesn't lie. Do ya, Mom?"

"Well—uh—this is not about me, dear. It's about Otto contributing to the delinquency of a minor. Now let's see," I said as I took my cell phone from my purse and tapped it lightly against my chin. "Shall I call Chief Hornsby-Anderson, Sheriff Johnson, or the Bedford Chief of Police? Seeing as how Otto picked you up in Hernia, drove halfway across the county, and dropped you off here, I'd say all three of them have the right to be involved."

It's been said that the flutter of a butterfly's wings along the coast of Africa can set into motion a chain of events that culminates in a hurricane by the time it reaches the coast of North America. I have no doubt that Otto was shaking in his shoes so hard that folks in San Francisco could hear their windows rattle.

"Ma'am, please don't call no one."

"Anyone."

"Them either. I didn't give this girl no cigarettes—I swear on my firstborn, the fruit of my groin."

"That would be loin, dear."

"Ain't that a cut of pork?"

"A pig's a pig, no matter how you slice it." I turned to Alison. "Well?"

"Big deal, so I already had the cigarettes. Still, he gave me a ride. That's illegal, ain't it? Ya know, like raiding and betting a runaway."

"That's *aid*ing and *a*betting. And you weren't running away—were you?"

"No." She sighed dramatically. "I already told ya where I was going."

"So you did. And you can tell me all about how, and where, you bought the cigarettes while Otto drives us back to where I left my car."

"Sorry, lady, but I ain't driving you nowhere. Gotta wait for the boss."

"Au contraire, Otto. Either you give us a lift, or I'm singing like a canary."

"Ya better listen to her," Alison said, "because she really sounds like a turkey with a sore throat."

"Why, I never!" Although perhaps I do. I joined the choir at Beechy Grove Mennonite one year, and attendance plummeted.

"Hop in," Otto growled, "but if either of youse opens your yap, out ya go."

"Deal."

On the way back to Hernia my precious charge admitted to swiping the cigarettes from Yoder's Corner Market. Then, much to my horror, she confessed to also stealing hair spray, gum, magazines, and a can of Vienna sausages.

"Why the potted meat, dear?"

"It was Lindsey Augsberger's idea. Ya see, Mr. Casey—that's my history teacher—is really mean to us, making us take pop quizzes and all. And he carries this really dumb suitcase thing with our papers and junk in it. But sometimes he forgets it, because it's the last period, and he's gotta go off and find Miss Hansen so the two of them can make out together in the copy room."

"They *what*?"

"Ya know, kiss and fool around. Anyway, so Lindsey comes up with this idea of putting something gross in the suitcase thing—"

"Attaché case?"

"Yeah, whatever. So I get some of them little sausages from the market and we put them in. First we take them out of the can, of course."

"Of course. What else would be the point?"

"Right. But this is on a Friday, see, and Mr. Casey goes home without the case. Then he gets sick, and is out a whole week. Meanwhile that case is sitting about six inches from a radiator, and since Mr. Ferguson—he's the janitor—doesn't hardly clean at all, and nobody says nothing to the principal's office, that thing starts to smell—"

"That will be all, dear."

"But I ain't finished with the story."

"Oh yes, you are. Besides, you might want to use the next few minutes to work on your apology."

"What apology?"

17

"The apology you're going to make to Mr. Yoder when you pay him back what you owe."

I glanced at Alison just in time to see her blanch. "Mom! You're kidding, right?"

"I'm as serious as a history test. How much money do you have?"

"I don't know. Maybe ten dollars—ya know ya don't hardly give me nothing for my allowance. Mary Jane says she gets—"

"Mary Jane milks cows, dear. You make your bed on days you feel like it."

She folded her arms across her blooming chest. "Not hardly. If I don't make it, you holler like I killed someone."

This mom stuff was not what I expected. Sure, there were bound to be days when one, or both, of us were out of sorts, but I didn't expect her to argue with everything I said. I hadn't dared talk back to my parents. I certainly never would have dared steal anything. And it's not that I wasn't tempted, mind you. That shiny new lunchbox with Dale Evans's picture on it called to me with its siren song from the McCrorys Five and Dime throughout the fifth grade. Of course Mama—not to mention Grandma Yoder—wouldn't hear of spending that much on something so frivolous. If a brown paper bag was good enough for the boy Jesus, it was good enough for me. I was practically willing to sell my soul for a sandwich container and a thermos with its own plastic red cup. For weeks that's all I could think about, especially at school, and my grades dropped precipitously. But my point is, I *didn't* steal it.

Alison was neither a cooperative nor a compliant sinner; I literally had to drag her into the market by a sleeve. When I let go she slumped just as surely as if I'd removed her backbone in one quick motion. Sam, who's had a thing for me even before my lunchbox days, didn't even notice the girl at first.

"My, my, what a fine-looking specimen of a woman," he said.

"Stop it, Sam. We're first cousins, for crying out loud."

"I hear that's legal down in South Carolina. Encouraged, even."

"You're a married man, Sam."

"Yes, but you're not. Even the patriarchs in the Bible had more than one wife."

"You forget, I'm engaged to be married to the handsomest man in the world."

"You've accepted my proposal?"

"No, and I wouldn't, even if you were the last man alive."

"You might change your mind after I'd had a chance to shower you with kisses, from the fuzz on your upper lip to the—"

"Ew, gross," Alison said.

Sam noticed her for the first time. "Ah, the little one. What is she doing out of school?"

"I'm wondering that myself."

"I'm not little," Alison said, and stamped her foot so hard a display of Little Debbie snack cakes collapsed and tumbled to the floor. "In two years I'm getting my driver's license."

"We'll see about that," I said. "In the meantime, dear, pick up the goodies."

"Aw, do I have ta?"

"Yes, and please hurry. You don't have all day."

Sam winked at me. "If she's squashed any of them, Magdalena, you're going to have to pay."

"Gross again," Alison said, and scooped up the jelly-filled rolls. Arms full, and unable to deposit the treats neatly on the display stand, she dumped them into a tub containing cans of tuna fish packed in water.

"Not there," Sam said.

Alison scooped up a dozen or so of the packaged treats and dropped them on the floor again.

"Alison!"

"Mom, you said yourself that I ain't got all day."

"Well, no matter what, you have time to apologize to Sam."

"No need, Magdalena. I was a teenager myself once. Hormones make you clumsy."

"Were that it was merely an estrogen surge. Go on, Alison, tell Cousin Sam what you're really sorry for."

"He ain't my cousin, Mom." It was the first time my stepdaughter had purposely tried to distance herself from me by playing the genetics card. Frankly, that hurt.

"Actually, he is your cousin. Your father and Sam are first cousins on his mother's side, and double second cousins once removed on his father's side. Add that all up, remove the 'removed,' and the two of you are brother and sister."

Sam laughed. "Something like that, I'm sure. Go on, little lady, tell me what it is you have to apologize for."

"Like I said, I ain't little."

"Alison!"

Sam put up a restraining hand. "That's all right, Magdalena. She's right; she's not a child." He smiled at Alison. "I'm sorry I called you that."

"Yeah, whatever."

"What are *you* sorry for?"

Alison hung her head and mumbled something that sounded like "If this is Belgium, I'll have pajamas for breakfast."

Sam cupped both ears. "Couldn't quite catch that."

"I'm sorry I stole a bunch of stuff from your store."

I've known Sam his entire life—he's six months younger than I—but I've never seen him so angry. Even when his wife, Dorothy, spent ten thousand dollars on a face-lift (a botched one, at that) and didn't tell him until after he'd opened the bill, he hadn't looked this upset.

"You stole from my store?"

"Yeah, but it was only cigarettes and sausages—dumb stuff like that. It wasn't, like, anything important."

"How many packages of cigarettes?"

"I dunno."

"A million?"

"No—sheesh! It was more like—uh—a carton."

Sam scribbled on a scrap of yellow paper. "That's over a hundred dollars' worth. Did you know that's a felony?"

"Uh—no. Is that, like, something really bad?"

"If I press charges—"

"Which you won't," I said, and showed Sam my teeth. It was the closest thing to a smile I could manage just then.

"The heck I won't!"

"Hey," Alison cried, "I'm gonna pay ya back."

"You're darn tootin'. But that's just for starters. Stealing cigarettes one day, and cars the next. That's how these things go."

"I won't steal any cars! I promise."

"The only way to make sure you don't steal my car someday is to have you shipped back to Minnesota from whence you came."

"I didn't whence anything; I only stole."

"Samuel Nevin Yoder," I roared, "how dare you threaten this child with repatriation?"

Alison's eyes widened with horror. "That ain't the death penalty, is it?"

"Absolutely not—well, for some it may be. For you it just means going home." I glared at Sam. "If you want trouble, Sam, that's what you're going to get. Just don't say I didn't warn you."

"Magdalena, didn't your mother—my aunt, may she rest in peace—teach you that you can catch more flies with honey than you can with vinegar?"

"She tried, but I never did see the point of catching flies."

Sam refused to crack a smile. "It's your call, Magdalena."

"All right. What kind of honey did you have in mind?"

"Our thirtieth high school reunion is coming up. I want you to go as my date."

"At the risk of sounded like a broken record—you're married."

"It's a reunion party, Magdalena, not an invitation to a drive-in movie. Dorothy won't mind. She already said she refused to go. In fact, she even suggested I take you."

"In a pig's ear." Although she had no reason to be, Dorothy Yoder is intensely jealous of yours truly. I'm sure it's because Sam talks about me too much. I mean, she has nothing to worry about. Her papa is rich—he bought the store for Sam—and she is basically an attractive woman. So what if, thanks to an incompetent surgeon, her nose slants across her face, her lips resemble a lightning bolt, and one bosom is so much higher than the other that water spilled on her chest runs sideways instead of down?

Sam picked up the phone, but his lecherous eyes were on me. "So it's the police, is it?"

I sighed so hard that my breath rustled the pages of a feed calendar on the wall behind Sam. "Okay, but you don't press charges, and you don't get to choose my outfit for the party" (Sam dresses Dorothy.) And you promise not to breathe one word of this to Gabriel."

Sam's grin is sure to be replicated by the Devil when he welcomes sinners to Hell. "I promise."

"Hey, wait a minute," Alison said. "I just thought of a deal-breaker."

"Not now, dear," I said. The precious child was looking out for me.

"But Mom, this guy—I mean, Mr. Yoder, Cousin Sam, whatever—might be a murderer. That should count for something."

I'd told Alison the basics about the Felicia Bacchustelli case. She'd have heard about it at school, anyway, given that in Hernia gossip travels faster than the speed of sound. I had not, however, said anything that would implicate Sam Yoder.

"Don't be ridiculous, dear. Sam isn't even on my list of suspects."

"Why not? He's got a motive, don't he?"

"He does?" The Bible *does* say that "a little child will lead them." It doesn't say where, and of course Alison is no longer little, but what do a few details matter when interpreting scripture? Context should take a backseat to cause, if you ask me.

"Think about it, Mom. This winery thing—who would it have hurt the most? Yeah, you, because ya own a high-priced inn. But who else?"

"The community, of course. Most folks here are very much against spirits of any kind."

"Ghosts too? Wow. But I'm talking about a business. The guys at Miller's Feed Store, they don't really give a hoot, because them rich wine drinkers that come to town ain't gonna buy no rakes and shovels, and the people who buy them now ain't gonna go nowhere else. So ya see, it don't make no difference to them."

"I see your point—so far. Go on."

"But everyone's gotta eat, right? And that's what Mr. Yoder mostly sells—food. Of course there's the other stuff; Mr. Yoder sells just about *everything*, if you know what I mean."

"I think she means welcome mats for Mr. Monthly Visitor," I said helpfully to Sam.

My translation, however, seemed to go over Alison's head. "Whatever. Anyhow, I heard that the winery was going to have a fancy restaurant. And ya can be sure that people would go there to eat out, on account it's the only game in town. No offense, Mom, but the PennDutch don't sell food to people who ain't guests."

"No offense taken, dear—except perhaps at your atrocious grammar."

"It ain't that bad. Anyway, where was I? Oh yeah, so everyone starts to eat out at the winery—maybe they call it Wine and Dine"—she giggled—"and that means they buy less groceries here. Even if they just go their for birthdays, or whatever, that would still be a lot of food they don't buy here.

"So ya see, Mom, it makes sense for Mr. Yoder to kill that winery woman. If she's dead, then maybe the brother-in-law will move away, and maybe the winery won't even be built. That means no restaurant, so everybody still buys their food here, and Mr. Yoder keeps on being rich like he is now."

I glanced at Sam, who seemed none too happy with this theory. "I guess you have a point, dear."

"No, she doesn't!"

"Who knows, I might even like to try the Wine and Dine—just for the dine, of course. The wine would be sin."

"Magdalena, don't be an idiot. About a third of my customers are Amish. They wouldn't go anywhere near an upscale place like that."

"What about the other two thirds? Most of those people do their primary shopping in Bedford. Even Oprah couldn't afford your prices on a regular basis. They use you for convenience. Let's say Jane Doe starts to bake a cake only to discover she's out of baking powder. Rather than run all the way into Bedford, she pays twice as much to buy it here. But then let's say there's another option: she can take the family to dinner, they can have cake for dessert, and no one has to wash the dishes. How sweet is that?"

Alison beamed. "Ya see, Mom?"

"Indeed I do."

Sam squirmed. "I dipped your pigtails in the inkwell, Magdalena. Okay, so maybe we no longer had inkwells back then, but I swear I cut one off."

"That you did. Is this supposed to help your case?"

"I don't have a case. *My* point is that you've known me my entire life. And yes, I'm a lecherous old geezer who doesn't deserve a wife as sweet and kind as Dorothy, but that doesn't make me a murderer. Come on, Magdalena. You more than anyone have got to know what's really in my heart."

"I lost my loupe. Without it, it's hard to focus on something that tiny. But I will agree that my gut feeling—at the moment—is that you're not a cold-blooded killer. You have cold blood, yes. You're just not the killer. Still, Alison has made a good case for you being on the suspect list. Sorry, dear, but I'm going to keep you on it."

My relative with the relative morals glowered at his pseudo-cousin once removed. "I'll waive payment for what she stole."

"You hear that, Mom? I don't have to pay!"

"Oh yes, you do."

"But why? Didn't ya hear what he said?"

"He's trying to buy a favor, dear. What he doesn't seem to understand is, a woman who has everything can't be bought."

She stamped her foot. At the rear of the store, an unstable pile of something crashed to the floor.

"Ya don't own me, Mom. Ya know that?"

"Yes," I said quietly.

"In fact, I don't even want ya to be my mom anymore. Go ahead and call my *real* mom and dad in Minnesota. See if I care!" She started crying, which made her even more angry—at herself.

"Now look what you've done," Sam said.

18

I slammed my checkbook on the counter and scribbled furiously. "Here's a thousand dollars. I'm sure that's more than enough to pay for what she stole. Use the rest of the money to take Dorothy out to dinner. Or buy her something nice. The Good Lord knows you owe her."

As much as our greedy grocer wanted to buy immunity from my investigation, his fingers wanted the money more. They crept across the counter like a strange hairy crab and snatched the check away while I was still signing my name. As a consequence, the R in Yoder is now permanently scrawled across his wooden countertop.

"Mom," Alison wailed, "ya ain't gonna make me pay back a thousand dollars, are ya?"

I snapped my pocketbook shut. "He's going to send me a proper bill. You'll pay me back whatever it is you owe him."

Alison sniffed loudly. I chose to interpret it as a perverse teenage way of expressing gratitude.

"Just remember, Sam," I said, "the law is generally more lenient on those who voluntarily confess their crimes."

I turned and strode away before he could respond. Alison, bless her heart, was right at my heels. The girl's a quick thinker. Having lost the first round in the battle to escape reparations, she'd already switched to "butter up Mom" mode.

Most of the way to the high school Alison praised my driving skills. When I didn't respond to this transparent tactic, she started in on complimenting my appearance. I am ashamed to say that I suddenly found myself on the slippery slopes of Mount Vanity.

"Ya know, you ain't nearly as old looking as most of my friends' mothers."

"I'm not?"

"Nah. I seen much worse. Corgi Wilson's mother has this wobbly thing under her chin."

"A wattle?"

"Yeah, and ya don't got that on account of ya don't got much chin. How lucky is that?"

"Indeed."

"And Deirdre Hockcomber's mom dyes her own hair, and it's really fake looking near the ends because it's so dark. But ya don't dye your hair, 'cause ya don't have to. They say mousy hair like yours is the last to turn gray. How about that?"

I turned right into the semicircular drive in front of the school. "You say the sweetest things, dear. But you're still going to have to pay me back."

"Man! No fair."

I bit my tongue while I found a parking place and was reasonably behaved while I marched Alison into the principal's office. I will admit to becoming slightly perturbed, however, when Mrs. Proschel, the school's new secretary, informed me that Principal Middledorf was home with the flu.

"The flu," I echoed. "Didn't he get a shot?"

"There wasn't enough serum to go around. It was in the news—I even saw it on TV."

"I don't watch TV. Besides, Herman's the principal of a school, for crying out loud. He's at high risk."

"To get sick, yes, but not to die. It's a matter of priorities."

"Priorities? You'd think the government would see to it that we had enough flu vaccine to keep high school principals from getting sick."

"Miss Yoder, I think you'll find that a majority of Americans support our country and the right of Halliburton to use American blood to safeguard its oil contracts."

"What?"

"It's called patriotism, Miss Yoder. The right to die for the American way of life. If we must force democracy on the rest of the world, so be it. Those people will thank us someday, don't you worry. Just as soon as they get essential services back, the letters of gratitude will start pouring in. In the meantime, the world is safe from weapons of mass destruction that could, and did, hit parts of Tel Aviv during the first Gulf War."

"Excuse me?"

"Have you considered moving to France, Miss Yoder?"

"Mrs. Proschel, I am as patriotic as you are— Did you say France? Well, I did take two years of French in high school, and I'm very fond of French fries. Oh, and would that mean I can stop shaving my legs?"

"Yuck," Alison said.

"You're not in the least bit funny, Miss Yoder. Thousands of Americans have given their lives so that we can worship the right God and have barbecues in our backyards without having to worry about our values being subverted by pagans. I must say I am surprised at your irreverence, you being one of the strict types of Mennonites."

"There is more than one God?" As soon as those words came out of my mouth, I was overcome by shame. Of course there is only one God, and that's the one in the Holy Bible. Still, the question has nagged at me from time to time. If there are no other Gods except for mine, how can mine be the *right* one? And if there aren't others, why does the Good Book bother to mention them?

"Miss Yoder, how dare you commit sacrilege in a public school?"

"I didn't mean to be sacrilegious," I wailed. "It's just that inquiring minds wanted to know."

"This is a Christian country, Miss Yoder. Comments like yours erode the spiritual fabric of this great land."

"But it wasn't always a Christian country. Freedom of religion was very important to the Founding Fathers, some of whom were Unitarian."

"Yes, they were," Alison said. "I learned about that for a book report."

Mrs. Proschel was livid. "You, Miss Miller, are truant."

"No, I ain't. I'm here."

"You may as well be; it's the end of fourth period. In fact, I'm going to mark you absent for the entire day."

Alison beamed. "So I get to go home?"

"You most certainly do not," I said. "Now run along, dear, and let me have a word with Mrs. Proschel."

Alison was more than happy to obey. Before the cantankerous new secretary could open her mouth, my pseudo-daughter had fled the office and disappeared among a throng of students who were just now changing classes. Alas, my reactions were not so swift.

"Miss Yoder!" the woman barked. "I am not through with you."

"Excuse me?"

"No doubt you think you're clever, cracking jokes all the time like you do. But you're not. It is high time that people like you face the truth: we are living in a new era. We have a mandate from the people to restore Christian principles across America and especially in the schools. That's how we build good citizens, Miss Yoder—with pliant minds that can be trained to walk the straight and narrow path. Put God back into school where He belongs, and this country finally has a chance again."

I patted my prayer cap in case Mrs. Proschel hadn't noticed that I'm a seasoned hiker on that straight and narrow path. "What about children who are Jewish or Muslim or even Buddhist? Where do they fit in the new era?"

"I am pleased to say, Miss Yoder, that the Hernia school system is one hundred percent Christian—if one includes those three Catholic girls that moved into that new house on the end of Hesper Street."

"We have a Muslim family living here now. I'm sure they'll have children some day."

My antagonist pursed her lips, as if consuming a particularly sour grapefruit. "Those people have no business being here. Our forefathers certainly never had them in mind. This country has enough trouble with the blacks without adding those swarthy Middle Easterners to the mix."

"Swarthy? Not that it makes a difference, but the Rashids have skin as light as yours."

Her dark eyes flashed. "My mother was Italian—from Sicily. That's different."

"Oh. Do you enjoy your job, Mrs. Proschel?"

"Certainly. Mr. Middledorf says I've taken to this job like a duck to water."

"Excellent. Then you shouldn't have any trouble finding another position."

"I beg your pardon?"

"You have two weeks' notice, Mrs. Proschel—starting today."

"Miss Yoder, what on earth are you talking about?"

"Your new job. You see, dear, I just fired you from this one."

Her mouth opened and closed like that of a baby bird demanding food. When no victuals were forthcoming, she began speaking.

"Y-y-you can't do that!"

"Of course I can. I just did, didn't I?"

"I don't work for you, Miss Yoder; I work for Principal Middledorf."

"*Did*. One phone call from me, and Herman will give you the ax himself. Do you prefer that?"

"You're not even on the Board of Education, Miss Yoder—are you?"

"No, but I am by far the wealthiest—some would say the most powerful—woman in town. It comes with certain privileges."

The dirty truth is that I once caught Herman Middledorf viewing a pornographic Web site on the computer in his office. Even though I promised never to divulge this secret—with the agreement that he straighten up his act—the man has a backbone slightly firmer than Jell-O and I felt certain he would be putty in my hands if I even hinted to go public with this juicy tidbit. The plain truth, however, is that I firmly believed that four out of five board members would be horrified to learn there was a bigot of Mrs. Proschel's ilk working for the school system. To be honest, the fifth member— and Gloria Reiger's identity is none of your business—was a bit iffy. Her uncle Mordecai was mugged by a gang of thugs while on a world tour. The assault happened in Oslo, and ever since the woman has harbored an unnatural hatred of Norwegians.

The light slowly dawned in Mrs. Proschel's brown eyes. "This is a perfect example of how far this country has fallen," she said vehemently. "There was a time when being white and Christian meant something."

"Shut up, dear," I said kindly, and took my leave.

"Someone's going to pay for this," she shouted at my retreating back. "You're not getting away with this, you know."

"Ooh, man, she sounds really ticked," I heard a student say. I'm pretty sure it was Alison.

I was ticked as well. It is a fact that anger begets anger. What follows therefore is an explanation—not an excuse—for what happened next.

No sooner did I pull out onto the highway and get up to speed then I encountered the world's slowest driver. Theopolda Livingood is so old she played with God as a child—His childhood, not hers. She is also so short she must sit on a stack of Pittsburgh phone books just to see over the dashboard of her car. Occasionally those tricky books slip out from beneath her, forcing Theopolda to steer by leaping up every now and then in order to see the road. Eventually the old dear grows weary from leaping and resorts to steering from memory. I kid you not.

Newcomers to Hernia have been known to call the police in alarm, claiming that there is either a runaway car or a very small child on the loose. A few less inhibited souls claim to have seen a ghost. Several drunks have been cured of booze by encountering Theopolda's seemingly empty car tooling about town.

Since Theopolda must expend all her energy just to peer through the windshield, checking her rearview mirror is simply not an option. As a consequence the centenarian is oblivious to the traffic behind her. She takes the entire road as her due and wanders back and forth across the lanes in bewildered abandonment. Every now and then she toots the horn for the sheer joy of it. Sometimes by mistake she slams on the emergency brake, which, come to think of it, would explain the slipping phone books.

At any rate, it is impossible to drive around Theopolda. As a result, the woman is Hernia's ongoing lesson in patience, a lesson most of us habitually fail. Even the Amish (women included) have been known to pull out their whiskers when trapped behind the happy wanderer.

Having no fuzz in need of extraction, I turned off onto the nearest side road, even though it wasn't the direct way to my destination: home. Thus it was without any planning—and certainly no malice aforethought—that I found myself passing by Zelda Root's house. Except for strained greetings upon chance encounters, my "new" sister and I had not spoken since the great revelation.

While I prefer to fret and stew about upcoming unpleasant situations, there is something to be said for impromptu problem solving: mainly that one doesn't have the time to get nervous. Not that I'm afraid of Zelda, mind you, but the acquisition of a sibling in middle age is, well, unnerving. The second I saw her house I made the decision to stop *and* to approach the visit as a dispassionate, but not uncaring, observer.

Now that my hitherto unbeknownst sibling was no longer employed by the Hernia police department, she was virtually without transportation. I'd recently heard that the rattletrap she'd driven since high school was as reliable as a weather report, which meant that it sat idle in her carport most of the time. It was there now.

Zelda didn't answer her doorbell, which was not a surprise. The fact that the door was locked was indeed unexpected—not to mention a mite dangerous. In Hernia unlocked doors permit neighbors to run in and turn off stoves or smoldering lamps without having to bother to look for the key. Fortunately, Zelda followed the practice of 88.8 percent of all Americans and hid it under the mat. (That figure, by the way, is made up, as are 64.7 percent of all statistics.)

Zelda's kitchen door is closer to her driveway than is her front door. It is the only one folks use, including Zelda. Always one to respect the privacy of others, I opened it a crack to make my presence known. "Zelda, dear," I called softly, "are you in?"

There was no answer, so I stepped in. Never the best of housekeepers, Zelda was nonetheless a biological Mennonite and thus incapable of sloth. It was, therefore, immediately obvious that something was dreadfully wrong. The sink was piled so high with dirty dishes that they spilled over onto the surrounding counters and even the floor. The refrigerator was standing open, empty except for an impressive collection of fungus species. The trash can was stuffed with frozen pizza boxes and emitting a smell rather like that of a dead sloth—I haven't smelled a whole lot of them, mind you—thereby negating my Mennonite gene theory.

"Zelda?" I called loudly this time. "Zelda!"

Still no answer. I steeled myself for what might well be a horrific discovery. I'd read about folks being found in advanced states of decomposition. Perhaps it wasn't the garbage can that was so offensive. Don't ask me why, but in looking back at it now, it never even occurred to me to call Chief Hornsby-Anderson. I did, however, grab a broom that was propped against the pantry door.

Just when I thought I had it together enough to proceed, I heard the strangest sounds coming from the general direction of Zelda's bedroom. When, a few seconds later, I identified the weird noise, my blood ran cold.

19

I couldn't believe my ears. The woman was still doing it! Melvin Stoltzfus had been arrested for murder—the murder of a Mennonite pastor, for crying out loud—and Zelda was still worshipping him. I mean that literally.

Zelda Root had long been in love with my erstwhile nemesis—our former Chief of Police—even though the maniacal mantis was married to my other sister, Susannah. Somewhere along the line Zelda stopped putting her boss on a pedestal and plunked him on an altar in her bedroom closet. Well, not him exactly, but bits of his hair and nail clippings, which she keeps in an urn. The altar—a long, narrow table covered with a white linen cloth—also supports a life-size photograph of Melvin's misshapen head and a pair of candles.

All this I discovered by accident one day, while searching the house on another murder case. Of course I was shocked to the tips of my stocking-clad toes, but I was absolutely stunned when I soon learned that Zelda's obsession with Melvin Stoltzfus had evolved into a religious cult.

Somehow an overzealous Zelda had convinced sixteen other human beings that the object of her devotion was divine. This was before Melvin's arrest and incarceration. When word of this bizarre religion became national news, as a result of his arrest, membership skyrocketed. Thousands of letters and calls poured in from around the country—although mostly from the blue states—overwhelming the faith's founder and the sixteen original disciples. In fact, Lance Imhoff, our mailman, refused to deliver all the sacks of mail to

Zelda's house, citing a bad back as the reason. Lance goes to my church so I know better: the man is simply afraid of what he calls "dealing with the Devil."

"O Holy Melvin," I heard Zelda chanting, "thy virtues are endless, thy promises sustain us in these, our darkest hours. O Great and Holy Melvin, send me a sign of thy favor. Assure us, your faithful followers, that thou rememberest us still."

I strode into the small bedroom where the blasphemy was taking place. Zelda was on her knees with her buttocks in the air and her head supported on cupped hands. In front of her on the homemade altar a dozen candles burned. The Noxema jar containing Melvin's bodily detritus was covered with a purple velvet cloth. Across it lay a single long-stemmed white rose.

Zelda seemed unaware of my presence. I would be lying if I said that I struggled with my conscience for more than a few seconds. A gal has to have fun, right? Besides, it was all horse pucky, and the sooner Zelda realized it, the better.

"Fear not, Zelda Root!" I said, speaking in as deep a voice as possible. "I rememberest thou still. How can I forget that prodigious makeup?"

"Oh Melvin," Zelda squealed in ecstasy, "thou dost answer me."

"Indeedost I doodost." Yes, I was being cruel, and not that it's anyone's business, but I have since repented. "Now, back to the subject of thy face paint. Dost thou not think it is too much?"

"Is it? I mean, is that what thou dost think?"

"Well, thou dost apply with it with a bricklayer's trowel. In fact, there are rumors that Jimmy Hoffa is alive and well beneath that glop."

"Really? Funny, that's what Magdalena Yoder always says—" Zelda's buttocks lowered as her head came up and then turned slowly in my direction. "It *is* you!" She struggled to her feet, not an easy task considering she was wearing cork-heeled espadrilles worthy of a streetwalker. "Get out of my house. Now!"

"I was only having fun, Zelda. Besides—"

"Blasphemous, that's what you are. I'm not going to listen to your excuses this time, Magdalena. If you're not gone by the time I count to three, I'm going to call the—well, I'll just throw you out myself."

"Your own sister?"

"Excuse me?"

"Your own flesh and blood?"

"Magdalena, as usual, you're not making a lick of sense. Have you been tippling again?"

"Both of those times were by accident," I wailed.

"Then you're just nuts."

"Then you're the pot."

She teetered backward, as if actually afraid of me. "Case in point, Magdalena."

"As in the pot calling the kettle black. It's you who qualifies for the loony bin. But never fear, big sister's here. I'll pick up the tab, on condition you attend all your therapy sessions. I know, a lot of psychiatrists have Gummy Bears for brains, but we'll find you a good one. The we, of course, being your other sister and I. Susannah doesn't have two nickels to rub together, but I'm sure she's an expert on quacks. At any rate, not to worry; your sisters will see you through."

"Magdalena, please step back. You're making me very nervous."

"*Moi?*"

"I don't have a sister. You know that. None of what you're saying makes any sense."

"I'm your sister."

"You see what I mean?"

"Zelda, I was planning to break this to you more gently, but you've left me no choice. So here goes: your mama and my papa were more than just friends. Thirty-five years later—that's right, isn't it?—voilà. You may call me sis, if you wish, but ix-nay on Mags. That's still reserved for Susannah—and Gabe. I trust you understand."

"Not a word. Would it help if I understood French?" Alas, she was being serious.

I sighed, unsure of how to make it any more clear. "Okay. Your mama had round heels and wore heathen underwear. My papa had lusty loins and a wandering eye. Together they did the extramarital Macarena, and then nine months later you came along."

Zelda's eyes widened as the meaning of my words penetrated her makeup. "Are you saying what I think you're saying? That my mother and your father had an affair?"

"Bingo." I held my arms open wide to receive my sibling who had been denied to me since her birth. I am not a hugger by nature, but I was more than willing to make an exception for my half sister—provided it was brief, and she didn't leave makeup behind on my clean broadcloth dress.

Zelda advanced as fast as her silly shoes would allow, eager to clasp me to her enormous bosom. I closed my eyes, the better to endure the hug.

"Hug away!" I cried bravely.

What happened next was so shocking that I couldn't even begin to process it until I was home, sitting at my kitchen table with a bag of frozen peas pressed against the left side of my face.

"Ach," Freni said when she got a gander at my slugged mug. She was standing in the kitchen doorway holding a pair of freshly plucked chickens. Incidentally, I am frequently asked by guests if chickens feel any pain during plucking. The answer is no. At least not nearly as much as they do when we slaughter them—which always comes first.

"It's worse than it looks," I said. "My lip bled for ages. My nose too. I wouldn't be surprised if my cheekbone is broken."

Concern was written all over my elderly cousin's face. "You were in an accident, yah? With the car?"

"No. My sister took a swipe at me. Her fist seems to have connected remarkably well."

"Susannah did this?"

"My other sister—Zelda Root."

Freni plopped the hens in the sink and slipped off her heavy wool cape. "So, how long do you know?"

"*Excuse* me?"

"I tell your papa and mama both that a secret this big they cannot hide forever. So now I am right, but they are dead. Where is the satisfaction in this?"

"*What?*"

Freni frowned. "Maybe she hit you in the ear too? I said—"

"My ear is fine! I just can't believe what it's hearing. Freni, are you telling me that you've known about Zelda all along?"

She shrugged. "She was my friend, your mama. My cousin too.

We had no secrets. And your papa—well, he kept no secrets from your mama. So then one day your mama tells me that your papa and Zelda's mama made warm the quilt in August. I promised your mama that I would never tell anyone, and I have kept my promise."

Perhaps my hearing was affected after all. "What's this about a quilt in August?"

Beads of perspiration popped up on Freni's brow. "Ach. It means to make new sweat when the chores are done."

"Apparently, but I still don't know what it means."

My kinswoman was now bright red. "It means to make the hair *strubblich* when there is no wind."

Strubblich means "messy" in Pennsylvania Dutch. Suddenly it was clear to me.

"They went swimming?"

Freni slapped a small but meaty palm to her forehead. "They do the honky-tonky."

"Ah! The horizontal hootchy-kootchy!"

"Yah, that's what I said."

The Bible—Mark 9:43-47—instructs us to lop off body parts that cause us to sin. It's a good thing most of ignore this verse; otherwise a fair number of male politicians would be singing soprano in their respective church choirs. If I took this verse literally I wouldn't have a face left. Still, I was tempted to cut off my ears with a paring knife, and not because they'd caused me to sin but because lately they'd been funneling unwanted information into my befuddled brain.

"I can't believe you've known this secret all these years and never told me."

"Your mama made me promise. I do not have the ship lips."

"I beg your pardon?"

"The loose ones that sink," Freni said, her patience wearing thin. "And you, Magdalena, who told you?"

"Doc Shafor."

"Ach! Who told him?"

"Papa."

"So then you told Zelda. Magdalena, why would you do such a thing?"

"Because Doc said she was really hurting and needed a big sister."

Freni plopped her squat but generous body into a chair. "Why does she hurt?"

"Because she is deeply in love with Melvin."

"Does Susannah know this?" she asked with remarkable calmness.

"Yes. But I don't think it bothers her. Susannah has always been sure of Melvin's love."

Freni shook her head. "Melvin's mama is my best friend, but still, I cannot understand why two women love that man."

"I'm with you there."

"But Doc Shafor is right, yah? It is your duty to love your sister. Even if she is Zelda."

"And even if she is idolatrous?" I clamped a hand over my miserable mug. I hadn't meant to go that far. There was no way Freni was going wrap her mind around the idea of a cult conducted from a closet in Zelda's spare bedroom. The poor woman still seemed surprised every time she flipped on a switch and a light came on.

"Ach, the Melvinites."

"You *know* about them?"

"Magdalena, I am Amish, but that does not mean I have noodles for brains. We pray for the Melvinites every day."

"But—but—"

"Yoder's Corner Market," she said, reading my mind, which might well be made of pasta, given its performance lately. "We hear all the gossip there. What we do not hear, the men tell us when they come back from the blacksmith shop."

I felt strangely betrayed. "I can't believe I didn't know you were aware of this. Why didn't you say anything to me? Why didn't you rant and rave?"

Freni shrugged.

"If I started my own religion, you'd be all over me like white on rice. Not that I would ever do so, mind you. I'm just saying 'if.' "

"I love Zelda because she is my neighbor—like the Bible says. But a crazy neighbor." She looked away. "You, I love like a daughter. A mama has a right to worry about her daughter."

Perhaps it was just the bruise on my cheek, but I felt like crying. Who knows, I might even have hauled my skinny keester off my chair long enough to hug Freni. Then, because we are both genetically programmed to eschew showing affection, we might well have self-destructed. Simultaneous spontaneous combustion, the fire marshal would declare it, after having poked through the ashes. For surely all that would have remained after such an intense conflagration would be Great-grandpa Hostetler's steel teeth (he sharpened them every Saturday, which was steak night) that I keep in the attic, and a fruitcake Cousin Alpharetta Augsberger gave me last Christmas. The latter has been regifted so many times that no one in the family is quite sure of its origins. One rumor has it that this dark, oblong object isn't even a fruitcake but a brick of some historical importance.

The story goes that during the American Revolution the item in question was hurled at our ancestor, Franklin Delano Yoder, by a patriot. Franklin, like many of the Amish, was a pacifist and thus viewed as a traitor by many of his neighbors. Even though Franklin was sorely tempted to toss the brick back at his tormenters, he slipped it into his saddlebag and rode off. "The brick stops here," he is purported to have said.

At any rate, before I could haul my patooty off my chair to hug Freni, the doorbell rang.

"I will answer it," Freni said quickly. She hopped to her feet and bustled off, leaving the door to the dining room swinging in her wake. I'm sure she was every bit as grateful as I was to escape the awkwardness of a full-frontal embrace.

I rearranged the bag of frozen peas while I waited for her return. Strangely enough, I wasn't angry at Zelda for attempting to alter my profile. But don't get me wrong: I was not about to offer her the other cheek. It's just that I understood where she was coming from. The Good Lord knows I was furious at Doc when he told me, and I might well have punched him had he been fifty years younger.

"Someone is here to see you," Freni said, bustling back into the room. She headed straight for the sink.

"Who?"

"English."

To the Amish, anyone not of their faith is English. By this method of reckoning a Buddhist American of Japanese descent qualifies as English, while an Englishwoman of the Amish faith—so far there aren't any that I know of—would not be considered English.

As a close relative and a conservative Mennonite, I am only quasi-English; it all depends on Freni's mood.

"Did you get a name?"

"No." She began scrubbing carrots that I knew for a fact had been washed previously.

I wasn't in the mood for Twenty Questions. Still wearing a bag of frozen veggies on my face, I went to see who it was.

20

Grape Parfait Pie

9-inch crumb crust (recipe below)
1 can (6 ounces) frozen Concord
    grape drink concentrate, thawed
    and undiluted
½ cup water
1 package (3 ounces) strawberry-
    flavored gelatin

1 pint softened vanilla ice cream
1 teaspoon grated orange peel
Sweetened whip cream
Candied violets

Heat Concord grape drink and water to boiling. Remove from heat and stir into gelatin; stir until dissolved. Gradually add ice cream, stirring until melted. Add orange peel. Chill until thickened, but not set (15 to 25 minutes). Spoon into prepared pie shell. Chill until firm. Garnish with whipped cream and candied violets.

Crumb Crust: Combine 1½ cups vanilla wafers, gingersnaps or graham crackers, ¼ cup sugar and ⅓ cup melted butter or margarine. Mix well. Using fork, press firmly against sides and bottom of 9-inch pie plate. Chill 30 minutes or bake at 375°F for 8 minutes and cool before filling.

MAKES 8 SERVINGS

21

"Well, I'll be dippty-doodled," I said to the unexpected visitor. "Come on in."

"Thank you," she started.

"Oh, a bruise!"

"It's nothing serious—just a little sisterly love. Pow! Right in the kisser."

"I do not understand."

"On more counts than one, dear. When I said I'd be happy to teach you to drive, I didn't mean today."

"Yes, yes, I understand this." Faya Rashid's eyes were darting around my snug little lobby as if it were the most interesting thing this side of the Museum of Bunions and Corns over in Harrisburg.

"The inn is an exact replica of the house my great-great-granddaddy Jacob 'the strong' Yoder built in the 1800s. The original blew down in a tornado a few years ago. Mercifully I was spared, although I did land facedown in a cow patty."

She nodded. "From McDonald's, yes?"

"Excuse me?"

"With the sesame seed bun."

"Not exactly. A cow patty is—well, we don't eat that part in America." I glanced over her head but could see no car in the gravel drive except for mine. "How did you get here, Mrs. Rashid?"

"I walk."

"Wow! That's a good five miles."

"I not walk all the way. I think maybe I am, but some nice Amish peoples, they give me a ride." She pronounced Amish as if it were "Aye-mish," which grates on my nerves so much I'm down to my last one.

"Well, that is very nice. May I take your coat?"

"Thank you."

It was a cloth coat, but I could tell by its heft that it had cost a pretty penny. I peeked at the label while hanging it and I was unable to recognize the brand name. That confirmed my suspicions.

Faya Rashid was altogether well turned out in a forest green skirt suit with pumps dyed to match. I know very little about gems, but enough to guess that the green stone in the pendant hanging from her neck was an emerald. If indeed Mrs. Rashid was finding Hernians slow to warm up to her, she might want to start by changing her wardrobe.

Any store that doesn't have "Mart" in the name is considered upscale by us locals. Natural versus man-made fabrics, we care not—although we're quick to seize an opportunity when we see one. When Clarence Girddlesmacker first saw polyester listed on a garment, he phoned the county agricultural agent to see where he could purchase polyester seed. The agent said he'd look around. "I got me a hundred acres I want to plant in polyester bushes," Clarence said to me at a church supper, his face shining with hope. I told him that if he had the patience to grow rayon trees, I'd be happy to give him the seeds for free. But Clarence changed his mind about farming and set off to seek his fortune in Washington, DC. Last I heard he was one of the president's advisers.

At any rate, I invited my elegant visitor to sit in the parlor, on the only comfortable chair. She looked around appreciatively, her gaze settling on a photo of a forebear in a simple wooden frame.

"Is that your father?" she asked. "His beard is very nice."

"It's actually my grandmother. She believed that if the Good Lord put it there, then there is where it should stay. Would you care for some hot chocolate?"

She smiled, revealing rows of pearly whites that would be the envy of any Hollywood starlet. "Yes. I like this American hot chocolate very much."

"Stay right there," I yelled as I boogied out of the room and back into the kitchen.

"Ach!"

Silly me. I should have known Freni would be standing in the doorway, her ear pressed flat against the lower panel. Thank heavens she's such a stocky woman. Anyone taller and lighter would have been thrown across the room. Freni, on the other hand, was like a stubborn doorjamb; I was just barely able to squeeze my way in.

"Sorry," I panted. "Now be a dear and make some hot chocolate for our guest. And serve one of your famous cinnamon rolls."

Freni rubbed the offended ear. "They are famous?"

"They're only the best in the world."

She beamed for second and then a cloud swept over her face. "What about her?"

"Her who?"

"That woman." The lack of a neck makes it hard to point with one's chin, but Freni did her best. "The Al Qaeda lady."

"*What?*"

"You think because I do not watch television, that I am ignorant of such things. But I read the newspaper, Magdalena. I know what is what."

"Mrs. Rashid isn't *what*, dear. She's a housewife from Lebanon—the same country, by the way, that provided cedar wood for King Solomon's temple."

"Like in the Bible?"

"You got it. I know she's Arab, not Jewish, but I bet she looks pretty much like Jesus's mother did."

"Yah?"

"So will you fix the cocoa?"

"Yah, I fix."

"Thanks. Oh, and if you must eavesdrop, open the door wide enough so you can see me coming. Or tuck the corner of a dishtowel through the crack."

Freni's face reddened. "I was not dropping the eaves, Magdalena. I was resting my head."

"Whatever." I patted one of her stubby arms affectionately. "Just bring the stuff out when it's ready."

She grunted her agreement and I sailed back to the salon. You can imagine my surprise when upon reentering this somewhat spartan space, I found it devoid of Middle Eastern women.

"Uh-oh." I dashed to the front door and peered through the peephole. There was no one on the porch or on the walk.

I returned to the parlor. What in a deviled egg was going on? Was I hallucinating? Was it time for me to hang up my brogans with gum on their soles?

As I stood there, flummoxed and contemplating the next stage of my life, the door that led from my private quarters opened, and out slipped Faya Rashid. She had her back to me as she closed the door carefully, lest it make a sound. When she saw me, she nearly jumped out of her designer pumps.

"Miss Yoder!"

"Mrs. Rashid. What on earth were you doing in my private quarters?"

"I—I—I had need to use the toilet."

"And did you?"

She nodded.

"You certainly were quick about it." Just how she had managed to reach the far end of my inner sanctum, line the toilet seat thoroughly with paper, do her business, wash her hands with soap and warm water for a minimum of thirty seconds, dry them properly, and return just after I did—well, all that was incomprehensible. A more brazen Magdalena would have demanded to inspect her hands, and pressed a tissue against the palms to absorb any remaining moisture. Alas, I am a timorous soul, which is probably why I will never amount to anything more than being a pseudo-sleuth.

"Miss Yoder, I hope I do not offend."

"Offend?"

"Perhaps it was not correct for me to use the toilet without permission."

"Don't be silly, dear. Did you leave a tip in the bowl?"

That gave her a start. "Tip?"

"Someone has to clean the bathroom, dear. That someone is me. I expect others to leave two dollars in the cut glass bowl on that little corner shelf above the sink."

She fumbled with the latch on her Gucci bag. Okay, maybe it wasn't Gucci, maybe it was Gnocchi. But I'm pretty sure it was Italian, and I'm ding-dong sure it was expensive.

"That's all right," I said, waving her back to her chair. "The first time is on the house. My cook will be bringing us the hot chocolate as soon as it's ready. In the meantime we can chat. Tell me again why it is you came all the way out here."

"There is something I did not say to you before when we talked."

"So spill it, dear. That means go ahead with your explanation."

"I came to bestow on you my gravest thanks."

"I beg your pardon?"

"My heartiest thanks, yes? The most sincere—from my soul."

"I'm sure you're very welcome, dear. But you thanked me back at your house."

"Yes, but then my husband called me to say that it was his wish that I should have the driving lessons. This I cannot believe at first, but he says, 'Yes, it is true.' He tells me that you go to the laundry mat and speak with him. He says that he has great respect for you, and this he wants for me as well. To be like you, yes?"

I patted my bun. How nice it is to be appreciated. Of course it wasn't the first time someone paid me a compliment. There was, for instance, that softball game in the 1970s when I caught a fly with my knees and advanced my team to the finals. Then in the late eighties I dug a woman's car out of a snowdrift (so I could have her parking space), and she said I was her guardian angel. The nineties were perhaps a bit slim. . . .

"Magdalena!"

I focused enough to see Freni standing in the doorway with a tray in her hands. Despite the distortion of her bottle thick glasses, I could tell that she was rolling her eyes wildly, fussing up a nonverbal storm.

"Freni, this is Faya Rashid. Faya, this is Mrs. Hostetler."

"Pleased to meet you," Faya Rashid said. She extended her right hand but withdrew it quickly when she realized Freni was unable to reciprocate.

"Hello," Freni said, and then thrust the tray at me.

I set the ebony tray with ivory accents on my sturdy, nononsense coffee table. The tray was a wedding gift to my parents from missionary friends of theirs. These friends had spent many years in what was then the Belgian Congo. I remember, as a little girl, listening to some of their tales: horrible, scary, and improbable stories of headhunters, and goat-swallowing pythons, and village chiefs whose wives were buried alive. I am pleased to say that all of this nonsense has been proven untrue by modern revisionist sociologists.

"Freni, dear, would you like to stay and have a cup as well?"

"Ach!"

"I'm afraid Mrs. Hostetler is a little shy," I said pleasantly to my guest.

"Ach!"

"It's a shame too, because she has the cutest stories to tell about her grandchildren. They're triplets, you know."

To her credit, Faya Rashid was nodding and smiling to beat the band. "Triplets—this means three, yes?"

"Three little angels," I said.

Freni beamed, her inner glow diffused as it was by a dusting of cake flour, giving her an ethereal look of her own. "Yah, they are very precious. Yesterday they help make the shnitz pies. '*Grossmutter*,' they say—that means grandmother in the dialect, yah? '*Grossmutter*, why must we peel first the apples?' So I say—"

The story was not only interminable but didn't seem to have a point. In many respects it reminded me of the dearly departed Reverend Schrock's sermons. Nevertheless, Faya Rashid nodded and giggled and oohed and aahed and went so far as to clap her dainty hands in apparent delight. Of course Freni drank in the attention as if it was mother's milk. At one point, my genetically impaired cousin put her stubby arm around Faya's slim shoulders. Frankly, that sickened me.

What kind of cousin, not to mention friend, is incapable of expressing herself physically to her own family but is a virtual slut with strangers? Well, I guess that answers my question. There certainly was no point in me hanging around. While I won't admit to pouting, I will confess to staying clear of Freni as much as possible the rest of the day.

22

I awoke the next morning refreshed and eager to grill the biggest weenie of them all. The fact that Ed Gingerich was old and a gentleman didn't mean he was innocent. Plenty of nice old men are killers. Okay, maybe they're not *so* nice, but you get my point.

After staying with me a few days, a very distraught Ed moved in with the Zooks, then the Mullets, then the Speichers, and last I heard the Litwillers. Belinda Litwiller is the world's worst living cook (a dubious honor previously held by Lizzie Mast), so it was quite possible Ed had already moved on, ahead of the gossip chain. Needless to say, I was pleased to find him still ensconced at the Litwillers, bundled up in a quilt and sitting in a rocker in front of a roaring fire.

"He doesn't say much," Belinda said, leading me to her guest. Thank heavens she hadn't noticed my fading bruise. "His lawyer calls every now and then—his stockbroker too. He talks then, but that's about it. Doesn't eat much either. Say, would you like something to eat? There's loads of stuff left over from lunch."

"No, thanks."

"You sure? John always used to say there's nothing quite like my cream of pigs' feet."

"I'm sure he did, dear."

"I used to serve it directly over toast, but now John wants it on the side. Except that he barely touches it that way. Says he's on a diet. I tell you, Magdalena, dieting is an unnatural activity. The Good Lord is going to punish us someday if we don't stop turning up our noses at food. Maybe send us a phantom."

"Excuse me?"

"A phantom—you know, when people starve."

"I thought that's what you said. Well, not to worry; I don't think there's a ghost of a chance that would happen. Oh, hi, Ed!"

Ed Gingerich was smiling, clearly happy to see me. This doesn't happen as often as one might think.

"Hi, Magdalena. What brings you out in the cold?"

"Just popped in to see how you're getting along. Is Belinda feeding you enough?"

"More than I care to eat."

"Are you sure I can't get you something, Magdalena?" Belinda couldn't be a more considerate hostess.

"Quite sure."

"I've got a nice pot of hog wart tea brewing."

"Pardon me?"

"Mama taught me how to make it. First you find a hog with lots of warts—"

"Truly, I'm fine. Belinda, I really need to talk to Ed alone."

"Say no more," she said, and like a considerate hostess, she made herself like hens' teeth—that is to say, scarce.

"Are you really all right, Ed?"

"I'm fine. Well, to be truthful, I could eat a horse. Just not if she cooked it. Say, is there any chance I could come back and stay with you again? Freni's biscuits are so light, you have to hold them down in order to butter them."

I settled into a nearby armchair. "Well, Ed, I'm actually glad you brought that up. I've been meaning to ask you a question, and now is the perfect time."

"Shoot." His eyes glittered behind the wireless lenses.

"You now have thirteen million dollars, Ed. Why aren't you staying in a hotel over in Bedford? In fact, why haven't you *bought* a hotel in Bedford?"

Ed took so long to answer I felt the need to run over and dust him. I resisted the Amish-Mennonite curse (if you see it, clean it) and amused myself by staring at the clutter on the mantel behind him. There was the usual assortment of framed photographs, but I found these particularly endearing. The Litwiller kids had all been through my Sunday school class and were as sweet as angels on sugar drips, but—and I say this with a charitable Christian heart—they defined the word "homely." And because I possess this charitable Christian heart, I won't go into any details. Suffice it to say the sons looked like long-necked rabbits that had recently undergone electroshock therapy, and the daughters, lacking necks, wore their heart-shaped pendants around their chins. Frankly, I was proud of the Litwillers for being proud of their children.

It was the knickknacks surrounding the family photos I found the most interesting. They included a ceramic castle of the kind normally found in fish tanks; a hornet's nest, still attached to a dead branch and propped against the wall; a bowling trophy inscribed to John Litwiller, Belinda's husband; a snowshoe with silk daisies woven through its mesh, also propped against the wall; and a plastic bust of ancient Egypt's renowned beauty, Queen Nefertiti. To my knowledge the Litwillers had never been abroad, much less to the Middle East.

"Sammy Litwiller won that bust at the country fair," Ed said, reading my mind. I had to give the man credit for being able to read small print from a distance. "He gave it to Belinda for her fortieth birthday, the only bright spot of her day. John and Belinda picked up the snowshoe on their honeymoon. They found it in an antique store on their way to a picnic. At the time Belinda wove real daises through the mesh. The silk ones you see now bring back memories. Like the hornet's nest does for their oldest son, Kyle. He was stung thirty-two times while—"

"I'm still waiting for an answer, Ed. Why are you mooching off of the generous folks in Hernia, when you should be living high on the hog with your *mucho* moola?"

"You sure do know how to turn a phrase, Magdalena."

"Compliment accepted. Now stop wasting my time."

"But you see, this is the reason. Discourse. My Fiona died forty years ago. I can't remember the last time I had a casual, extended conversation. But living with these families—it's been Heaven on earth for me. Even talking to you is balm for my soul."

Perhaps that's what my sister means whenever she tells me "you da balm." "I hope you're reimbursing these kind folks."

"Oh, I am. They're being well taken care of."

"Like you took care of me?" Ed hadn't even given me a wooden nickel.

"Don't you ever shake out your throw rugs, Magdalena?"

"Of course I do—occasionally."

"I left you a check under the large braided rag rug in your parlor."

"You *did*?"

"A considerable amount, I'd say."

"How considerable?" It is hard to disguise greed. After all, it is the strongest emotion in the world, propelling, as it does, most wars.

"Magdalena, haven't you heard? A gentleman never tells."

I couldn't believe my ears. "And a Mennonite farmer doesn't use innuendo, for crying out loud. That's a Presbyterian trait!"

Ed smiled. "I'm—I mean, I was a farmer, not an artifact. I think you'll find the sum I left you quite sufficient."

I stood. "In that case, thank you. It was a pleasure having you."

"You mean that?"

"Of course. For a man, you kept your room fairly tidy, and most important you chew with your mouth shut—sadly, a virtue not practiced by many these days."

Ed threw off his quilt and stood as well. He was dressed in an expensive ensemble of matching shoes, shirt, and pants. My knowledge of clothing labels does not extend beyond Haynes Her Way which, in the brief form, just barely qualifies as sturdy Christian underwear. I was never much interested in sewing, although I wield a pretty mean darning needle, therefore my modest Christian outerwear are all made by a local Amish woman. Now where was I? Oh yes, I may not be skilled at brand name recognition, but I know quality when I see it. Ed Gingerich's outfit cost a pretty penny.

"You look snazzy," I said.

He gave his outfit the once-over. "What? This? These are just some things I picked up in Pittsburgh on one of my many trips to see my lawyer."

"By the way, how is that going? Any chance of overturning the sale?"

"They're still looking into it. But so far it looks good. The Bacchustellis misrepresented themselves—there's no denying that. But these things take time."

"Why Pittsburgh? Aren't there any good lawyers in Bedford?"

"I'm sure there are. But for something this important, it made sense to bring in the best."

I nodded. "And by the best, you mean Sand, Hammerhead, and White, right?"

He nodded in turn. "Best of the best. Cream of the crop."

"Do they handle murder cases as well?"

"I'm sure I don't know. Is there something you're not telling me, Magdalena?"

"I guess you haven't heard. A woman was killed early yesterday morning, and it would appear that I am one of the suspects."

"You don't say!"

"Oh, but I do. This isn't the first time—or the second, for that matter—that it's happened, but believe me, it never gets any easier."

"I'm sorry to hear this. Who are you accused of killing?"

"Someone you knew very well—at least much better than I did."

"Peggy Roughgarden?"

"No. It's— Wait just one Mennonite minute. Why on earth would I want to kill Peggy Roughgarden?"

"After what she said about you at the covered dish dinner last month, I don't much blame you. Of course murder is a sin, so I didn't mean that literally—but still, what she said was really unforgivable. You know what I mean."

"I do? No, I don't. What did she say?"

"Well, it was really more how she said it. I'm sorry, Magdalena, I can see that I shouldn't have brought it up."

"Just give me a hint," I cried. "Please, pretty please, with a bow on top."

"I can't. It wouldn't be right."

Being a farm girl, born and bred, I knew there was no sense in beating a dead horse. But I also knew—thanks to my French guests—that a freshly dead horse can be turned into steaks or, at the very least, dog food and glue. I was far from through with the topic of Peggy Roughgarden.

"I respect your desire to protect my feelings, Ed. Unfortunately, I have no choice but to tell you what I came to say."

"Go ahead." He seemed resigned rather than curious.

"The murder I mentioned happened on your farm—your former farm. The body was discovered lying face up in a flooded and frozen foundation ditch. A footie, I believe it's called." I was playing ignorant in order to build up suspense.

"Footer."

"Are you sure? That doesn't sound right."

"Positive. Don't make me wait, Magdalena. Who was it?"

"Felicia Bacchustelli." I leaned forward, the better to observe any reaction.

Ed's face ran the expected gamut of emotions: surprise, disbelief, shock, even anger.

"You don't think I did it, do you?"

"I didn't say I did."

"Who would want to kill Felicia?"

"I would—but I wouldn't. I mean that it appears that I have a motive, but I don't. Do you know what I mean?"

"I'm not sure I do."

"Well, it's this whole competition thing. No doubt some folks will think that I killed Mrs. Bacchustelli because I was afraid that Grape Expectations would take business away from me—which it wouldn't, because my guests are a totally different crowd."

Ed licked lips that were as dry and cracked as hen's feet. "What would my motive be?"

23

"Revenge. The Bacchustellis lured you into betraying the community for thirty pieces of silver. Metaphorically speaking. In real life you lucked into more moola than an old coot like you could ever spend. But it cost you the respect of the community. The only way to regain that is if Grape Expectations pulls up stakes and moves out of here. But what if they don't? I spoke with Vinny Bacchustelli yesterday—helped him pick out a casket—but he didn't say anything about leaving. Frankly, I don't think he's the type to back out of anything. Even when it involves the death of his sister-in-law."

To my consternation Ed wiped a tear from his cheek. "Have you already tried and found me guilty, Magdalena?"

"By no means! Ed, I'm sorry. I really am. You put me on the defensive, and I guess I sort of overreacted."

Ed rubbed his other cheek with the back of a speckled hand. "It's all right. I figure this makes me a member of a very elite group."

"Excuse me?"

He smiled wanly. "A Magdalena Yoder apology—there can't be too many recipients of that. Am I right?"

I am quite capable of giving tit for tat. "Did you want the medal, dear, or will the certificate be enough?"

I'm sure Ed would have volleyed a clever retort had not Belinda burst into the room carrying a tray loaded with comestibles. Although dismayed, I made a move to help her.

"Magdalena, now you sit right back down and have some breakfast. You too, Ed." She shoved aside some magazines, placed the tray on the coffee table, and began pointing at the various items.

"Found out I was low on hog wart tea, so I made you each a nice cup of hot Colgate."

"I beg your pardon?"

"You take two tablespoons of toothpaste—mint works best—three teaspoons of sugar, a pinch of cinnamon, boiling water, of course, and—"

"I'm allergic to cinnamon."

"Me too," Ed said, not missing a beat.

Poor Belinda was crestfallen, but she did her best to assume a hostess smile.

"I've got flax seed muffins, grapefruit squares, and if you want something a little hardier, there's pickled herring with peanut butter wraparounds. I make the flat bread myself with oat bran. John and I have the lowest cholesterol scores our doctor has ever seen."

"You really shouldn't have gone to all this bother," I said. "I really have to be going. But Ed here was just saying how much he craved one of your wraparounds."

"Really? Because I've never made them for him before."

"Then he's in for a treat."

Ed treated me to a look that undoubtedly curdled every drop of milk for miles around. If offered coffee I would have to drink it black—or not at all.

I chose the latter. "Belinda, you've been the hostess with the mostest, but I really ought to be running."

Her face fell. "But you can't. The main course will be ready in about twenty minutes. You can smell it now, in fact."

I twitched my sniffer. One of the advantages of having a nose this large is that I am usually the first, in any given group of people, to smell something. Apparently not this time, because Belinda was right. The heavenly aroma of an herb-roasted chicken was not only detectable but nearly overpowering. How could I have missed it? But still—who on earth, besides Belinda, serves a multi-course breakfast?

"What is the main course?" Ed asked.

"Texas chicken."

"Really?" I said. "Are Texas chickens any different than their Pennsylvania counterparts?"

Belinda smiled at my ignorance. "It's armadillo, Magdalena. The finest ones come from someplace called Longview, Texas. They ship them packed in dry ice. I usually order a dozen at a time. The company includes a booklet of recipes, but I've only ever tried one. You serve it in its own shell, garnished with acorns. First you grind up the meaty parts—"

"Gag me with a spoon," I said, borrowing from my sister's colorful Presbyterian vocabulary.

Poor Belinda appeared stunned by my callous comment. It behooved me to repent immediately.

"Sorry, dear, if that sounded harsh. What I meant was that— well, does one eat them with a spoon?"

"Exactly." Her eyes shone with renewed excitement. "Magdalena, you've eaten armadillo on the half shell before, haven't you?"

I licked my lips, which is not the same as lying. "Alas, no time for delicacies today," I cried, and scooted my scrawny patooty out the front door without further ado.

I had a question knocking about in my smallish brainpan, somewhere beneath my prayer cap, a question for the brutish chauffeur, Otto. But I had yet to eat, and a hungry investigator is a crabby investigator and likely to elicit anger rather than information. Therefore I had a moral imperative to stop by the Sausage Barn and load up on pacifying pancakes and assuaging sausages.

Although the days were getting longer, and the shadows getting shorter, this morning was cast in a panoply of grays. Driving up Highway 96 was not the pleasure it usually was. The mountains appeared low and gaunt, their bare trees like the claws of dead, upturned ravens. The new Mozart CD I'd been anxious to play was disappointingly funereal. All this is to explain my state of mind when I saw the tall figure draped in flowing black robes and shuffling along the edge of the road.

"Oh, Lord," I gasped, "must you take me now?"

The Good Lord, as usual, took His own sweet time to answer. In the meantime I slowed so that I was driving alongside the figure in black. I even lowered my window an inch, lest I be required to make conversation with the ghoulish stranger. One must always appear dignified, especially in death. It would indeed be in bad form to race down the highway with the Grim Reaper loping along behind in mad pursuit. Such a sight was certain to scare small children and put the hens off laying.

"Lord," I begged, "can we please get this over as soon as possible? I'm not very fond of pain, as you well know. And please see that my family is cared for. Both Gabe and Alison come across as a lot stronger than they really are. As for Freni, I'm the daughter she never had. She's going to take it really hard."

"What about your sister?" the Reaper rasped.

"Susannah?"

"Do you have another?"

I stopped the car. The Reaper stopped as well.

"Actually," I said, "I do have another sister. And I have a feeling she might be a mite relieved if I were to say good-bye to this cruel world—one less sticky relationship with which to deal. But as for Susannah, I don't think my passing will affect her one iota."

"What makes you say that?"

The raspy voice sounded familiar. Perhaps I'd been premature in my assessment. Could it possibly be . . . ? No. Susannah swaddles herself in colorful wispy chiffons. She wouldn't be caught dead—no pun intended—in black rags. And a hood? I don't think so. My baby sister refused to wear a veil at both her marriages on the grounds they messed up her hair too much.

"I asked you a question," the Grim Reaper said. He—it *is* a he, isn't it?—tapped a long narrow foot clad in a plain black lace-up shoe.

Holy guacamole! Nobody has feet as narrow as Susannah's. Realizing that it was my sister, I lowered the window all the way.

"Susannah! What on earth are you doing in that getup?"

"I'm in mourning, Mags. Or haven't you figured that out?"

"Mourning for whom?"

"My Melkins, of course."

"Hop in," I ordered.

She wasted no time. In fact, I've never seen her move that fast, unless it was at a fabric sale at Material Girl.

Immediately I regretted my own haste. My sister smelled like a farmer who'd been baling hay all day.

"Uh, be a dear, will you, and sit in the back."

"Mags!"

"All right, but keep your window down." I pressed the pedal to the metal. "What's this all about, Susannah?"

"I told you. I'm in mourning for my sweetykins. I'm not going to shower, brush my teeth, or even wear makeup for thirty days."

I jiggled a pinkie in my right ear, just to make sure it was in working order. "Did you say 'no makeup?' "

"Look at me, Sis."

I glanced at her face, which was turned toward me. It wasn't my fault I lost control of the wheel, and my side mirror dinged Catherine Beiler's mailbox. I hadn't seen my sister's naked face since she was eighteen and theoretically free of our mother's strictures. I'd totally forgotten that without war paint she was the spitting image of Granny Yoder.

"I know," she said, "it's really awful, isn't it?"

"Catherine Beiler will never notice. Last year someone stuck a plastic sunflower in her petunia bed. It's stayed there for six months. But if my car's been damaged— Never mind. Susannah, what were you doing walking along the highway like that?"

"Because I no longer get to use the cruiser, and my old clunker is officially now a junker. It wouldn't even start this morning. I couldn't get anyone to give me a ride."

"Where are you headed?"

"Bedford County jail."

"But that's twelve miles away. Probably more, since it's on the other side of the city."

"I was hoping someone would give me a ride—and you did. Mags, you wouldn't believe how rude people can be. Honking their horns, shouting really nasty things. You'd think I killed someone."

"Reality check, Susannah. You're dressed like the Grim Reaper. Besides, your sweetykins *did* kill someone. He murdered a pastor, for crying out loud."

"Mags, he hasn't been tried yet. He's innocent until proven guilty."

"But he confessed! Plus which, he tried to kill me as well. Where's your loyalty, Susannah?"

"Don't you see? I *am* being loyal. I promised to cherish and love him until death did us part—which it hasn't done yet."

"Tell that to Reverend Schrock's wife. Death departed her husband, and she loved and cherished him so much that she went around the bend when he was murdered by your husband."

"Mags, I'm not going to take this. Stop the car. I want to get out."

"Too bad, dear. I have to go to Bedford anyway. Besides, I have something really important I need to talk to you about."

"Save it, Sis. I don't want to talk about how you and the Babester can't agree on who officiates at your wedding. At least you have a choice. My hunky-dunky doesn't get any choices now."

Hunky? How deluded can love make one? The only hunky thing about Melvin Stoltzfus was the hunk of coal he had for a heart. And shouldn't that be chunky, not hunky? And what, pray tell, does dunky mean? Unless, she meant to say donkey—ew! Papa used to own a pair of donkeys: Matilda and Herman. He got them as payment for a year's worth of fresh milk from another farmer who'd fallen on hard times. Although Matilda was a bit stubborn, she was extremely gentle. Especially with children. I remember Papa leading her around the barnyard, me on her back. I must have been four. Herman, on the other hand, was as mean-tempered as a summer day is long. He was also in possession of a considerable male attribute that led this four-year-old to ask questions my very flustered papa wouldn't answer. The thought of my spindly brother-in-law being similarly endowed was enough to make me want to poke out my mind's eye.

"This has nothing to do with Gabe, dear. This is earth-shattering news that involves you."

That did it. "Me?"

"Yup."

The bundle of black rags bounced in expectation. "Spill it, Sis. You know how I hate surprises."

"Indeed, I do. That's why I'm going to wait until I have a tummy full of flapjacks."

"The Sausage Barn?"

"Do you know any other place where one can live as dangerously and not break any laws?"

She giggled. "Fat's where it's at, right, Mags?"

"It's good to hear you laugh, Susannah."

My baby sister grabbed the rearview mirror and turned it toward herself. "Do I really look so bad, Mags?"

"Like death warmed over. In fact, I thought you—"

"Don't look now, Mags, but there's someone following us."

24

I snatched control of the mirror away from her. Susannah, whose first smile occurred when observing her own reflection, snatched it back.

"I said don't look now."

"Then why do you get to look? Never mind. Who is it?"

"How do I know? It's just somebody in a car. I can't see their face."

"How do you know they're following us?"

"Because when you stopped to pick me up, this same car was behind you—way behind you. But it stopped too."

I grabbed the mirror again. "That could just be a coincidence. Maybe the driver stopped to change a CD. That is the safe way to do it, you know."

Susannah rolled her eyes. She has the ability to roll them so far back the irises disappear. The effect now, given her macabre hood, was bone-chilling.

"Oh, Mags, you're usually the one to jump to conclusions, but sometimes you miss things that are as plain as that nose on your face. I bet you wouldn't see a tiger if it jumped out of the bushes and bit you. Believe me, that guy's tailing us."

I eased back on the accelerator. The vehicle behind us appeared to slow as well. I then stomped on the brakes. So did our follower—and by then I was convinced that my sister was right. Well, the Good Lord didn't give me big feet just for standing. I gripped the wheel tightly as I pressed the pedal so far into the metal it nearly disappeared into the floorboard.

Highway 96 has more twists than a Slinky. We sailed around some, screeched through others, and it wouldn't be much of a stretch to say that our tires connected with asphalt only half of the time. All the while my sister emitted high-pitched noises, the likes of which I haven't heard since my honeymoon with my pseudo-husband, Aaron Miller.

About a quarter mile before the Sausage Barn I made a flying right turn onto Applegate Lane. Very few folks other than the ones who live along this road are aware of its existence. That's because the entrance to Applegate Lane is all but obscured by a pair of enormous rhododendrons that billow over the roadway and are trimmed only when the few residents of this back road have difficulty entering the highway. Susannah, much to my disappointment, was not only familiar with Applegate Lane but whooped with delight.

"Wahoo! You go, Mags!"

I braked as quickly as was possible. A second later I could hear the car following us roar by.

"We've lost them," I said. "At least for now."

"I tell you, Mags, I didn't think you had it in you."

"I'm full of surprises, dear. Apparently, so are you. How did you know about this place?"

"How did you?"

"This is still inside—although just barely—the town limits, thanks to our land-grabbing ancestors who set the boundaries two hundred years ago. When I was on the planning commission, we had to approve the houses built out here. Now you answer me."

"My Mellykins and I used to make out here all the time. When we were dating, of course. After we got married, we made out in our home. We usually started on the couch, but then—"

"I get the picture. Please stop before I have to plunge my car keys into my ears."

"Sis, you never did like Melvin, did you?"

"Never."

"Not one teeny-weeny bit?"

"Not even one molecule."

"Why?"

What was there left to say that I hadn't said a million times over the years? Susannah already knew—or at least she'd been told—that

I found the mantis repulsive in every conceivable way. Perhaps what irritated me the most about the man was his arrogance. In his mind he was always right; everybody else was wrong. Never mind that an eel skin purse has more brain power than the miserable mantis. Here, after all, is a man who once tried to milk a bull and who regularly sent his favorite aunt in Scranton packages of ice cream by UPS. I know, this must sound harsh and not at all Christian, but believe me, my description has been charitable to the extreme.

"Why?" I repeated.

"You heard me." Susannah glowered at me from beneath her hood. I never thought the day would come when I thought she looked better in makeup than without. The only way out of this conversation was to derail it.

"Don't you want your surprise?"

Her face—what I could see of it—softened. "Of course I want it."

"Then let's am-scray," I said, and saw that we covered the distance from Applegate Lane to the Sausage Barn in record time.

Wanda Hemphopple was her usual disagreeable self. "Back so soon?" she snarled.

"You know the mantra, dear. Fat's where it's at. I just can't stay away."

"Who's your friend?"

"Su—"

"Suzie Reaper," Susannah said in an unnaturally high voice.

Wanda cocked her head. "You been here before?"

"No."

"That right?" Wanda clamped my arm with talons of steel and yanked me away from Susannah.

"What on earth!" I protested.

"Shhh!" The woman with a life-threatening hairdo dragged me outside before continuing. "Magdalena, I know you and I don't see eye to eye on most things—"

"Try again, dear. Mine is the eye of a needle, yours is the eye of a hurricane."

"Whatever. Look, I'll give you dinner tonight free if you'll take that street person somewhere else for breakfast."

"She's not a street—"

"Dinner free for the rest of the week."

"Beverages included?"

"Absolutely."

"Lunches too?"

"Okay. Now, go in and get her?"

"What about breakfast?"

"Oh, why not. Now hurry!"

"I don't think so. I can afford to buy my own meals, thank you."

"But you led me to believe—I mean, you said—"

I jerked free from her grip, but she has the tenacity, if not the looks, of a bulldog. The talons just dug new holes in my arm.

"I'm not playing games here, Magdalena. I can't have that person in there now."

"That person?"

"Your friend. Miss Reaper. You have got to take her someplace else. Please? *Please*?"

"What gives? And you better tell me the truth."

Wanda sighed so hard and long that a patch of ice at our feet began to melt. "All right. It's the Board of Health. Apparently there's been some kind of complaint—I can't imagine what—and those fools have decided to pay me a surprise visit. You know how it is."

"All their visits are surprises, dear. That's how the system works."

"Yes, but—never mind. My point is that your guest, while I'm sure she is the nicest person, looks a bit—uh—unsanitary."

"Unsavory, perhaps, but not unsanitary. I assure you that Ms. Reaper is scrupulous about washing her hands." That I knew for a fact.

"You may be right, but—"

"Speaking of butts, I need to set mine down. I noticed that booth seventeen was empty, so I'll just show myself to it." I wrenched away a second time and threw myself against the door. "Ta, ta, and no need to thank me."

Although Susannah was tapping her foot impatiently, she was still standing by the cashier stand. You can be sure, however, that every diner in the place had his or her eyes glued on the messenger of death. Mrs. Wattlebaum, who has been pushing the century mark for a ridiculous number of years, appeared especially terrified. The poor dear is afraid to reveal her true age lest Willard Scott wish her a happy birthday on television. Mrs. Wattlebaum read somewhere that the centenarians Willard acknowledges all die within a decade.

"Sis," Susannah hissed, "what are these people staring at?"

"Death warmed over." I grabbed her by bell-shaped sleeve and dragged her back to booth seventeen. I may be skinny, but Susannah is a smoker and weighs as much as a tumble weed.

"What did Wanda want, Mags?"

"It's nothing. But just in case she hassles us— Why, Wanda, dear! Did you follow me just to take our order?"

"That's right. Knowing you, Magdalena, I'm surprised you didn't head straight for the kitchen, just to get me in trouble." She whipped out a pad and a pencil so short it was running out of periods. "What'll it be?"

"My usual."

Wanda nodded, her eyes shifting to Susannah.

"She'll have my unusual," I said.

"Your what?"

"The opposite of my usual: eggs runny, pancakes burned, and bacon so crisp it shatters just by looking at it."

Wanda scribbled a notation. "Don't leave this booth," she whispered, and then threatened me by lowering her head and waggling her beehive practically in my face.

"Sis," Susannah said when she was gone, "you remembered how I like my food!"

"You've been married, Susannah, not out of the country. Now take a deep breath—one of those yoga things you're always yapping about—because what I'm going to tell you will knock your socks off."

"I haven't worn socks since the eleventh grade. Besides, you don't wear socks with sandals."

"Is that a fact? I'm sure I wouldn't know, seeing as how I wear sturdy brogans, like the Good Lord intended."

"Which aren't in the least bit sexy."

"Sexy shoes, indeed. Don't even get me started—oops, too late. Take high heels, for instance. They make your feet hurt, so you take them off, and then, since you're already half-undressed, you take everything off, and that leads to the horizontal hootchy-kootchy, which leads to unmarried mothers, which leads to undisciplined children, which leads to crime. If you boil all that down you're left with the simple equation: high heels lead to murder. If you ask me, any shoe with a heel higher than an inch should be outlawed. Now, where was I?"

"You're about to knock my low-heeled sandals off."

"Right. Susannah, there's no way to sugarcoat this. So here it is: Zelda Root is your half sister."

My sister stared at me for an interminable length of time. Then her eyes began to twinkle, and the corners of her mouth turned up.

"You finally did it, Mags. You had the humor transplant I told you about."

"What?"

"It was only a joke, Sis. But somehow you actually found a doctor who could do it. Did it hurt? Better yet, how much did it cost?"

"I'm not joking! She really is your half sister. If you don't believe me, just ask Doc Shafor. Better yet, ask Zelda."

"Now you're going too far, Sis. Jokes are funnier when they're short."

"I'm not joking."

"Come on, give me a break."

"Papa was a two-timing adulterer, for crying out loud!"

It isn't my fault that I was blessed with a pair of lungs capable of seeing me to the top of Everest without an oxygen tank. Every adult in the restaurant looked our way, including Marlene Mandelbrot, who wears a permanent neck brace. She was going to have some explaining to do to her insurance company.

"Mags, I can't believe you'd say such a horrid thing about Papa. If you're going to make something up, make it up about Mama."

"Mama?"

"She was always looking sideways at Mrs. Bumblegrass, my high school guidance counselor. I swear, Mags, I used to wonder if the two of them weren't up to something."

I gasped, so great was my shock. "Mama was a virgin!"

"Right, and I'm the pope."

"Wrong color robes. Look, Susannah, leave Mama out of this. And I am not making this up. Papa really did have an affair with Zelda's mother. That means she's our half sister. Like it, or not, we've got another sibling."

The transformation that my sister's face underwent was both startling and fascinating. I've met Jim Carrey—he once stayed at the PennDutch—but he couldn't hold a candle to my Susannah's rubbery mug. First amusement, then disbelief, followed by doubt, then finally horror as the truth I'd spoken permeated her very core.

"Oh my gosh!" she shrieked, raised both hands, and slammed her fists into her chest.

The truth is, my sister did not use the word "gosh." I won't repeat the word she said, because I'm sure you know what I mean. Much more interesting is the fact that her chest exploded, and something black, hairy, and evil burst forth into the light.

25

Lavender Frappe

1 can (8 ounces) frozen Concord
   grape juice concentrate, thawed
   and undiluted
1 can (6 ounces) frozen apple juice
   concentrate, thawed and
   undiluted

3 cups water
¼ cup lemon juice

In bowl or pitcher, combine all ingredients and blend thoroughly.
Pour into freezer container and freeze until mushy. Beat with a fork
and return to freezer. Freeze until firm. Scoop into glasses to serve.

MAKES 8 SERVINGS

26

Shnookums, my sister's wretched excuse for a dog, stood blinking for a few seconds in the middle of the table. No one knows for sure which breed he is, seeing as how Susannah adopted him from a "high-kill" shelter. I've always maintained that he was half bite and half sphincter muscle. A charitable veterinarian once postulated that the pitiful pooch might be half teacup Chihuahua and half Yorkshire terrier. Whatever his bloodlines, he's one hundred percent terror. Never did such a spiteful, ill-tempered creature walk the face of this earth—not that he's ever had to do that, mind you.

Susannah, like myself, is flatter than wallboard. There's plenty of room for the mangy mongrel to ride around in her bra, and that's exactly what he does. Except for lunging at folks, his wickedly barbed jaws snapping, the poor excuse for a rat never has to move. I'm not exactly sure how my sister attends to the needs of his sphincter half, and I'm not eager to find out.

At the risk of eliciting sympathy on his behalf, I must report that the curmudgeonly canine was yelping piteously, having just been pummeled by his owner's fist. You can be sure that our table was still the center of everyone's attention.

My poor sister, bless her heart, was beside herself with anguish. "My baby! My precious Shnooky-wooky. What have I done?"

Shnookums responded by throwing back his head and howling like a dog a hundred times his size. I dare say he sounded almost as loud as a beagle.

"Lester, it's a singing rat," an enormously fat woman said, gasping between words. She tried to squeeze free from her booth, but the table in between her and freedom had other ideas. Her children, already quite chubby, sobbed as her elfin husband tried in vain to pull her loose. Judging by her weight and his antics, I took them to be tourists from Ohio.

"Baby, look at Mama," my sister ordered her odiferous offspring.

The odious creature would not obey. His snout pointed to the ceiling, Shnookums was far too busy vocalizing to hear his mistress's voice. What then was a loving sister—like *moi*—to do?

"Shut up, you miserable excuse for a dog," I said, not uncharitably. To ensure I got his attention, I clapped my hands with some force.

Apparently I clapped too hard. How was I to know? At any rate, the miniature mutt not only ceased howling, he took off like a rocket propelled missile, streaking across tables and leaping over the backs of seats with all the agility of a cat. Although I'm quite sure that cats and dogs cannot interbreed—it's undoubtedly illegal in several states—the possibility of this happening, however small, might be worth investigating. That might explain some of the weird behavior the beast has engaged in over the years.

Alas, with no coaching from me, Shnookums headed straight for Lester's wife. The poor woman shrieked, as did her jam-covered children, which only served to excite Shnookums all the more. The last I saw of my honorary nephew was his sphincter disappearing through the swinging doors that led to the kitchen. The distant clatter of pots and pans, as well as muffled oaths, confirmed that his presence had been noted by the cook and quite possibly by the health inspectors.

Susannah, who had, up until now, been all but immobilized by shock and concern, sprang suddenly to life. She would have made a mad dash after him, but I gallantly blocked her. I made her sit and followed suit.

"Let him be for now. They'll realize soon enough that he's at least part dog. They might even give him a bone. You need to sit back down and process what I just said: Zelda Root is our sister."

Poor Susannah looked as white as the mold on the tomatoes she keeps in her vegetable bin.

"Mags, are you a hundred percent sure?"

"I'm afraid so. Doc Shafor got it straight from the horse's mouth—in this case *mouths*. Papa and Mrs. Root went to see him about an abortion, but he refused. Would it help, Susannah, if you talked to him? Maybe there are questions you'd like to ask."

"But he's a creepy old man. I mean, isn't he always putting the moves on you?"

"Well, yes—but he's an exceptionally good cook. And I'd be happy to go with you."

"I'll think about it, Sis." She was silent for a moment. "Is Zelda younger or older than me?"

"Technically that would be 'I,' as in 'than I am.' But never one to split hairs—"

"Mags!"

"The truth is, I don't really know. We'll have to ask her."

"I hope she's younger. I always hated being the baby."

"You know, Susannah, it might be fun having another sister. We could have sleepovers, make popcorn and s'mores, go swimming in Miller's Pond late at night—not skinny-dipping, of course, although we could wear skimpy Presbyterian underwear. We could even rent a video. I wouldn't mind watching one, as long as there was no swearing, no violence, and everyone stayed properly clothed as the Lord intended."

I stopped enumerating the good times that lay ahead, not because I'd run out of fun things to do, but because a shadow had fallen across our table. I looked up to Wanda's do swaying menacingly close to the genuine faux Tiffany light fixture.

"Well, I hope you're happy!" She was clearly anything but.

"Excuse me? We're having a family discussion here."

"You're going to have to take it somewhere else."

"We haven't even gotten our food yet."

"There isn't going to be any food."

"You can't deny us service—that's discrimination."

"Yeah," Susannah chimed in, "that's discrimination against an old-fashioned Mennonite woman and a poor widder woman. We can sue."

Wanda looked like she would sooner crumple than argue. I braced myself to catch her should she fall. If my spindly arms couldn't support her weight, maybe I could at least prevent the lethal beehive from hitting the floor.

"They're closing me down," she said, her voice barely more than a whisper.

"Who?" I said. "The Board of Health?"

"I was in the kitchen when that awful beast"—her chin pointed at Susannah—"burst through the door. I tried to convince them it wasn't a rat, but they didn't believe me. They said that even if it is a dog, that's against health regulations. They said they're going to shut me down." The mighty Wanda began to whimper.

I like my foes to be stalwart, able to give tit for tat. When the fight goes out of them, it goes out of me. Sometimes even, as much as I struggle against it, a latent maternal instinct kicks in, and I come to the aid of my former combatant.

"We'll just see about them shutting you down." Having yet to consume a bite, I slid easily from the booth, maneuvered carefully around Wanda and her teetering tower, squeezed past the billowy Buckeye tourist (who'd been finally pulled free by her elfin husband), and trotted to the kitchen. Susannah, who is always up to a good show, skipped along behind. She was, of course, eager to get back her bosom buddy.

"Well, well," I said, giving the two inspectors the once-over, "look who we have here." There was no need for a twice-over, because I knew both men very well. Albert had been a classmate of mine from kindergarten through high school, and Patrick I'd once hired to do odd jobs on the farm before I converted it to an inn.

"Magdalena," Albert said in acknowledgment. It was not the first time my name had been used as a swear word.

Patrick looked startled to see me. "What are you doing here, Miss Yoder?"

"I came to retrieve my sister's dog."

"I don't see a dog," Albert said. "I do, however, see a rat."

"Don't be silly, dear. Rats are much bigger than that."

"I'm still writing it up as a rat."

The cooks, recent immigrants from China, spoke nary a word of English and appeared quite unperturbed by the commotion. (The waitresses, by the way, convey their orders by circling pictures of the various dishes.) In fact, they seemed much more interested in

Shnookums. Lee, the head cook, had one eye on the mutt and another on a pot of similar size.

"Don't even think about it," I said, and waggled a finger in warning. "Susannah," I continued, "get Shnookums and then leave, will you please?"

"But Sis—"

I would have repeated my request, but Wanda was already in the doorway, her anxious face trained on me. A good show, like a tree falling in the forest, must have an audience to be fully appreciated.

"Very well, stay." I turned back to Albert, who appeared to be the one in charge. "Does the Board of Health know about your record, dear?"

His face colored. "Excuse me?"

"Car theft, wasn't it? No, it was armed robbery. How silly of me—it was both! You stole Jenny Bonecutter's mom's car and knocked off a 7-Eleven in Bedford. If I remember right, your haul was less than twenty dollars."

"Dude," Patrick said, "is she telling the truth?"

"Forsooth, the dudette doth tell the truth, Patrick. We lost the homecoming game on account of our star quarterback was behind bars."

Albert was not amused. "I was a minor, Magdalena. My record's been expunged."

"Ah, so it has. Which brings me back to my original question: did you tell the Board of Health?"

"That ain't none of your business. Besides, it don't change nothing. Patrick here can write Wanda up, even if I get canned."

"Now see what you did?" Wanda wailed.

"Never fear, Wanda dear," I said through gritted teeth. So much for the thanks we get for trying to help others. "Patrick won't be writing up anything. Unless, of course, he wants the whole world to know what I caught him doing in my barn one fine day."

Patrick had flame red hair, which clashed horribly with the blotches of magenta that spread across his boyish cheeks. "I been thinking, Albert, and this here ain't no rat. It's gotta be some kind of dog. Look what it's trying to do to the dust mop."

We all looked. It wasn't a pretty picture. I'm sure that somewhere in the Bible it's listed as a sin.

"And anyway, this kitchen ain't really that bad. Ain't nothing like Gerber's Grill, that's for sure."

"Yeah," Albert said, and stashed the clipboard under his arm. "We got ourselves a bigger fish to fry." He laughed loudly and poked Patrick with his elbow. "Grill—fry. Get it?"

"You're too witty by half," I said, and pointed to the door.

When they were gone Susannah grabbed her loathsome lothario and stuffed him down the front of her ghoulish garb. Meanwhile I stood guard over the kitchen until I heard the front door close behind the health inspectors. Then I turned my attention to Wanda.

"You don't need to thank me, dear. But a free meal now and then would be nice." I flashed her an impish, albeit somewhat gummy, smile.

"In a pig's ear!"

"I beg your pardon?"

"There wouldn't have been any trouble to begin with if your crazy sister hadn't brought that creature into my restaurant."

"I'm not crazy," Susannah said. "I'm eccentric."

"You have to be Southern to be eccentric. You, Mrs. Stoltzfus, are every bit as loony as a lake in Maine. Just like that killer husband of yours."

"How dare you!" I said, my hackles hiked. "No one gets away with attacking my flesh and blood—except for *moi*."

"What are you going to do, Magdalena? Kill me like you killed that woman from Grape Expectations? Is murder now your family pastime?"

Wanda's taunts were too much. And after all I had just done for her! Sometimes a gal can get pushed too far, even a good Christian woman like myself.

"It was me," I said.

"What was you?"

27

"I'm the one who put that hot dog in your beehive."

Wanda turned the color of raw bratwurst. "*What* did you say?"

"I slipped the weenie down your bun."

The restaurateur had to brace herself on the edge of the sink to keep from falling. I can't say as I blame her. I'd done a truly horrible thing; perhaps the worst thing I've ever done. Even worse than inadvertently marrying a bigamist.

It was the same homecoming game Patrick had spent behind bars. I was sitting in the bleachers, directly behind but a tier higher than Wanda. She'd always been mean to me, hanging out as she did with Mary Jane Yocum, my chief tormentor. In those days every girl, not just Wanda, wore her hair in an elaborate beehive held together with tons of bobby pins and gallons of hair spray. But Wanda's beehive was by far the largest and most elaborate.

My date that evening was Oscar Mayer. For the record, I had every intention of minding my own business, but even before I had a chance to sit down—hot dog and cola in hand—the girls started in with their jokes about yours truly. Wanda was the loudest. My revenge was both delicious and served up warm. When everyone's attention was focused on the opening kickoff, I slipped my wiener from its bun and poked it down a hole I'd observed in the top of my tormentor's hive. The astonishing thing was that no one noticed.

For days Wanda paraded up and down the halls of Hernia High with a decaying meat by-product in her hair. The smell in our homeroom grew rank, but this was a school after all, and one filled with adolescent boys. Not to mention Yoder with the Odor. It was only when flies, not bees, began to buzz around Wanda's hive that Mr. Pruett, our physics teacher, sent her to the nurse. Later, word got out that when the nurse extracted what was left of poor Oscar, Wanda became hysterical, convinced that it was her brain that had been removed. (Lest one feel too sorry for Wanda Hemphopple—née Hormelheimer—she was the schoolyard bully who sat on other girls' lunches and wrote wicked things about them with her lipstick on the toilet stalls.) Her IQ plummeted, along with her self-confidence. Alas, this wonderful improvement was short-lived. When Mrs. Bumblegrass, the guidance counselor, finally persuaded Wanda that the gray matter she'd lost was merely a hot dog and not her brain, Wanda instantly reverted to her obnoxious self.

"It was *you*?" Wanda said, her voice trembling.

" 'Twas I. But I'll have you know, I've already paid for it. I can still recall how hungry I was that night, because said weenie took my last nickel."

"Wow, Sis," Susannah said. "I never knew you could be so cool. You've got to admit, Wanda, that what Mags did took a lot of nerve."

Wanda raised her hand as if to strike me but instead patted my back. "Your sister is right; I've got to hand it to you, Magdalena. You're one in a million. Nobody else had the nerve to stand up to me in those days."

"Nobody else had a death wish."

"Too true. What surprises me is that you still have it."

"I do? Oh—yeah. You must be referring to the bacon I dropped in there a few minutes ago."

"Bacon?" Wanda bent over and swatted at her elaborate do. Sure enough, after a few seconds it fell out, along with a key, a pencil eraser, a small bottle of antibacterial cleaner, a wad of gum, a phone card, three pennies, and a nickel.

"Magdalena, you're going to pay for this!"

"I'm only responsible for the bacon. But hey, you better check out that nickel. It's an Indian Head. It could be worth a pretty penny, unlike those pennies that are pretty common—you know what I mean."

"I know that if you don't leave these premises by the time I count to ten, I'm going to wring that scrawny neck of yours and then have you arrested for trespassing."

Relieved of any vestigial guilt and admired by my sister, I felt lighter than air. Thus I had no problem sailing out of the Sausage Barn with my dignity intact. Susannah, her pooch restored safely to her bosom, swished happily along behind me like a three-dimensional shadow. Our meal, alas, was left behind at the Sausage Barn.

I told Susannah that I *might* take her to see Melvin, if she accompanied me on my errands. Given that the woman was unemployed and the love of her life was behind bars, she had no excuse not to go with me. I only had two rules—no smoking in my car, and four-legged creatures should be neither seen nor heard.

We drove in amiable silence the rest of the way into Bedford. Either luck was with me or my guardian angel woke up from her nap, because I found a parking spot just across the street from the Bacchustellis' condo.

"You going to wait here, or come with?" I said to Susannah.

"Is he cute?"

"Is who cute?"

"The man you're going to see?"

"His sister-in-law just died, for crying out loud!"

"I'm a widder woman. I can give him comfort." Her words were weighted, heavy enough to topple over on a soft mattress if given the chance.

"You are *not* a widow woman!"

"Jeez Louise, you don't have to get so bent out of shape."

"Susannah, you're my sister and I love you very much, but if anyone else made such an insensitive comment, I'd be all over them like crust on a pie."

"What if it was a pumpkin pie, and only had one crust?"

"Stop it!"

"Oh, I know what your problem is. You're having man troubles again."

"I most certainly am not—and what do you mean by 'again'?"

"Whenever you and that hunky doctor of yours fight, you get all prickly."

"You would too if you couldn't find anyone to perform the ceremony— I mean, I do not!"

"So that's it. A silly ceremony is all that's standing in the way of happily ever after?"

"I'd hardly call it silly. Do you know that he actually had the nerve to ask me to convert?"

"Cool."

"How can you say that? You know how I feel about being a Christian."

"Yeah, but I think it would be cool to have a Jewish sister. Moses had one. Jacob had a couple, didn't he? Heck, maybe even Jesus had one."

"It isn't going to happen, dear."

"And he isn't going to become a Christian either, is he?"

"Not a chance."

"Well, Sis, you can't have it all."

"Who says?" I wailed.

"You've got to stop wailing, Magdalena. Only sirens wail."

"That's not true at all. They don't call that wall in Jerusalem the Siren Wall."

"Whatever." I'm sure my sister didn't have a clue as to what I meant.

"Is happiness too much to ask?" It was, of course, a rhetorical question.

"For you, maybe. You're too picky, Mags. If happiness came along and sat right beside you, you'd tell it the seat was taken."

"I would not."

"You overanalyze, and you constantly moralize."

"I do not."

"You've got a hunky guy who's deeply in love with you, and yet you have to think of ways to complicate the situation."

"That isn't so."

"Oh, yeah? Then why don't you just live in sin?"

"Because it's wrong."

I got out of the car, and much to my surprise, Susannah did as well. Perhaps it was just my imagination, but it seemed like she needed my company. Even if she didn't, it was gratifying to know that she preferred me to my car's stereo.

"Who are we going to see?" she said, walking so close that had I stopped abruptly, we would have both fallen to the pavement like a pair of unsupported tent poles.

"Vinny Bacchustelli."

Susannah gasped and clutched at my coat sleeve, nearly taking me down. "He's the brother-in-law?"

"Yes. Do you know him?" Silly question. I'm not saying my sister is a tramp, but she knows every good-looking man in Bedford County—and come to think of it, half the homely ones as well.

"Nah. I'm still a married woman, Mags."

"Knock me over with a feather and call me Ima Jeanne. Since when did you stop looking at good-looking men?"

"Since I married Pooky Bear. Really, Mags, I'm not the hooch you think I am."

"The what?"

"The hooch—one of the fallen women, as you like to call them."

"Sorry." I said it without a lot of feeling, because my insensitive sibling had just referred to that miserable mantis of hers as Pooky Bear, a name I invented for my pseudo-husband, Aaron Miller. Sure, Aaron was the slime on the sludge on the ooze at the bottom of the pond, but my pet name for him evoked better times and therefore was—as much as a non-Christian thing can be—sacred.

"No need to be sorry," she said blithely. "I just wanted you to know that I've changed."

I must say her words were some comfort. If only she'd see the light and dump the cold-blooded killer she was married to.

Archibald Arms has got to be the most luxurious condominium complex west of the Susquehanna. The intertwined As on the outer door are genuine gold leaf, applied by a Greek monk who is an expert iconographer. There was even an article about Father Gregory in the paper.

The lobby floor and central staircase are marble and so highly polished that one gets the impression that they are perpetually wet. Women visitors, as well as bagpipe players, are advised to wear suitable undergarments.

The two-story chandelier (which a local wag dubbed "death on a chain") was assembled from a single casting of Belgian bronze and seven thousand Austrian crystals. The front of the building was constructed after the giant light fixture was in place. The first time the chandelier was turned on, Bedford experienced a three-hour blackout.

The doormen and -women wear red coats that come to their ankles and sport eighty-eight brass buttons apiece. In addition, they must each wear a black satin stovepipe hat and doff it every time they open the outer doors to greet a guest. The front doors, by the way, were carved from Indonesian teak and depict exotic tropical scenes. There are those who are certain they see a naked David Bowie cavorting about beneath the palms. One church even sued to have the doors sanded down. Alas, I have spent many hours studying said doors and can't see anything but skinny palm trunks.

Needless to say, the lobby—which is open to the public—has become something of a local attraction. On weekends folks come from as far away as Johnstown to frown at the doors before having them opened by hat-doffing red-coated yeomen.

Fortunately Tuesdays are slow days for tourists, and except for a couple from England, we had the lobby and its attendants to ourselves. As the others were leaving, I overheard the husband speaking loudly to his wife.

"I daresay," he dared to say, "that was even better than the changing of the guards back home."

She was quick to respond. "Yes, much better. We didn't have crowds of silly Americans to contend with."

I cleared my throat in order to get their attention. "With which," I said pleasantly.

The wife, who looked surprisingly familiar, was decked out in a massive flowered hat and white gloves. "I beg your pardon?" she chirped.

"Never end a sentence with a preposition. You should have said 'with which to contend.' "

The woman appeared unreasonably annoyed at my charitable explanation. "Philip, we simply must hurry back to our entourage."

"Of course, dear. But may I remind you it was your idea to shake off Scotland Yard for an hour so we could do some sightseeing on our own."

I gasped. "Now I know who you are! You're Her Majesty, the Queen of England, aren't you?"

"We are not amused," the petite woman said, and practically pulled her husband down the front steps and toward the street.

"We're not amused either," Susannah said. Despite some people's opinions of her, my sister has many fine qualities, and loyalty is one of them. Apparently, so is popularity.

Three doormen rushed to be at our service, each calling out my sister's name. In turn, Susannah gave each of them a movie star kiss. By that I mean she loudly kissed the airspace in front of both proffered cheeks, but didn't do any actual laying on of lips. But even this nonphysical demonstration of affection flew in the face of our genetic heritage, and so I can only assume it is something she learned during her brief stint as a Presbyterian.

"Whom do you wish to see today, Susannah?" The questioner wore a chapeau almost twice as tall as the other stovepipe hats, so I took him to be the head doorman.

"The usual, Derrick."

The *usual*?

Derrick, if that was indeed his name, stepped over to the nearest wall and pressed one of many buttons on a brass panel.

"Yes?" a male voice said.

Derrick mumbled something unintelligible and then smiled at Susannah. "You know the way," he said.

"What was that all about?" I demanded as soon as we stepped into the privacy of an elevator.

"You'll see."

"I want to know now."

Susannah rammed the penthouse button. "Are you impressed yet, Mags?"

"I still can't find a naked David Bowie— Wait just one potato-peeling minute! One of those palm trees *isn't* a palm tree. Am I right?"

"You're a hoot, Mags, you know that?"

"And a holler. But am I right?"

"I haven't a clue what you're talking about, Sis. What I meant was, are you impressed that all the doormen know me?"

"Well, now that you mention it—"

The elevator door opened, taking me by surprise; it opened directly on the penthouse. I must confess that I reared back like a mare startled by a snake in the road. Only it wasn't a serpent that I beheld.

28

I was gazing at paradise itself. Who knew that such luxury existed? I shall spare you most of the details, even the memory of which causes me to lust. Suffice it to say the carpet was so thick that having stepped on it, my feet disappeared from sight. Every hard surface that should have been wood was gold instead, and where simple Christian plaids would have sufficed, silk brocade and simmering satin had been put to sensuous use. When I looked up at the ceiling I saw clouds—painted clouds to be sure—but so high they might well have been the real thing.

"Nifty, isn't it," Susannah said, just calm as she could be.

"You've been here before?"

"Yup—well, I've been to the servants' wing. It's almost as nice."

"But—"

"Hello, Miss Yoder. Hello, Susannah."

Had I been alone, I might have jumped to the conclusion I was having a religious experience and it was the Good Lord speaking. I might even have concluded that I'd died and gone to Heaven and was now standing at His front door. Alas, the real Heaven—it pains me to say this—might not include Susannah. Although hopes for her salvation dimmed when she joined the Presbyterians, since leaving them she has surely been on the wide, fast track to the other place.

At any rate, since I wasn't alone, I merely jumped out of my left brogan. "Susannah, did you hear that?"

She giggled. "Of course."

"But I don't see anyone. Do you?"

"You're on a surveillance camera, Mags."

"I am?"

"Sure. You don't think someone this rich wouldn't have top-notch security, do you?"

"But this is rude. What if I'd been picking my nose when the door opened?"

"Don't be silly. There are cameras in the elevator too. Besides, Vinny could just as well have been standing in front of the door to meet you."

"In which case I'd politely look away," Mr. Bacchustelli said, appearing from nowhere.

At the risk of sounding easily startled, I feel obligated to reveal that the man's sudden appearance caused my right foot to leave its brogan. As the carpet pile totally hid my tootsies, I decided to worry about my shoes later.

"Mr. Bacchustelli," I said somewhat sharply, and then remembered that I was speaking to a bereaved man. Using a tone that was pleasant but still conveyed my disapproval of magic, I continued. "I trust that all the funeral arrangements have been made to your satisfaction."

"Yes, they have. Again, thanks for your help."

"It was my pleasure. Uh—you know what I mean."

"Miss Yoder, Susannah, would you care to come and have a seat?"

"Don't mind if I do," Susannah said, and then without further ado sailed off into one of the vast rooms that opened onto the equally vast sitting area. In her flowing black rags she looked for all the world like a witch without a broomstick.

"I can only stay a minute," I said. My eyes, I'm quite sure, betrayed me. How comfortable were those gilded couches piled high with silk pillows? Would I be allowed a close-up look at the coffee table, which was essentially a large, intricate carving protected by a glass top?

The grieving brother-in-law ushered me to the nearest couch, with which my bottom eagerly connected. It was indeed comfortable—especially when I arranged the pillows like so. As for the coffee table, I was dying to ask the price. Never had I seen such detailed carving. Even Blind Noah, who's been carving cuckoo clocks since he was a boy, is incapable of work that exquisite. Well, perhaps by now he might be, were he not missing three fingers and a thumb.

"Would you care for a drink, Miss Yoder?"

Mr. Bacchustelli was not only rich, but he could also read minds! I was, after all, quite parched.

"Don't mind if I do."

"Is it still cold out?"

"Very. It's going to be a three sheep night."

"I beg your pardon?"

"Oh, it's just an old saying around here. It means that it is so cold, you'd have to take three sheep to bed to keep you warm."

He chuckled. "Sheep, eh? I'd always heard it was dogs."

"Don't be ridiculous. Who ever heard of taking a dog to bed?"

He laughed again. "Well, since it's that cold, I recommend we drink Irish coffee."

"I don't suppose you could rustle up a mug of hot chocolate instead. And don't forget to pile those miniature marshmallows on top—although the regular size ones will do in a pinch."

"I'm sorry, Miss Yoder, but we don't keep either cocoa or marshmallows on hand."

"Then Irish coffee it is!" To tell the truth, it was shaping up to be a long, hard day and I could use a boost. A nice cup of exotic European coffee sounded like just the ticket.

"Whipped cream on top?"

"Yes, please." I'd never had coffee with whipped cream on top. How clever of the Irish.

Mr. Bacchustelli pressed a button on the wall, spoke in low tones into a circle of small holes, and then sat back on his own couch with a smile. "Miss Yoder, I'm glad you stopped by. I was about to call you, anyway. Have the police made any progress in their investigation?"

"Well, these things always take more time than people realize. I assure you, Mr. Bacchustelli, that I've been working as fast as I can."

"What do you mean by 'I'? Are you the only one working on it?"

"I'm sure that's not the case. No doubt the others are handling the forensic aspects. The only reason I'm doing preliminary interviews is because I know the locals."

"I see," he said, although he sounded like he didn't.

"I have some leads. As a matter of fact, that's why I'm here."

He stiffened a little, but that may have been because a uniformed maid materialized out of nowhere. She was bearing a tray upon which beckoned two very tall glass mugs containing the Irish coffee and topped with towers of whipped cream.

Without being told, the maid approached me first. Perhaps it was rude of me, but I didn't wait until my host had been served before taking my first sip. I like my hot beverages scalding—just a bubble away from boiling. Hot enough to scour loose the phlegm, as Papa used to say. Papa, however, would not have approved of this coffee.

I'm sure Ireland is a beautiful country, and I've known many fine folks of Irish descent, but just between you and me, they can't grow coffee there worth beans. My goodness, was this stuff terrible. All the Irish whipped cream and sugar wouldn't have made it palatable. The only way not to appear rude was to consume it as fast as I could while it was still hot. My throat would be phlegm-free for months.

Apparently Mr. Bacchustelli had never seen someone drink a cup of coffee that fast. "Wow," he said, "that's really amazing."

I smiled weakly. "That just goes to show what I thought of it."

"Would you like another?"

"Well, as delicious as that was—"

"Go ahead, take mine. I've had too much caffeine today as it is."

I was suddenly feeling peculiarly light-headed. Oh, what the hay, as Susannah sometimes says. If gulping down another mug of noxious brew would make a grieving man feel better, then I'd be a pretty poor excuse of a human being if I didn't cooperate. And why not, anyway? My throat was already acclimated to the heat.

"Open the hatch and down it goes, but where it goes, nobody knows." I gulped the second mug of noxious brew even faster than the first one.

"Miss Yoder—"

"Did someone call my name?"

"Miss Yoder—"

"That's my name, all right. Don't wear it out."

"I think maybe you shouldn't have had that second drink."

"Nonsense, dear. Just because it was vile is no reason for me to be rude. Or should I have said 'wretched'? Because 'wretched' and 'rude' alliterate, you see. Alliterate—now that's an odd word. Who do you suppose sat back on their duff, on a divan spilling over with puffy pillows, and said, 'I think I'll invent a word and call it "alliterate" '? I bet it was Samuel Johnson—or Sammy, as I like to call him."

"I'm getting your sister Susannah."

"Not Susannah—Sammy!"

"Stay right there."

"Where else would I go?" I was, after all, feeling deliciously relaxed. In fact, so much so that I swung my bare feet up on the couch and decadently draped myself across down-filled pillows whose silken covers had been made at the expense of thousands of silkworms. What had I been thinking when I decorated the PennDutch in austere, bone-bruising furniture? Why practice living in Hell, when it is possible to achieve a little bit of Heaven on earth? What an exciting thought! The possibilities were endless. Out would go the margarine; in would come the butter. Out would go the cheap paper towels; in would come the thirsty, quilted variety. Out would go the plastic flowers; in would come the fresh. Out would go my crabby, mean-spirited acquaintances; and in would come—"

"Mags!"

"Sammy!"

"No, it's Susannah, Sis. Who's Sammy?"

"The man with the Johnson—I mean Johnson. Did I already say that?"

"Mags, you're drunk."

"Am snot."

"Are so. Vinny said you drank two Irish coffees in less than two minutes."

"Hideous stuff—they should stick to corned beef and cabbage. They grow much better cabbage than they do coffee."

"Mags, it's called Irish because there's whiskey in it."

"Don't be silly. You know I don't drink alcohol. It's a sin. So why is it that Jesus drank wine? And don't give me that grape juice argument. If it was grape juice he'd turned that water into, the Bible would have said so." I looked at Vinny to see if he had the answer. But forget answers. Here was one handsome man.

"Look at me, Mags."

"I'd rather look at Vinny. Vinny, Vinny, Vinny. Did you know it rhymes with 'ninny'?"

"You're drunk, and I'm going to take you home. Otto will drive."

"Otto? Now isn't that a coincidence? Otto is the reason I came here. Otto, Otto, Otto—just like that dog in the funny papers."

"It ain't a dog's name," Otto growled.

"Yes, it is. He's kind of a cute dog too. Even wears army clothes. You ever wear army clothes, Otto?"

Susannah held my face in her hands, forcing me to look at her. "Where are your shoes?"

"They're lost."

"Lost? Where?"

"If I knew, they wouldn't be lost, would they?" I felt the sudden urge to sing. *"They're little black shoes who have lost their way—"*

Susannah grabbed me by my armpits and hauled me off the comfy couch. "Mags, you're making a fool of yourself."

"There's no fool like an old fool."

"Come on, it's time to go."

"No, it ain't—I mean, isn't. I have to ask the dog a question. That's why I came here."

"There's no dog here."

"Otto, then."

"Ask me what?" Susannah might have been right; I haven't encountered many dogs that could actually speak.

"I want to know what you were doing in Hernia early yesterday morning."

"Hernia?"

"Silly name for a town, isn't it? Our great-great-great-grandpa named it. He wanted to name it Hemorrhoid, but he didn't know how to spell it. Now, where was I?"

"Something about Otto being in Hernia yesterday morning," Mr. Bacchustelli said helpfully. "I'd like to know the answer to that as well."

Otto blushed. "I was seeing Susannah."

"Seeing her about what?"

"Boss, do I have to tell you in front of her?"

"Yes."

"I spooga nightowl wi Susnah," he mumbled.

"I only speak English," I said somewhat crossly.

"That was English."

"Then repeat it clearly," Mr. Bacchustelli said, also sounding a bit cross.

Otto was the crossest of all. "I *said*, 'I spent the night at Susannah's.'"

Now Susannah was blushing. "I can explain, Sis."

29

"In English as well, please."

"I've been lonely with my Pooky Bear gone. Then one day I met Otto and we hit it off right away, and since he was lonely too, I didn't see any harm in it. We're friends, Mags, nothing more. Sometimes I visit Otto here, back in the servants' quarters. That's how come I know my way around."

Otto turned even redder. "I ain't lonely, boss."

I struggled to make sense of what was being said. English or not, the conversation was difficult to follow. Who knew that two cups of coffee would make me so sleepy?

"Uh—what I want to know," I said, "is—uh—why Susannah was walking along the highway today. Why didn't she—uh—ride into town with you?"

"Drop it, Mags," Susannah said, her nails digging into my arm like a raptor's talons.

"You know," Otto said, "I'd like to hear the answer to that too."

Susannah didn't give him a chance. Using her black artificial nails, she pulled me from the sumptuous penthouse before I even had the chance to thank Mr. Bacchustelli for the disgusting beverage he'd had the audacity to serve.

The second the elevator doors closed, she let me have it with both barrels. "How dare you embarrass me like that?"

"Like what?"

"Otto is not supposed to know that I'm on my way to see Melvin."

"Why not?" I jabbed at the lobby button but somehow missed.

Susannah punched the correct one. "Because he's jealous of Melvin, that's why."

"He's jealous of a killer? Killer—now that's a word I don't get to say every day. Killer, killer, killer. It rhymes with Miller, even Phyllis Diller."

"Give me your keys, Mags."

"What for?"

"Because you're drunker than a skunk."

"Hey! I resemble that remark—I mean, *resent*."

"Your keys." Her talons, which had released their prey when the elevator doors closed, gripped me again.

"All right, hold your horses!" I searched my purse in vain for the keys. Is it my fault that many items, such as church bulletins, facial tissues, or tubes of lotion, become amorous in my pocketbook and reproduce? Finally, I gave up and dumped the contents onto the elevator floor. If Susannah was dead set about getting the keys, let her find them herself.

Susannah claims that seconds after I emptied my purse, my eyes rolled back in my head and I slumped to the floor. She claims that I lay there, passed out, until Derrick the bell captain helped her carry me to the car. For the record, this is utter nonsense. I did not pass out. I was completely aware that Derrick carried me to the car and laid me in the backseat. I may, however, have fallen asleep shortly after that.

When I awoke I was at home in my bed. Sitting on my bed, just inches from my head, was the Babester. He was grinning like a Cheshire cat on steroids. Given that Quasimodo was ringing church bells in my head, I feel that I had a right to be irritated.

"Gabe! What in the world are you doing here? And what's with that silly grin. You look like a horse getting its teeth examined."

"I love you too."

"And for crying out loud, what am I doing in bed?"

"I'm afraid you were drunk again, hon."

"Don't be ridiculous! You know I've never had a drink in my life—except for the time I inadvertently drank a pitcher of mimosas."

"What about the hot toddies?"

"Inadvertent as well."

"Hon, do you know what an Irish coffee is?"

"Disgusting?"

"That would be the whiskey part of it."

"There really was alcohol in the coffee?"

"Bingo."

"But I had only two cups."

"Public opinion aside, you're not accustomed to drinking. Besides, I heard you gulped those two cups down like your mouth was lined with asbestos."

"Who told you that? Susannah? Because she wasn't even—"

"Hon, I didn't come here to get on your case about drinking. I want to talk about us."

"Us?"

"There is still an 'us,' isn't there?"

"Of course there is—isn't there?" Granted, the last time Gabe and I spoke we were both hot under the collar, but I never once doubted that we would eventually work things out. But even *if* we couldn't, it would be me who called it off, not him. The thought that he might be the one to end things was terrifying. It would have frozen my blood had it not been for all that alcohol, which just goes to show you that imbibing that whiskey had actually turned out to be a blessing. And if something was a blessing, it obviously couldn't be all bad. . . .

"Earth to Magdalena. Come in, please, Magdalena."

"What?"

"I asked you if you were feeling well enough to come over to the house for supper."

"Uh—when?"

"Now."

"*Now?* It isn't even lunchtime yet."

"Hon, you've been asleep for six hours."

"But I'm sure I look awful. I feel like something the cat dragged in, ate, and then threw up."

"You look fine."

"Just fine?"

"Okay, ravishing. In fact, if I didn't know you to be a woman of high moral character—the occasional tipple aside—I'd ravish you right here and now."

"You mean that?" Yes, I was taking a risk, but if he answered correctly, he would gain a whole lot of brownie points.

"Absolutely. Magdalena, I can't put my finger on it exactly, but as beautiful and alluring as you've always been, lately you've become even more so."

Alluring? *Moi?* Big old horsey-faced, heifer-footed me? Even a million points was not too much for the handsome doctor/mystery writer from the Big Apple.

"What about Alison?" I said.

"Susannah made arrangements for Alison to spend the night at her friend Kumquat's house. By the way, hon, what kind of parents would name their daughter Kumquat?"

"They're actually very nice people, dear. The Kuhnbergers didn't have Kumquat until rather late in life. She's the apple of her father's eye. Anyway, what about my guests? I need to be here for them. Even a quiet bunch like this can get rowdy if there's no one here to ride herd."

"Been there, done that, ride 'em cowboy."

"Excuse me?"

"Freni served while I babysat. To tell the truth, they really weren't all that bad. Miss McGee from Charleston took her teeth out at the table, which absolutely horrified Mr. Guggenheim from Minneapolis, who said he'd always heard that Charlestonians were so well mannered, to which Miss McGee replied that she was from Charleston, West Virginia, not South Carolina, and that in West Virginia it was considered good manners to take your teeth out before cleaning them at the table." Gabe laughed heartily.

"That Miss McGee is quite a cutup, isn't she?"

"So you'll join me for dinner?"

He didn't have to twist my bony arm. "Give me twenty minutes?"

"Take thirty." He leaned over and kissed me lightly on the forehead before striding manfully from the room.

Overcome with joy, the second the latch clicked shut I did sheet angels in bed. (For those of you who've lived sheltered lives, sheet angels are similar to snow angels, but without the snow, of course.)

Then without a second to spare I leaped out of bed, forewent Big Bertha, my sinful Jacuzzi tub, and raced through the shower. Then came the difficult part—dressing.

A casual observer might conclude that all my clothes are the same. However, nothing could be farther from the truth. I own blue broadcloth dresses, blue wool dresses, blue wool blend dresses, blue polyester blend dresses, blue rayon dresses, blue nylon blend dresses, and for those rare times when I'm feeling a bit racy, blue mercerized cotton dresses with white rickrack along the edges.

Wearing silk, by the way, is like playing with fire, and therefore the fabric should not be found in a good Christian's closet. This is only my personal opinion, mind you. But consider the fact that Hollywood stars wear silk, and it is common knowledge that many of them have the morals of a tomcat on Viagra. Better to wear nylon and sweat like a Swede in a sauna than be seduced by silk. And as if avoiding temptation was not reason enough for not wearing silk, then consider that fabric's origins. What woman in her right mind would wear a dress made from caterpillar secretions?

At any rate, that evening I selected a fairly new, store-bought frock constructed of the finest mercerized cotton. My prayer cap was, of course, white; my hose tan; and my second pair of brogans (my best were still lost somewhere in the penthouse carpet) black. Although it is no one's business, my sturdy Christian underwear were white and, although not new, expertly mended.

Feeling rather alluring, I went so far as to pat some unscented, colorless face powder on my nose. With a proboscis as prominent as mine, failure to do so can result in temporarily blinding those around me. I had a hunch that after dinner Gabe would attempt to position his own proboscis close to mine—perhaps even to engage in a little lip-lock—in which case it wouldn't do to have the landing strip obscured.

With less than a minute to spare I breezed out the front door in high spirits. "Valeriee, valerah," I sang in my not too unpleasant, albeit quavering, voice. It promised to be a memorable evening.

Dr. Gabriel Jerome Rosen opened the door before I had a chance to knock. This was just as well. Over the years my knuckles have permanently disfigured the doorjamb.

"Hi, hon." He leaned forward and gave me a peck on the cheek.

I savored his warm masculine smell, mingled as it was with something that said loving from the oven. The Babester, when he wants to be, is a dynamite cook.

"Well?" I said.

"Well what?"

"Well, what do you think of this dress? It's practically new."

"Your mercerized cotton is mesmerizing."

"I'll take that as a compliment," I said, and sailed past him into the living room.

It was a living room I'd seen a million times. The Millers, the former owners, had lived across from us Yoders for several generations. The last Miller to reside there was Aaron, my pseudo-husband, now happily my ex. Aaron's parents had been consummate pack rats, with no sense of style. After their death Aaron hired a one-eyed interior decorator from Pittsburgh to turn the chaos into a manly bachelor pad. The transformation was so remarkable that locals were actually willing to pay to see it. It is a little known fact that this was the original *Queer Eye for the Straight Guy*. Gabe has made only a few subtle changes, honing the Pittsburgh decorator's taste with a Manhattan sensibility.

My betrothed led me directly to the dining room, where the table had been attractively set for three. "Here, darling," he said. "I want you to sit at the head of the table."

"And the righteous get to sit at either side?"

"What?"

"Never mind. Why three place settings? Is the third for the Prophet Isaiah?"

"That's Elijah, hon, not Isaiah. And it's for Ma."

My blood ran so cold it even froze in a few extremities.

30

Concord Bavarian

2 envelopes unflavored gelatin
½ cup Concord grape drink
1¼ cups milk
½ cup sugar

Dash salt
1 tablespoon lemon juice
1½ cups heavy cream, whipped
½ cup Concord grape preserves

Sprinkle gelatin over Concord grape drink to soften. Meanwhile, scald milk. Stir in sugar and salt. Add gelatin mixture and stir until dissolved. Blend in lemon juice. Chill until slightly thickened. Fold in whipped cream. Pour into 4-cup mold. Chill until firm. To serve, unmold gelatin onto serving plate. Spoon Concord grape preserves over mold.

MAKES 6 SERVINGS

31

Surely he didn't, did he? No, even Gabe couldn't be that dense. The Bible says the truth will set us free. Why then does it seem like all the truth does is make for upset stomachs? I would do my best to postpone the inevitable.

" 'Ma' as in 'Ma, what a lovely table'?" I said in my best fake Southern accent.

"My mother, hon. She has to eat too, doesn't she?"

I didn't dare tell him that was debatable; I was pretty sure demons didn't have appetites. "I thought this was for us—to talk over things."

"It is. But Ma has a few things she wants to say as well."

"Gabe, this is not going—"

The door from the kitchen flew open, and Ida Rosen stood there in all her four feet, eleven inch splendor. Perhaps she didn't see me, given as how my head tends to perch above the clouds. If she did, it did nothing to ameliorate her behavior.

"Oy, does this shiksa give me a headache, or vaht?"

"Ma!"

"Alvays late, this one. Is it too much to ask that she should call? My knishes are burned and the brisket is like shoe leather. Gabeleh, vaht do you see in this voman?"

"Ma, she's standing right here!"

"Vhere?"

"Up here in the clouds," I said.

Ida scanned the room, one hand over her eyes, until she focused on my knees. Then she followed my slim proportions skyward, like Jack climbing the beanstalk. Finally Ida clutched dramatically at a chest ample enough for a dozen Yoder women.

"You shouldn't sneak up on an old lady."

"Sorry, dear. I'll bring the marching band next time."

"So vaht's mit der sarcasm?"

"It just comes naturally."

"Again mit der sarcasm. Gabeleh, a thousand good Jewish girls in New York I could have arranged for you, and not one of them has a tongue like this."

"I'm actually quite fond of her tongue," my beloved said, much to my amazement.

Mrs. Rosen mumbled something in Yiddish, which, by the way, shares some words with Pennsylvania Dutch, given that both languages have German roots. Alas, thinking my parents' ways were quaint, I'd ix-nayed on utch-Day while growing up. Of course I picked up a few words anyway; nothing really useful. At times like this being essentially monolingual was both a curse and a blessing.

"Gabriel! Do you vant that I should have another heart attack?"

"You never had a first one, Ma. That was indigestion."

Ida turned to me. "My son the heart doctor, and vaht does he know about hearts? Nothing about a mother's heart." Her eyes gleamed as she thought of a new way to torture me. "So, Miss Yoder, vhy is it you have no children of your own?"

"I'm not married."

"Vaht you vere, yah?"

"It lasted only a month." In case she didn't yet know—which was highly doubtful—there was no point in telling her the marriage was bogus.

"Ma!"

"*Nu?* So I don't have a right to know these things? Look at those hips—a bar mitzvah boy has vider hips than that. Gabeleh, maybe she isn't fertile. Vhat then vill I do about grandchildren?"

"I'm forty-eight," I wailed. "That manure wagon pulled out of my station a long time ago. If Gabe wants children, he'll have to get a pet—just not a cat. Alison is allergic to cats. That's why I got rid of Little Freni. Speaking of hearts, that just about tore mine in two.

There's not a day that goes by that I don't miss playing with my pussy."

The glitter in Ida's eyes only intensified. "Manure vagon? Vaht does this mean? So she's meshuga too?"

"Let's eat," Gabe pleaded.

"Yah, so *now* vee eat. Never mind that everything is ruined because she talks too much." The miserable munchkin trudged back into the kitchen to fetch our dinner. I'll have it be known that I tried to help, but she adamantly rebuffed me.

I watched in awe as Mrs. Rosen brought *twelve* steaming platters and bowls to the table, none of which appeared burned or as tough as shoe leather. The Good Lord knows I didn't dare refuse to sample any of the dishes, but by the time we were through passing things around, my plate was piled three layers high.

"Dig in!" Gabe said, and did so himself without waiting for grace.

I said a silent prayer of thanksgiving, to which I attached a silent plea for strength. But no sooner did I bring the first forkful to my mouth than Ida shot me a look that could bring a Texas Ranger to his knees.

"Vhat? You don't like my *tsimmes*?"

"You're whatsis?"

"Candied carrots," Gabe said, his mouth full. "Jewish style."

"I'm sure they're very good, Mrs. Rosen, but I thought I'd start with this." The this in question appeared to be stuffed cabbage, but I wasn't about to make assumptions.

Ida clucked, sounding for all the world like my favorite hen, Pertelote. "You're starting with *that*?"

I dumped what was on my fork and stabbed a carrot.

"Oy," Ida said, "so now she doesn't like my stuffed cabbage."

"Ma!"

Clearly I was in a lose-lose situation. While I may be shaped like a post, I like to think I'm not quite as dumb as one. Only a certified idiot would hang around for further abuse.

"If you'll excuse me," I said, and stood.

"Vhat?" Ida turned to her son. "Gabeleh, she should have done that before we sat down."

"Ma, please—"

"No, *Gabeleh*, your ma is right. I should have taken care of business before I sat down. So now I'll do it standing. You, Mrs. Rosen, are the third rudest woman I've ever met. And you, Gabriel Jerome Rosen, are the second biggest mama's baby I've ever met. I'd rather have a root canal—without laughing gas—than eat supper with you two tonight."

Ida gasped. "Vhy only the *third* rudest? You see, Gabeleh, how she treats me?"

"Ma, stop it!"

Ida gasped louder. "My heart."

"Your heart is fine, Ma. But mine won't be if Magdalena leaves now."

I laid my napkin on the table with considerably less flare than I'd planned. "That's all right, Gabe. Give her what she needs—attention. I'm out of here."

"You're not leaving, hon. Not until I've said what I'd planned all along to say tonight."

"And what would that be? That after we're married your ma and I will share the same kitchen and live happily ever after?"

"Don't be silly," Ida said. "You don't even cook."

"Shut up, Ma—please." Beads of perspiration dotted my fiancé's forehead. He closed his eyes before continuing. "Magdalena, I've decided I'm going to convert to Christianity."

"*Oy veys meer!* My heart! This time it really is my heart."

I was dumbfounded by Gabe's offer. "We need to talk outside," I said when I could speak again.

"Vhat? And leave me to die here alone?"

"You won't be alone, Mrs. Rosen. You've got all this food to keep you company."

Gabe looked at me and then his mother, and when he turned back to me he grabbed my hands. "Yes, outside."

Ida tried to follow us, but after pushing me gently onto the porch, Gabe shut the door on his mother and held it closed with both hands. "Hon, I meant what I said inside."

"Does this mean you believe that Jesus is the Messiah? The only begotten Son of God the Father? Your personal Lord and Savior?"

"Do I have to?"

"To be a Christian you do."

"You sure?"

"Positive. Being a Christian is all about faith."

"Hon, you know I love you. But I can't force myself to believe something. I don't know that anyone can."

Of course he was right. If a man pointed a gun at me and told me that he would shoot me unless I believed that Jesus was *not* the Messiah, I'd be out of luck—unless I lied. The fact that Gabe offered to pretend to believe for my sake, knowing how much it would upset Ida, was a testament to his love for me.

But what about the apron strings of steel? I'd need a wire cutter to sever those. And please allow me to make one thing perfectly clear: I didn't for a minute think that Ida's possessive nature had anything to do with her fitting the stereotype of the Jewish mother. I plain, flat-out don't believe in stereotypes, because my mother, Mennonite to the core— Well, never you mind about my mother. Any unflattering talk about her is likely to result in Hernia being visited by an earthquake, pestilence, or a swarm of penny-pinching tourists.

"Gabe," I said, "I understand your point—"

"And, hon, I don't want you to get the wrong idea. Just because Ma's like that—"

"Don't worry your hoary little head. Our mothers are sisters under the skin—except that my mother is dead, and yours isn't. That, and the fact that if my mother was alive she'd stand ten inches taller than yours, and could out-guilt Ida with her tongue tied up with licorice sticks."

"Then I'm glad you understand, hon."

"I do. What I don't understand is how you let her manipulate you like you do."

"But I'm her only son."

"She has daughters."

"Yes, but ever since Pa died—well, you know how it is."

"I'm afraid I don't. My parents died at the same time. Besides, call it conceit if you will, but I never could stand to let other people push me around, including Mama. Somehow I always thought that I mattered too much—to myself, if to no one else."

"I know. That's one of the things I love about you." Gabe put his arms around me and held me close. I'm sure to some the gesture might have appeared obscene, like getting halfway to second base.

The truth is we were keeping each other warm on a cold winter's night.

I'm sure Gabe was about to enumerate more of my admirable qualities had we not been interrupted by a pair of headlights bobbing hither and thither as a car advanced up the long gravel drive. The lane has some dips, but it's fairly straight. Judging by the erratic driving, I decided the visitor was Doc Shafor.

Sure enough. The battered old Chevy jerked to a stop amid a spray of stones, and out popped a dapper-looking doc. Despite the frigid temperature he was minus a coat, but his weskit vest sported a pocket watch chain, and his remarkably small feet were encased in spats.

"Get a load of that," Gabe said. "When is the last time you saw spats on anyone other than Scrooge McDuck?"

"Doc has a whole collection." I gently extricated myself from Gabe's warm arms. "Hi, Doc."

"Don't let me stop you kids."

"We were only hugging."

Doc slapped Gabe on the back. "You're one lucky man, Doctor. I've been aching to put my arms around that lovely lady since she turned legal."

Although I was quite used to Doc's outrageous comments, nonetheless, I could feel myself blushing. Thank heavens the porch light was dim.

"Doc," I said, "how would you like to put your arms around a lovely woman on an exotic tropical island?"

"Magdalena, I thought this moment would never come. Glory hallelujah, and pass the moonshine."

"Not me, Doc! Ida Rosen."

"Yeah. Well, I'm just an old man on a fixed income. I could take her about as far as the Maryland border—maybe a tad further if you chipped in for provisions."

"The entire vacation would be my treat, Doc."

"In that case, I've always had a hankering to visit the U.S. Virgin Islands."

I may be a simple Mennonite woman, but I read voraciously. Besides which, I excelled at geography when I was a girl. The U.S. Virgin Islands were far too close for what I had in mind.

"I hear they're overrun with tourists, dear. Where's the romance in wall-to-wall people? No, I'm thinking of someplace truly exotic—like Bora-Bora."

"As in the next island over from Tahiti?"

"That's the one. I read someplace that there is a resort with glass-bottom huts built out over the water. One can lie in bed and look at brightly colored tropical fish."

"You'll spring for that?"

"Absolutely. Doc, you've been there for me so many times I've lost count. It's time I tried to pay you back. And anyway, what good is money if you can't spend it? Especially on friends."

Doc's eyes gleamed like a cat's. "You're one heck of a woman, Magdalena." He tapped Gabe on the shoulder. "You'd be a fool to let this one go."

"I know," Gabe said. "But before you two get carried away, I think you should know that my mother hates flying—"

The door flew open, slamming into my beloved's behind. "Vhat he said is not true! I love to fly." Ida waved her stubby arms, nearly hitting me in the face with a fistful of liver spots. "See? I fly like a bird."

"Ma," Gabe gasped, "you were listening at the door?"

"*Nu?* I'm your mother; I gave life to you."

"Indeed, you did," I cried gaily. "So, are we all agreed?"

Alas, my betrothed looked as if we'd all agreed to enter a boiled turnip–eating contest. No doubt it was the thought of his mother doing the box springs bossa nova in Bora-Bora that made him unhappy. *That* was something his mother and mine did not have in common. Despite having given birth to two children, Mama was a virgin when she died.

"Then it's all settled," Doc said.

"Great." I gave Ida a broad smile so that she would find it easier to thank me.

"Gabeleh, is this woman trying to get rid of me?"

"No, Ma—"

"Actually, I am. I can't wait for you to leave so I can throw your son to the ground and make mad, passionate love to him." I clapped both hands over my filthy mouth. I couldn't believe I'd actually said those words, which, by the way, I'd read in a romance novel Susannah loaned me. It just goes to show why the Good Lord wants us to wear sturdy Christian underwear and not those easy to rip bodices depicted on the covers of titillating books.

Doc grinned. "Ouch. It makes me hurt with envy just to hear this kind of talk. Ida, will you throw me on the floor of our glass-bottom hut in Bora-Bora? But throw me gently. We wouldn't want the glass to break."

"Yah, no problem."

"Ma!"

"Vhat? A mother shouldn't have any fun?"

I grabbed Gabe's hand. "Come on, let's give the lovebirds some time alone. Will you walk me back to the inn?"

"But Ma's supper— Oh, the heck with Ma's supper." Gabe squeezed my hand and then pulled me close so that he could put his arm around my bony shoulders.

Although the night was bitterly cold, I felt snug and warm all the way home. We stood for an eternity on the kitchen steps, unwilling to part. In the end it was the incessant ringing of the wall phone inside that spurred us to say our good nights. What might have ended with Gabe rounding second base, well on his way to third, got him barely past first. Contrary to the rules of the game, he insisted on carrying his bat with him, and in an upright position to boot—although that is neither here nor there.

"Yes," I snapped into the receiver after the millionth ring.

"I know who killed Mrs. Bacchustelli," a strange woman said quietly.

32

"Who is this?"

"Magdalena, don't you recognize my voice?"

"*Mama?*" Just so you don't think I'm strange, my much deceased mother once communicated with me before. It wasn't with words—she made her wishes known by a rain shower on a perfectly sunny day—so I wasn't sure what her celestial voice sounded like.

"You're such a hoot, Magdalena. I'm glad we're best friends."

"We are?"

"Maybe we should save the joking for later, Magdalena. What I've got to tell you is pretty important."

"Tell away!"

"Remember how you asked me to keep my ears and eyes open and report anything—anything at all—that might have to do with Felicia Bacchustelli's death?"

Agnes Mishler! Of course. I did indeed ask her to keep me informed—but not when I'd finally decided to allow Gabe to reach second base.

"Yes, I remember."

"Well, I was minding my own business when I saw this car pull up, and guess who got out?"

"The mailman?"

"Don't be silly, Magdalena. What would the mailman be doing out at Grape Expectations?"

"What were *you* doing out there?"

"Releasing Felicia Bacchustelli's soul from the dead."

"I beg your pardon?"

"In many cultures it is believed that the soul of a departed person lingers near the place where the death occurred. This is especially true if the person has been murdered. I took the liberty of seeing to it that Felicia Bacchustelli's soul realized it was free to go."

"And just how did you do that?'

"I simply told her so—that she was free to go. And I left a few coins and some chocolate and water so that her soul would have sustenance on its journey."

"Provisions? She wasn't going to Maryland, for heaven's sake."

"Magdalena, you're not mad, are you? I mean, we're still friends, aren't we?"

"As much as ever, dear. Do you mind terribly if we get to the business of the car?"

"The car?"

"The point of your call," I wailed.

"Oh yes. There I was, minding my own business, when suddenly Hiram Stutzman drives up. Hiram doesn't see me because it's dark out and I'm wearing black sweats. I know, you're supposed to wear white when dealing with the dead, but you see, I didn't want to confuse Mrs. Bacchustelli. I mean, what if she thought I was You-know-who and came toward me instead of going to the light?"

There was no point in telling my new best friend that there could be no confusing a very stout woman with the Lord. "Let's skip along ahead, dear, shall we? What did Hiram do after he got out of the car?"

"He got a gun, that's what. And he aimed it right at—"

The next thing I heard sounded like a bolt of lightning. Of course it wasn't lightning; there wasn't a cloud in the winter sky. But what could it be?

"Agnes? Agnes, are you still there?"

She did not respond.

"Agnes, can you say something? Make a sound—anything. Let me know you're all right."

Call it instinct, call it intuition, call it a hunch—just don't call it psychic ability, because that, I'm pretty sure, is a sin—but I knew deep down in my rangy bones that Agnes Mishler, Hernia's diva of gossip, was dead. I had the same feeling at the exact time that my parents were crushed between the milk tanker and the semi-truck loaded with state-of-the-art running shoes.

I hung up and dialed Chief Hornsby-Anderson.

We pulled into the clearing at the same time. Because it was cold, I waited until she got out before doing the same. By then the moon had risen, and her badge glistened in its light. Something else glistened as well, and it took me a few seconds to recognize it as a gun. Taking a cue from nature, my blood ran cold.

"Miss Yoder," the chief said, acknowledging me with a brisk nod. "I prefer that you wait in your car."

"Nonsense. I mean, I'm coming with you. Agnes Mishler counted me as a friend. Not many people do that."

The chief sighed. "Are you always so strong willed?"

"Hardheaded is the preferred term. Sounds more feminine, don't you think? And the answer is yes."

"Then stay behind me. Keep in my shadow."

That was easier said than done. Chief Hornsby-Anderson is six inches shorter than me and takes baby steps. I, on the other hand, have the gait of an Arabian—the horse, not one of the Saudis. It wasn't my fault that I kept bumping into her and, worse yet, stepping on the backs of her shoes.

"Miss Yoder, please—"

"Call me Magdalena. Or, if you prefer, you may continue to call me Miss Yoder. In fact, call me anything you want—although calling me Mrs. Rosen would be a mite premature. Just don't call me late to dinner." In retrospect my verbosity was due to heightened emotions. Trust me, it isn't easy searching for the body of a friend, even a recent one like Agnes.

"Miss Yoder, please keep your voice down."

"Aye, aye, sir."

The chief stopped abruptly, and I didn't. For a moment we staggered and clutched at each other like heathen dancers who'd consumed too many hot toddies. The chief, being more agile and a good deal younger, stabilized first.

"*Please* stay right where you are, Miss Yoder."

"No problemo, your chief chieftainship." Perhaps it was best that I stay behind. The Bible tells us not to be a stumbling block to others. Heaven forefend a young impressionable soul should drive by and see the chief and I doing the vertical hootchy-kootchy by the light of the silvery moon.

While I shivered—from cold, not fright—Hernia's finest, armed with the largest flashlight I'd ever seen, did a remarkably thorough, albeit quick, search of the area where Felicia Bacchustelli had been found. She did not, however, find any sign of Agnes Mishler. Nonetheless, I complimented her on her efficiency.

"Thanks. To tell you the truth, I was a little nervous about shining this light at the trenches."

"In case you should find poor Agnes lying in one of them, as dead as last week's pot roast?"

"No, the dead I can handle. It's the undead that give me the willies."

"The undead?"

"I know, that's not a very scientific term, is it? You see, in California my partner in the homicide division was Linda Lopez. One of the cases we handled was that of a woman who'd been murdered and thrown into a farm pond by her lover, who owned the farm. We'd been tipped off by a neighbor who claimed to have witnessed the event. The pond was dragged and then drained, but still no body. Then we had a torrential rain that left about six inches of water in the pond bed, because the drain had been resealed. Linda went out there one last time because she couldn't shake this feeling that the woman was still there.

"The pond had a dock that extended about twenty feet over the water, and on a moonlit night just like this—but not as cold, of course—Linda looked down from the dock and saw a reflection in the water. But it wasn't her face, she saw, but that of the murder victim."

"Stop. This is too creepy."

"Anyway, you see? When I looked in the footers, I was afraid that I might see Mrs. Bacchustelli's reflection staring back up at me instead of my own."

"Don't stop altogether. Did you ever find the woman's body?"

"Yes. But it wasn't until almost a year later. The farm had been sold and the pond drained again—this time to build a strip mall. The corpse was found about a foot beneath the muck. You see, the farmer hadn't just thrown his lover into the pond, he'd actually managed to bury her at the bottom."

I shuddered. "Does this sort of thing happen often in California?"

"Every day."

Dense may be my middle name, but I know sarcasm when I hear it. "Agnes might have been calling from home," I said. "There really was no way to tell."

"Let's drive out to her place," the chief said. "We'll take my Crown Vic."

We got in the squad car but not without checking the rear seat first. Just for fun, since someone else was driving, I adjusted my seat all the way back and hoisted my hooves up unto the dashboard. Yes, it was an immodest thing to do, but sturdy Christian underwear can hide a multiple of sins. Besides, I was never allowed to do this as a teenager. A gal has a right to have fun sometimes, doesn't she?

"Miss Yoder, please take your feet off the dash."

"What if I take off my shoes?"

"Feet belong on the floor."

"Yes, ma'am."

"Miss Yoder, why is it you don't have caller ID?"

"Where's the fun in that? Having it would be like finding out the sex of a baby before it's born."

"What about telemarketers?"

"Nothing could be more fun."

"I beg your pardon?"

"The trick is to listen intently—well, pretend to, at least—to their entire spiel. Then when they're done, you say, 'I'm sorry, but I have a hearing problem. Could you repeat that, please?' "

"You don't!"

"I most certainly do. And let me tell you what—"

"Miss Yoder, don't you find this a bit childish?"

Never underestimate the value of a quick change of subject. The more obscure the topic, the better.

"Did you know that the loggerhead turtle is the official state reptile of South Carolina?"

"What?"

"Make your next right, dear. That will take us directly to Agnes Mishler's house."

The chief shook her head to clear it of confusion dust. "Thanks."

Slightly irked at having been called childish, I decided not to warn her about Agnes's quirky uncles. Assuming she hadn't yet heard the gossip, she might be in for a little surprise. Sure enough, about a hundred yards from the Mishler brothers' home, she stomped on the brakes. Had my tootsies still been on the dashboard, I'd be picking shards out of my feet to this day.

"What in the devil is that?"

33

"What, dear?"

"That! What are those naked women doing outside on a night like this?"

"They're not women; they're overweight men. And I think they're playing badminton."

"You sure? About them being men?"

"It was easier to tell when they were thin. Especially in the summer."

"There has got to be an ordinance against this type of behavior."

"There is one against public indecency, but this is a private road."

The chief shook her head again. "And to think we Californians are supposed to be kooky."

"The land of fruits and nuts," I said agreeably.

She scowled. "Aren't you calling the kettle black?"

We pulled into Agnes's driveway, and that's when my heart sank. Agnes always keeps a security light burning by the front door. It's not her uncles she's afraid of but bears and kooky Californians who have come east to find themselves. The light was off tonight, as apparently were all the lights in the house.

"You stay in the car," the chief said. "And keep the doors locked, no matter what."

"Aye, aye—I mean, yes."

Wielding a flashlight the size of Delaware, our new Chief of Police, Olivia Hornsby-Anderson, strode bravely to the house. I saw her ring the bell a couple of times and then knock. When no one answered the chief walked around to the front-facing garage and, standing on her tiptoes, peered through a narrow window that spanned the topmost portion of the door. After giving me a thumbs-up, she jumped back on the porch and rang the bell again.

When a reasonable length of time had passed, the chief, who was remarkably spry, jumped off the porch and worked her way around the house, shining her beacon into all the windows. Back on the porch, having completely circled the house, she simply turned the front doorknob and let herself in. That's when I hopped out of the car.

Call me foolish, but aren't rules meant to be broken? Besides, this wasn't a rule; it was an order the chief had given me. At any rate, the second I got up on the porch, the front door opened with a bang and out staggered the chief, shaking like a leaf and as pale as the skin behind my knees.

"Miss Yoder, I told you to stay in the car!"

"What?" Playing hard of hearing need not be reserved just for telemarketers.

"Get back in the car!"

"What?" By the time I could hear her, it was too late for her to do anything about it but complain.

"Miss Yoder—"

"What's wrong? Why didn't you go inside?"

"I did."

"You know what I mean."

"Uh—okay, I'll tell you. But this has nothing to do with my effectiveness as Hernia's Chief of Police."

"Spill it, dear. If I were a cat, you'd have used up seven of my lives by now."

"Well, you see—okay, I'll come right out with it. I'm claustrophobic. There, are you happy?"

"Is that all? I thought maybe you found Agnes lying on the floor dead or something."

"Miss Yoder, you don't mind having a look around, do you?" She thrust the monstrous torch at me. "You'll need this; the lights won't come on."

Of course I minded doing the chief's job for her. No sane person would agree to wander the maze inside Agnes's house with just a flashlight to illuminate the way. But Agnes had called for my help, and besides, I left sanity at the door the day I fell in love with Aaron Miller, my pseudo first husband.

"Is the back door locked?" I asked sensibly. After all, there was no point in winding through the maze in Agnes's living room if the kitchen door was unlocked.

"Yes, it's locked. Magdalena, are you sure you don't mind doing this? I know it's asking a great deal, and you're not even an official policewoman, but you're so—so—well, confident. I have complete faith in your ability to take care of yourself."

"I don't mind at all," I said, and squared my bony shoulders. Confidence, I've learned, comes from self-esteem, but it can also derive from the way we act. In other words, you become what you appear to be.

While I may have appeared to be confidence personified, inside I was a shaking, quivering bowl of unsolidified headcheese. Agnes's maze was creepy enough in the daytime with the lights turned on. A good Christian should never undertake a dangerous endeavor without praying first, so that's exactly what I did. My fear was not abated, so I kept right on praying, my head bowed and hands clasped, like the Good Lord intended. Did you know that there are some Episcopalians who don't even close their eyes. . . .

"Miss Yoder, are you all right?"

"Fine as frog's hair, dear."

"I beg your pardon?"

"Okay, okay, I'm going on in. You don't need to push me."

"I'm not touching you, Miss Yoder."

Perhaps it was the hand of God then. Building on that, I imagined God's protective hand gently pushing me along through the winding passage that cut through Agnes's clutter. When I got to the fork in the road, the Good Lord gave me a nudge in the right direction.

I know that God really doesn't have a body—at least not exactly like yours and mine. But the funny thing is, as I was being propelled forward by the hand that really didn't exist, I started to believe I could see it. The fingers were long like Mama's, but the nails were bitten short like Papa's. Maybe they were reaching out from the beyond to help me when I needed it most. Who knows?

At any rate, although I felt protected, worming my way back to the kitchen, when I finally got there my self-centered little heart leaped into my throat. Lying facedown on the linoleum floor, the beam from my flashlight casting a pale yellow circle on her back, was the lifeless form of Agnes Mishler. Don't ask me how I knew she was dead at that point, but I did. Just as I knew that the Lord was still with me, I knew that Agnes wasn't.

A slight shift of the torch beam revealed the black polymer handle of a cheap butcher knife. So much for the method employed in Agnes's demise. I swung the heavy flashlight around the room, the dim yellow circle it produced glancing off various objects like a stone ricocheting across Miller's Pond: the refrigerator, groaning under the weight of magnets; a vintage metal bread box held together by rust; the bottle of wine Agnes had offered to share; the stiff gray strings of a dry mop head leaning against a corner. But no killer—at least none that I could see.

Still, it would be stupid to stay a second longer, and you can bet your bippy that I didn't. Hansel and Gretel could not have opened the back door any quicker. A greyhound chased by a hungry cheetah couldn't have raced around to the front of the house any faster. I nearly knocked the chief over as I leaped on the porch.

"Miss Yoder—"

"I was right! She *is* dead on the floor."

"You're sure?"

"Yes—at least about the floor. And I'm pretty sure about the dead part too. There's a butcher knife sticking out of her back."

"I'm calling Chris for backup," she said as much to herself as she did to me. "The sheriff too. After all, this isn't even in the town limits—"

"Yes, it is. It's just like Grape Expectations. Our founding fathers had great expectations—no pun intended—when they set the town boundaries. Some folks say they would have annexed western Maryland as well had it not been for all the rowdies down there."

"I'm still calling the sheriff. I'll ask him to issue an APB on Hiram Stutzman—"

"It wasn't Hiram."

Chief Hornsby-Anderson stood with her mouth open wide enough to catch a nightjar. That is a dangerous thing to do, especially if one is allergic to feathers. Sometimes even if one's not.

"Delores Wrensberger choked to death on a whip-poor-will," I said kindly.

"What?"

"It was awful. She'd pretty much swallowed it whole, except for some of the tail feathers—"

"No, what did you say about Mr. Stutzman?"

"I said that he didn't kill poor Agnes."

"But she said his name just before you heard the gunshot."

"I'm not sure it was a gunshot. Not anymore."

"Miss Yoder—"

"Look, Chief—may I call you that? Or would you prefer Chieftess?"

"Chief is fine. So is Olivia."

"If Hiram Stutzman killed Agnes Mishler, it would be because the queen of nosy had the skinny on him. But he didn't, because if he had, he'd have smashed that bottle of wine to smithereens, which, of course, he didn't."

"Is that Pennsylvania Dutch?"

"No, it's common sense."

"I see." She cogitated for a moment. "What would you suggest we do next, Miss Yoder? I mean, I know what I'm going to do, but I'm curious as to what you think we—I mean, I—should do."

Believe me, I wasn't feeling a speck of schadenfreude. Chief Olivia Hornsby-Anderson had come to Hernia with sterling credentials. This was her first murder case here. But was it her first *ever*? If so, that would explain how it is we were able to afford her. Stupid me. I'd been so excited to get a woman applicant for the job that I'd only glanced at her performance rating, not the record itself. Haste makes waste, Granny Yoder always used to say as she scurried about our house, waving her cane at whomever was displeasing her at the moment.

"If I were you—which, of course I'm not—I would do just as you said. Call the sheriff. Also call the Hernia Rescue Squad. Tell them to bring the ambulance. Then I'd wait right here by the squad car—better yet, inside—while I sent Miss Yoder—that would be *moi*—next door to interview the Mishler brothers. Maybe they saw something that is pertinent to the situation."

"Miss Yoder, you're a mind reader! That is exactly what I was going to say next."

"Then there is no need to say it, dear."

I waited until she was safely locked inside the Crown Vic before tiptoeing through the pine trees that separated the two Mishler homes.

34

The Mishler brothers had taken their act inside but had yet to put on any clothes. Nonetheless, when Big Goober opened the door, he didn't seem even a trifle embarrassed.

"We've got company," he called to his brother, Little Goober. "It's Magdalena Yoder."

Not that I looked closely, mind you, but their nicknames have nothing to do with their respective anatomies. It may well be, however, that these appellations have affected the men's personalities. Their given names, by the way, are Zibeline and Aubergine.

Little Goober dashed into the room with surprising speed for a sixty-some-year-old. Nude but not rude, he proffered a pink hand for me to shake. Rude but not crude, I politely declined, citing a possible cold virus as my reason.

"Would you like to sit down?" Big Goober gestured at a pair of plastic-covered sofas.

"Thanks, but no thanks. I can only stay a minute," I said.

"Would you like some hot chocolate?" Little Goober asked. "Agnes said you that you are very fond of it."

I'd expected to find the brothers' residence toasty warm, to make up for the heat lost during their outdoor shenanigans. But it was downright cold in there. Perhaps they preferred a colder house so as not to shock their systems so much when they went outside. At any rate, one certainly couldn't fault the Mishler brothers' hospitality—although on the other hand, drinking a beverage, even a hot one, made by a naked man was unappealing.

"No thanks. Like I said, I can only stay a minute. I just have a question or two to ask."

"This sounds serious, Brother," Little Goober said to Big Goober.

"It is," I said.

"We're within our constitutional rights," Big Goober said. "This is a private road. We own all the land from Remount Road down to here. Even the parcel with Agnes's house. What we do in pursuit of happiness is nobody's business, because nobody, except for us, is supposed to be on our land."

"Agnes doesn't own her house?"

"She owns the house, just not the land. Not until we die. Then she owns the whole kit and caboodle."

"Relax, fellas. I'm not here to complain about your nudity. Trust me, I've seen it all before, and on a grander scale. I just want to know if either of you heard a gunshot this evening."

Little Goober grinned. "Of course we did. Me and Brother were shooting bottles off the stump. Just like we do every evening after supper."

"But in the dark?"

"Makes it more fun that way. Of course you have to be careful doing the happy dance if you win, 'cause it can make for a pretty nasty cut. See?" Little Goober lifted his right foot and held it against his left knee.

I made the mistake of looking at the sole of his foot. Unfortunately, my eyes refused to stop there.

"I've seen nastier," I said. "So, you guys didn't hear any other shots?"

"Should we have?" Big Goober asked. "Is Silas Hemphopple still shooting deer out of season?"

"He is. But that's not what concerns me now. While you were shooting, did you see any cars drive up to your niece's house?"

"No."

Big Goober gently elbowed his brother aside. "We saw the police car. But that's it. Is that how you got here, Magdalena?"

"I'm afraid so. I have some bad news for you guys. Maybe you should sit down."

Despite the fact that both Goobers were well into their sixties, perhaps even seventies, they sat like obedient schoolboys. I forgot myself for a second and started to sit on the couch opposite them. A grease smear tipped me off just in time.

"Agnes has been injured."

Big Goober reacted first. "How bad?"

"She might be dead—but maybe not. I don't know. I found her lying on her kitchen floor. There was a butcher knife— Well, it didn't look good."

They staggered to their feet. "We've got to get over there," Little Goober said.

"Wait." Big Goober turned to me. "I think I heard another car."

"When?"

"During supper. Brother and I always watch *Jeopardy* when we eat, so that had to be between six thirty and seven."

I glanced at my watch. It was seven thirty on the dot. It was all jelling, except for one thing. How could Agnes have called me from the construction site? I slapped my forehead with an open palm.

"Dummkopf!"

"Magdalena, Brother and I do not tolerate folks calling us names."

"Sorry, Goobers, that was meant for me. I'm such an idiot."

"You shouldn't call yourself names either, Magdalena."

"Because there's already too many people calling you names," Little Goober said solemnly.

"What? Who calls me names?"

"Everyone—"

"Sometimes Brother speaks first and thinks later," Big Goober said. "You understand that, don't you, Magdalena?"

"Why, I never!"

"See what you've done, Brother?" Little Goober said. "You've gone and made her mad."

"I am not mad. Look, guys, we need to focus on Agnes. Can either of you think of anyone who might have had it in for her?"

"Everyone." This time it was Big Goober who generalized.

"Can you be more specific?"

"Well, as you know, our niece likes to—uh—"

"Interfere," Little Goober said.

"Right. She's kind of nosy. Gets that from her mama's side of the family. Come Halloween it's her house that gets TP'd, not ours. You asked about cars, Magdalena. Well, there was this real fancy car come out here about lunchtime. Don't remember the exact time, but it come before *All My Children*."

"I just adore Erica Kane," Little Goober said.

"Move it along, Big Goober," I said gently. "I need to get back to Agnes's house. So do you."

"Okay. There was a man in that fancy car, but he wasn't one of our own."

"He was English?"

"Yeah, that Iraqi fellow who owns them dry cleaning stores. I've seen him a couple of times in Yoder's Corner Market." Both Goobers, by the way, deign to dress when they come into town. The alternative is Hernia's hoosegow, a damp and chilly place certainly not amenable for sitting around in the altogether.

"He's not Iraqi—he's as American as you and I and apple pie. And his ancestors came from Lebanon."

"Big diff."

"Actually, it is."

"Whatever you say."

"How long did Mr. Rashid stay?"

Big Goober scratched his nose. "Can't say exactly, but it must have been during *All My Children* when he left. Brother eats raw carrots every day for lunch, so I gotta turn up the TV pretty loud. Anyway, I looked out the window when the show was over. By then the car was gone."

They were anxious to check on their niece, and so was I, but I wasn't quite through. "How do the two of you get along with Agnes?"

You could have knocked Big Goober over with a feather. Little Goober plopped back on the plastic-covered sofa on his own accord. Both men turned milk white, but only as far as their shoulders.

Big Goober found his tongue first. "Are you making some kind of accusation, Magdalena?"

"*Moi?* Why would I do such a thing?"

This time Little Goober won the draw. "Because you're a nosy busybody with a razor sharp tongue who helps the police out since the only ones Hernia can afford are too dumb to know their noses are attached to their faces."

"Uh-oh," Big Goober said, taking a step back from me. "I'm afraid this is one of those times Brother speaks first and thinks second."

"Sticks and stones may break my bones, but a good orthopedist can mend them. But your relationship with Agnes appears to be irreparable. For one thing, she claims that the two of you are as broke as beggars and that this is really her house."

Big Goober's eyes narrowed. "Does she have proof?"

"Let's say she does."

"Our brother had no right to give her our house," Little Goober said. "She already had one that he gave her when she turned twenty-one."

Big Goober glared at Little Goober. "You spoke first again."

"I don't care. This is a free country, isn't it? She can't evict us just because we choose not to wear clothes."

The wail of our town's ambulance seeped through the crack at the bottom of the door and around ill-fitting windows. I waited until it died down before responding.

"Not only can she evict you," I said, "but if she's right about ownership, consider it a done deed."

"I hate her," Big Goober said.

"Enough to try to kill her?"

His eyes disappeared behind slits. "I'm going to ask you to leave, Magdalena."

"Very well." I walked with exaggerated slowness to the door. "You boogers—I mean Goobers—coming with me?"

"No."

"I would have," Little Goober said, "but then you pis—"

"—tachio ice cream," I cried, clapping my hands over my ears. Unfortunately, as often happens when I clap my ears, I boxed them as well with a ten-pound purse.

Hernia's heroic EMTs are nothing if not efficient. By the time I returned breathless to the crime scene, Agnes was loaded into the van and hooked up to a tangle of tubes. The chief, who was standing by the rear doors, welcomed me anxiously.

"I was getting worried, Miss Yoder,"

"I'm a big girl, or haven't you heard?"

"So they tell me."

"What's her condition? Is she dead?"

"She's lost a lot of blood, but there's still a pulse. The knife is still in her, by the way."

So much for my psychic ability. Oh well. We Mennonites take seriously the biblical prohibition against witchcraft and by extension seers of any sort. Scratch any fortune-teller and you're much more likely to find a lapsed Presbyterian than one of the Plain People.

"Chief, you might want to question the two Goobers."

"Excuse me?"

"Her uncles. Big Goober and Little Goober. Their Christian names are Zibeline and Aubergine."

"Those are Mennonite names?"

"Their mother was a pagan from Paris, for what that's worth. Their father was one of the few local Mennonites who didn't claim conscientious objector status during World War Two. Anyway, after the war he brought her back from Europe. But after giving him three sons she returned to Europe, and he never heard from her again. He even hired a private detective to hunt her down, but to no avail. Rumor has it that she may really have been a German war criminal and fled back home when the noose here started tightening. One theory even has it that she was Eva Braun."

"Hitler's girlfriend?"

"Yah-voll."

"Forgive me, Miss Yoder, but you people have got to be the biggest gossips in the world."

"Thank you. You should hear what they say about you—oops."

"Maybe some other time. So tell me, why should I be interested in interviewing Miss Mishler's fraternal uncles?"

"Because they hate her guts. And that, my dear, is not gossip."

"They said that?"

"Big Goober's exact words—though I may have added the guts."

"Thanks, Miss Yoder. You've been a big help, just like I knew you would. Have you ever considered applying to a police academy? Because if you ever do, you have my recommendation. And I'm sure Sergeant Ackerman would be happy to endorse you as well."

"Hmm. Would I have to share a locker room with sweaty young male cadets?"

"I'm sure they have separate facilities. At least we did in California."

"In that case I'll pass. Now, chief, if you'll excuse me, it's been a long day."

"Indeed it has. Enjoy your evening, Magdalena."

I had no intention of enjoying my evening. My investigation into the death of Felicia Bacchustelli had only just begun.

35

Concord Grape Cake

*1 package (18½ ounces) white cake
mix
1 envelope (2 ounces) whipped
topping mix*

*4 eggs
1½ cups cold Concord grape juice
Confectioners' sugar*

In large mixer bowl, combine cake mix, whipped topping mix, eggs
and 1 cup cold Concord grape juice. Blend until moistened. Beat 4
minutes at medium speed. Pour into greased and floured 10-inch
tube pan. Bake at 350°F for 45 minutes or until cake tests done. Cook
in pan 15 minutes. Turn out onto wire rack. Using metal skewer or
straw, poke holes in surface of cake. Carefully spoon remaining ½
cup Concord grape juice onto cake until it is absorbed. Cool cake.
Sprinkle with confectioners' sugar before serving.

MAKES ONE 1-INCH CAKE

36

Only a rube would drop in on someone without calling first. I held my coat tightly closed against the wind with one hand and rang the fancy-schmancy doorbell with the other. I must say I was shocked by the rapidity with which it was answered.

"Miss Yoder, it's only you."

"Yes, Ibrahim. But this time I'm big as life and twice as ugly."

"You look the same as before." He made no move to invite me inside.

"Who is it, Ibrahim?" The dulcet tones of Dr. Faya Rashid were comforting.

"It's only Miss Yoder," I said.

She appeared at the door, slipping beneath her husband's arm. She was breathtakingly beautiful in a cornflower blue silk ensemble that complemented her olive skin. Her raven hair was swept off her neck, displaying to its full advantage a pair of diamond chandelier earrings. Never one to even contemplate a romantic liaison with someone of my own gender . . . well, never you mind.

"Come in, Miss Yoder," she said.

Her husband stiffened. "But, Faya, we are eating dinner."

"Where is your hospitality bone, Ibrahim? There is plenty of food."

"Perhaps our *guest*," he said, his words sagging with sarcasm, "has already eaten. This is late, even for us. And I don't know if she cares for lamb. Most Americans don't, you know."

Faya grabbed my free hand. "Do you like lamb, Miss Yoder?"

"It's not ba-a-ad."

"You see, Ibrahim?" She pulled me inside. "Come, you must eat with us."

"Don't mind if I do," I said, peeling off my coat.

"Excuse, please, while I make the place set." She scurried off, her flowing silk ensemble following a nanosecond behind.

"What's this all about?" Ibrahim growled when we were alone.

"I was hoping you'd tell me. My sources say that you paid a visit to Agnes Mishler's house today."

"I'm sorry—whom did you say?"

"Agnes Mishler, the town gossip. About this tall"—I gestured—"shaped like a five-hundred-pound bag of potatoes. I'm not being judgmental, you understand. I'm merely stating the facts."

"I'm afraid I don't know the woman."

I looked at him with cold beady eyes. It's a look I've honed over the years by practicing daily in a mirror. Believe me, given my normally sunny disposition, it hasn't been easy.

"They probably don't serve lamb in the hoosegow."

"I beg your pardon?"

"And thank goodness most prisons these days issue orange jumpsuits, or scrubs, instead of those horrible stripes. With your physique I'm afraid you'd look like a lopsided barber pole. I mean that charitably, of course."

He leaned so close I could smell cloves on his breath. "What's with this prison nonsense?"

"It's no nonsense, dear. The state pen is where you could end up if you obstruct this investigation. Your wife is so beautiful; a girlfriend named Mike would just not be the same."

"Okay," he growled, "I went to see Miss Mishler, but I didn't harm a hair on her head. I just told her that I would appreciate it if she kept her darn mouth shut. Faya is having a hard enough time adjusting to life in America without the town gossip implicating us in a murder."

Before I could growl back at Ibrahim, the lovely Faya swept back into the room. "Everything is ready. I shall spread the food now, okay?"

"Spread away," I cried with forced gaiety. The truth is, however, that I believed Ibrahim. Call it instinct, if you will. I didn't especially care for the man, but that was another issue altogether. What was called for now was an attitude adjustment on my part, and Faya's spread might well be what the doctor ordered.

And quite the spread it was. There was the aforementioned lamb in a yogurt sauce; rice cooked with plump golden raisins; okra stewed with tomatoes; cucumber, tomato, and onion salad; hummus and freshly baked pita bread; and for dessert baklava so sweet it made my teeth ache just to look at it.

The sumptuous meal was followed by coffee served black in thimble-size cups. The scalding liquid was so thick it plugged the cavities created by the baklava. Fortunately the concentrated caffeine packed quite a punch, revitalizing me. Three more cups and I was raring to go.

I have been called impulsive. It is one of the nicer things folks have said about me. It seems that I just can't help jumping to conclusions and immediately acting on them. I can only conclude that I must be right most of the time, or I wouldn't find this behavior beneficial. In the paraphrased words of my good pal Dr. Phil, it must be paying off.

At any rate, instead of heading back to the PennDutch Inn to interact with my guests, or back to the Babester's house to react to my future mother-in-law, I rather stupidly got it into my head to pay a home visit to Hiram Stutzman. Perhaps the stupidest part was that I didn't take the time to inform anyone of my intentions. If Hiram really was guilty of killing two women, I could be the charming third.

There appeared to be only one light on in the Stutzman home, emanating faintly through a back bedroom window. How horrible it must be to live by oneself in a home that had once been brimming with life. If I was Hiram, I would consider turning the house into a thriving bed and breakfast . . . He better not dare! The nerve of that man.

The Stutzman house has a perfectly functioning doorbell, but where's the fun in that? Besides, he had an ill-fitting storm door that, when rapped sharply with walnut-hard knuckles, made more noise than a horde of Hell's Angels on muffler-deprived choppers. After several minutes of gratifying din, Hiram flipped on the porch light and peered through a front window. He had his hand over his lust-inducing eyes, presumably to help him see beyond the glare of the glass. I gave him a jaunty salute.

After a few seconds the front door jerked open, and then the storm door. "I know better than not to invite you in. I'm surprised there aren't helicopters already circling overhead."

I had to squeeze past him to gain entrance. "They're waiting for my distress signal. Would you mind speaking closer to my purse?"

"As a matter of fact, I would. Magdalena, you're wasting your time and mine."

"Ah, but I'm wired by Levantine coffee—although it could have been merely Colombian—just prepared by a beautiful young woman from Lebanon. Have you ever had lamb cooked in yogurt?"

"Spill it, Magdalena. You didn't come here to talk about food."

"You're quite right." I looked around. The house looked re-markably clean for one run by a man living alone. Frankly, that was a bit worrisome. In my experience it's the neat freaks who are wound the tightest. If a house doesn't have at least one dust bunny hiding under the sofa, run for the hills. "My, what a pretty couch that is. Did it come in other color combinations?"

"Say what?"

I stooped and tapped on one of the wooden legs. "Maple?"

"Magdalena, what are you doing?"

I stooped farther and thanks to the protection offered by my sturdy Christian underwear was able to thrust my bony behind high in the air. If Hiram Stutzman thought I was trying to entice him, he had another guess coming. However, as I eventually discovered—once I got my patooty higher than my shoulders—there was no need to worry: a dust bunny the size of Wisconsin greeted me.

"Definitely not maple," I said. It took me a full minute to straighten into an upright position. "I'm here to ask about your whereabouts today."

"Is that all? Why didn't you just phone?"

"Phone, shmone. I much prefer to interface with people."

"You much prefer to interfere in people's lives. If you must know, I drove into Bedford to buy some socks."

"*Socks?*"

"Do you know a place in Hernia that sells socks?"

"Proceed."

"I did a couple of other errands as well—filled up on gas, picked up a few groceries. On the way home I swung by Grape Expectations. I hadn't been out there since Ed sold his farm. I wanted to see what there was—and yes, get a feel for where the murder had been.

"The first thing I saw was a sign advertising the winery that was to be built. Magdalena, I couldn't help myself. I got out my hunting rifle and shot the dot right off the 'I.' Then I came back here, milked and fed the cows, finished cleaning up the dairy room—the health inspector is coming out tomorrow—and then finally sat down with a TV dinner in my bedroom. And since I know you're going to ask, I do have a permit to carry my rifle in my pickup."

"Choose your words wisely," the great Chinese sage Ming Dalina once said, "because you may have to eat them, and not all of them taste good." Heeding Ming Dalina's superb advice, I actually thought before I spoke.

"Hiram, did you run into Agnes Mishler today?"

"Was she in Bedford? I didn't know that was her. All I know is that a woman cut right in front of me, barely missing my car by an inch. So yes, I leaned on the horn. It was the driver beside me who flipped her the bird."

"What bird?"

"Half of a victory sign."

I made a victory sign and then folded my middle finger. "I don't get it."

"That's to your credit, Magdalena."

I taxed my brain and thought again. Either Hiram was diabolically clever, placing Agnes in Bedford rather than Hernia, or his response was one of confused innocence. But Agnes had distinctly said Hiram had gotten out of his car at the construction site, a gun in his hands—and then bang.

What might Agnes have said if that knife hadn't stopped her? But that was it! It was a knife, not a bullet. Agnes Mishler might well have been telling me the story of Hiram shooting the sign when she was stabbed from behind. As for the loud noise, could that possibly have been her hitting the floor?

When all was said and done, what really happened was something only the killer knew, and even then it was quite possible he—

or she—hadn't been in the room long enough to hear Agnes's prelude. The important question for me was: did I believe Hiram Stutzman? Again, it was time to defer to the wisdom of the great Ming Dalina. "Trust your gut feeling," she is purported to have said, "especially if you have just eaten at a questionable restaurant."

Call me a fool, or a sucker for Hiram's hangdog expression, but what I now felt in my gut was that he was incapable of murder. A lifelong Mennonite, Hiram was not raised in an eye-for-an-eye culture. The death penalty, whether right or wrong, was an anathema to him. It was clear to everyone who knew him—except suspicious folks like me—that Hiram had externalized the deaths of his family. Yes, he was a broken, disturbed man. He was not, however, a walking time bomb like I'd imagined earlier.

"Hiram, when you stopped to shoot at the Grape Expectations sign, did you not notice anyone else around?"

"There *was* no one else around."

"Actually, there was. Agnes Mishler was there to release the soul of Mrs. Bacchustelli."

"What?"

"My sentiments exactly. Apparently Agnes was a pseudo-Buddhist—or something like that. Anyway, she called me to say she saw you get out of your pickup with your gun."

"And then what?"

"That's it. Those were the last words she said."

"Did you call her back?"

"Yes, but I got a busy signal. As it turns out, she's dead."

The shock on his face wasn't just my imagination. It was the same look Mama had on her face when Cora Beth Nuenswander stood up in church and started speaking in tongues. We Mennonites don't go in for that practice by the way, unless we're talking to foreigners. No, what shocked Mama—as well as the older half of the congregation—is that Cora Beth was speaking in Pennsylvania Dutch, a language she hadn't bothered to learn from her parents, *and* what she was saying was abominably filthy. At any rate, Mama's look had been one of utter disbelief, as was Hiram's.

"What do you mean, dead?"

"How many meanings are there? She was dead—like a dead flower, a dead animal, a dead person."

"Did she have a heart attack?"

I had one more test for him. "Yes."

"That doesn't surprise me. Carrying around all that weight had to be hard on her heart."

I nodded and then ambushed him with my next question. "So, whose knife was it?"

"What? Magdalena, you may not know this, but over the years I've come to your defense when people have said you're crazy."

"They *what*?"

"Some people have even given you a nickname."

"The great Ming Dalina?"

"No, but that's close. Mag*nuts*ia. That's what they call you."

"Who? When? How dare they?"

"And now that you're engaged to this Jewish fellow from New York, they're come up with a new name—Bonkers for Yonkers."

"He's not from Yonkers; he's from Manhattan!"

"Magdalena, take it from someone who has been there: a good therapist can do wonders."

"Why, I never," I said, and without uttering a word of farewell, stormed out of the house.

The nerve of that man! Who was he to talk? It was him the populace feared—him, and Wanda Hemphopple's tower of doom. And who else had the nerve to call me psychologically challenged? Not Agnes Mishler, that's for sure. And not her naughty nude uncles. If the good citizens of Hernia wanted to see walking, talking nut cases, they best hightail their highfalutin hinnies down to Charleston, South Carolina. Trust me, I've been there. But at least those folks have the good manners to call their whackos eccentric—not hurtful things like Mag*nuts*ia.

Tires squealed and gravel pinged as I barreled out of Hiram's driveway. Once on the highway I pressed the pedal to the metal, and by the time I reached Dead Man's Curve I was traveling at a speed appropriate only for the salt flats of Utah. Heaven help the pair of eyes I saw staring at me from the middle of the road. Heaven help me.

37

These were not cat eyes, nor did they belong to a wild animal. They were human eyes, about three feet above the highway, and they belonged to Hiram's youngest child, Eliza. She was dressed in her Sunday best, holding her doll Amy with her left arm, and sucking on her right thumb. She was both substantial and ethereal; she looked three-dimensional, yet my headlights seemed to pass right through her.

I'd heard many tales of Eliza sightings since her tragic death at that very spot, but of course I hadn't believed them. It's not that I don't believe in ghosts—it is not a commonly held Mennonite belief, mind you—because I have seen Granny Yoder's ghost a number of times. But bearers of these tales have most often been teenagers given to wild imaginings, or adults whose grip on reality has been noticeably and publicly slipping.

There was no time to ponder what that said about me. All I could do was close my eyes before impact—if, indeed, impact even applied here. Which it didn't. I sailed right through the spectral being without feeling the slightest bump. When I glanced in the rearview mirror a second later, Eliza Stutzman was still there, but she had turned and was watching me drive away.

As I approached Slave Creek I slowed considerably, as the bridge across it has been needing repairs as of late. Along with the deceleration, my blood pressure came down considerably, and by the time I reached the PennDutch I was my same old self.

* * *

By now Freni had finished the evening's dishes and gone home. My guests, tired from their excursion into Bedford, had already gone to their rooms, with the exception of the woman from West Virginia. She'd fallen asleep at the quilting stand I keep in the dining room. Taking great care not to wake her, I removed my comfortable clod-hoppers and tiptoed into the parlor. There I proceeded to roll up the carpet and search for the envelope that Ed Gingerich had purport-edly left for me.

It wasn't there. Neither was it under the furniture. It was, of course, possible that one of the guests had discovered it and helped his, or her, self. It was also possible that Alison—and I shuddered to think this—had stumbled across the check and not told me. It was, however, impossible for Freni to have found the money while clean-ing and not to have shared her discovery with me. My cousin is so honest she once made her husband, Mose, hitch up the buggy and drive the twelve miles into Bedford so that she could return an extra dollar she had received as change at Pat's I.G.A.

At any rate, there were the two aforementioned possibilities, nei-ther of which seemed as likely as the possibility that Ed Gingerich had been lying. If he wasn't lying about leaving the money, he was at least lying about the amount. A sum that would have impressed me, like he claimed, would have sent a guest packing with glee or Alison into orbit on her way to a mall. And if Ed was lying about the money—well, you can see where I was going, can't you? Right back to my car, which, thankfully, was still toasty warm inside.

I spent the drive to Belinda's mulling over my various theories and their respective suspects. Of all of them, what made the most sense was the one I'd already formed about Ed. Here was a man who'd taken a bite out of the forbidden apple, regretted the conse-quences, and then in an attempt to undo what couldn't be undone, had chopped down the apple tree and chucked it from the garden al-together. Too bad for him, some of the apples had been knocked loose and were rolling back in.

Yes, like Hiram, Ed had been born and raised a pacifist, but the mere fact that he had been greedy enough to sell his farm to grape growers meant that he was already outside the Mennonite mold. Ed, I concluded, might well be capable of murder.

Belinda answered the door in a pink chenille bathrobe and

curlers in her hair. I couldn't recall seeing curlers on anyone for the past twenty years, thank heavens, and recoiled in surprise.

"You didn't think it was naturally curly, did you, Magdalena?"

"Well, uh—aren't they hard to sleep in?"

"They're torture. But a little hardship is good for the soul, right?"

"Absolutely. I've got a hair shirt, size eight, you can borrow, but my bed of nails is already spoken for."

"You're teasing, aren't you?"

"Possibly. May I come in?"

She swung the door open wide. "I'm having myself a little nightcap. Would you care to join me?"

Who knew Belinda was a tippler? "What's in it?"

"An old nightcap. Pure cotton, of course. I cut it up into tiny pieces, simmered it for six hours, and then ran it through my food processor three times. Then I added a little hot milk, some artificial sweetener, and a dollop of vanilla extract. You can't even tell it used to be a nightcap. But it's got a lot of fiber in it, and you'll be regular again first thing in the morning."

"Sounds fascinating, but I think I'll pass. Is Ed Gingerich here?"

"Actually, he's out back chopping firewood. You can go through the house if you want or around the side."

"Thanks. I'll just go around." I took three steps and turned. "Oh, one more thing. I'd go easy on the vanilla extract, or you might wake up tomorrow with a killer headache."

"If I do, I'll just have a little hair of the dog that bit me."

I shuddered knowing that Belinda had indeed once clipped a poodle that bit her. "Well, toodle-loo, dear," I said cheerily and without further ado trotted around back to find Ed.

One has to admire the residual strength of elderly farmers. I found Ed swinging that ax with the oomph of two Gabes and the precision of a plastic surgeon. I watched silently for a moment, gratified to see that a life of discipline and hard work paid dividends other than basal cell carcinoma.

When he paused to rest, I purposely stepped on a twig so as not to startle him. "Ed," I called softly.

He turned. "Magdalena!"

"As big as life and twice as ugly."

"My wife—may she rest in piece—used to say that. Only in her case it was true."

"That's an awful thing to say."

"Fiona wouldn't have minded a bit. That woman had a quick wit and a self-deprecating sense of humor." He sighed. "It's hard to find that in a woman these days."

I nodded sympathetically. I certainly didn't have a funny bone in my body. In fact, the rather odd shape of my elbows confirms that.

"Ed, dear, I checked under the braided rug in my parlor, and there wasn't anything there."

He rubbed his chin with a calloused hand. "That's odd. Do you think someone might have taken it?"

"No, I don't."

"What are you saying?"

"That maybe you forgot. I do that all the time, by the way. I intend to do something and somehow skip ahead in my mind and think I've already done it."

"I know what you mean, although I can picture myself lifting up a corner of that rug and tucking the envelope under. Braided from lots of scraps, but predominantly green and blue, right?"

"Correct. Listen, Ed, be a dear, will you, and call your bank in the morning. See if the check has been cashed."

"Good idea. Thanks for letting me know."

"No problemo." I smiled broadly. "Oh, by the way, I called George Sand, of Sand, Hammerhead, and White. I gave him your name by way of introduction. I told him I was in need of a good attorney—you know, on a retainer, just in case one of my guests ever decides to sue me. You don't mind, do you?"

"Of course not."

"Somehow I didn't think you would. The call was, of course, a waste of my time. He said he's too busy representing Charlie the Tuna to take on a new client."

Ed tossed the ax toward the woodpile. It landed in a pile of leaves. "Like I said, they're the best. I consider myself really lucky to have gotten in with them when I did."

"You can say that again. After Charlie, they'll be handling a case for the Little Mermaid, and then Neptune—"

"Okay, so I never filed a suit with them. What does that prove?"

"For one thing, you don't know anything about sharks. And for another, it confirms that you're a liar."

He had the nerve to look me straight in the eye. What's more, he had the gall to not say anything further. Believe me, there is nothing quite so defeating as silence. It was time for me to go fishing, and I knew just the bait.

I took a deep breath before casting out my line. "Why Felicia and not Vinny?"

"What did you say?"

"A bullet can kill a man just as easy as it can a woman."

"Yes, but it was Felicia who refused—" His jaws snapped shut, but the bait was already headed for his gullet.

I took a step back. "Refused what? She seemed like such a sweet girl." Trust me, the Good Lord has a special category for lies that protect the common good—at least I hope so.

"Sweet? The little witch wouldn't let me out of the deal. Said 'over my dead body,' as a matter of fact. Vinny I could talk to, but not her."

"It wouldn't have done you any good, Ed. Even if you'd managed to get your farm back, your reputation is shot."

"That's what you think. Not everyone is as unforgiving as you. I was duped, that's what they're saying. Or have you been too busy talking to listen? No, what they won't forgive—if they ever find out—is that I own a third of Grape Expectations."

My jaw dropped, and I had to waste precious seconds picking it up. *"You what?"*

"You're out of farming, Magdalena. You've forgotten how dicey it is making a living in this business. Too little rain, too much rain, early frost—there is nothing you can count on. And those government subsidies that everyone thinks we get somehow end up in the hands of the big corporate farms. To make a long story short, I've been operating in the red for the last ten years. Heck, I haven't bought a new pair of shoes in three years."

"Spare me your sob story and get back to you owning a third of Grape Expectations."

"It was Felicia's idea: my land in exchange for my debts being paid off and one third of Grape Expectations. Anyway, she had what she thought was a brilliant marketing plan, combining wine tasting with the Plain People experience. Snobby yuppie gawkers is how she characterized our future customers. People who wanted to combine pretension with cultural awareness. I was to provide the latter. You see, next door to the wine-tasting room we'd have a mock-up of an Amish home with nubile young women dressed in traditional garb selling cheeses, quilts, and homemade furniture. There'd even be a so-called Amish wing of the lodge. Face it, Magdalena, your PennDutch Inn was about to become redundant."

"Why, I never!"

"But I'm not all bad, you know. I thought about it—the Amish gimmick part—and decided it wasn't right. Not in conjunction with a winery, for heaven's sake. So I asked them to buy me out, and when they refused—it was mostly Felicia—I told them they could just have my shares."

"Like Judas trying to return his blood money."

"Exactly— Hey, I don't like that remark. Anyway, they wouldn't take my shares. They said a deal is a deal, and unless I cooperated, they would expose me to the community and say it was all my idea. When I couldn't think of any other way to stop Grape Expectations—"

"Without more bad press, you mean."

"I did what I could to save the Amish in this community from commercial exploitation. And don't jump to conclusions, Magdalena, because I really didn't intend to kill Felicia Bacchustelli. I only meant to scare her. I used to do a lot of hunting when I was younger, and I was always a pretty good shot. But I miscalculated this time—so you see, it was an accident."

I was appalled but not shocked by his state of denial. Unfortunately, I've been around murderers enough times to know that, for the most part, they feel that they can justify their behavior. There aren't a whole lot of folks who wake up in the morning, rub their hands together diabolically, and say, "I'm going to commit an evil act today."

"Ed, did you practice knife-throwing as well?"

"Pardon me?"

"There's not a whole lot of room in Agnes's kitchen to toss a knife without hitting her. Are you still going to try to blame that on an accident?"

He stared at me, pulling the silent treatment again.

"I know it was you, Ed. You may as well come clean."

"For your information, Magdalena—not that you'll believe me—my intention was just to sound her out. To learn what she did or didn't know. Well, she knew too much. In fact, that busybody was on the phone when I got there."

"Talking to me, in fact."

"I didn't have a choice, Magdalena. I had to silence her, but I'd left my gun in the pickup. The knife was hers."

"So it was her fault you stabbed her?"

"You talk too much, Magdalena."

"Is that a threat?"

"Chopping wood is a good way to clear your head. I came out here to think, to figure out what to do next, and then you show up. And you don't stop talking. You're making me very nervous, so I'm saying things I don't mean to say. This *is* your fault, Magdalena."

"Give it up, Ed. Turn yourself in. You're only going to dig your hole deeper."

I saw Ed pick up a heavy stick of firewood. I even saw him pull back his arm. I did not, however, see him throw it.

38

I woke up with a headache the size of Montana, while my body felt like it was lying under the state of Texas. It took me a few seconds to realize that I was at the bottom of a woodpile, and that said pile was in a pickup truck and moving along the highway at considerable speed.

It was also extremely difficult to breathe, what with my face pressed into the bed liner and the weight of a maple tree compressing my lungs. I did not cry out, if only because it took too much energy. It was also futile. But the worst aspect of this horrible situation was that I soon found that I could not move. My arms, as well as my legs, were restrained—not by ropes or handcuffs but by the sheer weight of the wood.

I was raised on Bible stories in which the protagonists prayed for help and, invariably, their prayers were answered. Even some of my own prayers have been answered. On the other hand, I know plenty of people who've prayed to be delivered from one problem or another, but whose prayers have appeared to go unanswered—at least in this life. And while I'm on the subject of prayer, let me make it perfectly clear that fervor and a positive outcome do not necessarily go hand in hand. Every now and then I'll read the testimony of a plane crash survivor who insists that the Good Lord saved him, or her, because they prayed "real hard," totally ignoring the fact that a hundred other passengers died. Quite likely there were some real hard prayers among the doomed as well.

I'm pretty sure, however, that it doesn't hurt to pray, and stuck under a cord of wood as I was, there was nothing else I could do. So

I prayed, and prayed, and prayed, all the way to, and across, the Maryland border.

Please don't get me wrong; there might be nothing wrong with some parts of Maryland and even a few of those Marylanders, but the word in Hernia is that it is a wild and desolate place populated by a rough-and-tumble bunch. Forsooth, I could smell the difference as we crossed that imaginary line. You can be sure that, not having brought any provisions with me, I became even more upset.

After about an hour of driving on paved roads—the pavement came as quite a surprise, mind you—Ed turned off on a dirt road. Whatever discomfort I was feeling up until that point was, by comparison, now trivial. The road was like an old-fashioned washboard punctuated by potholes dug by Paul Bunyan. I would have bounced right out of that truck had it not been for all that wood on top of me. The last pothole I remember was so deep that for a few seconds I thought sure I heard the dulcet sounds of Chinese being spoken. Before I could call upon my new Asian friends for assistance, we bounced out of the hole. So high did we bounce that some of the wood actually spilled over the sides of the truck bed. It wasn't much, I'll be honest about that, but enough to make the entire pile shift. The next thing I knew I was fighting and clawing my way to the top with all the ferocity and strength of a grizzly bear, thanks to the miracle of adrenaline.

Then I was out! There was no time to assess or attend to my multiple wounds and abrasions. Throwing myself on the mercy of God, His angels, and whatever lay at the side of the road, I leaped over the nearest railing.

You can imagine my relief when my senses reported that I had landed in a thicket of some sort and not on a rock or at the bottom of one of those infamous Maryland abysses. The bushes were actually rather soft, and cradled as I was in their broken stems, I thought it wise to rest a minute before continuing with my escape. What I didn't count on was the fact that adrenaline rushes are often followed by an intense need to sleep.

The next thing I knew it was morning and I was being prodded by a walking stick. I looked up to see two pairs of human eyes, one obviously rather curious, the other strangely blank. They belonged to a man and a woman, respectively.

"What is it?" the owner of the blank eyes asked.

"A woman in a bush," her male companion said.

"What's she doing in a bush?"

"I was trying to catch birds," I said. "There were two in here just a minute ago."

"Huh?"

"My wife doesn't understand humor," the man said. "She used to work for *Kirkus*."

I struggled free from the bush's scratchy embrace. I'd never felt so stiff and bruised in all my born days. At least I was alive and someplace where English was spoken.

"Where am I?"

"Goiter, Maryland."

"Excuse me?"

"Go ahead, make fun of the name," the woman said. "Everyone does. At least we don't sleep in bushes."

"Where are you from?" the man asked.

"Hernia, Pennsylvania."

He chuckled. "Good one."

"I don't get it," his wife said.

I forced a smile. "I really am from a town named Hernia, Pennsylvania. You see, I jumped off a truck last night, having just clawed my way through a load of wood—that's why I was asleep in the bush. Anyway, I'd been taken prisoner by an old Mennonite man who'd killed two women, all because he was greedy. You haven't seen a strange pickup truck today, have you?"

"No, ma'am. But some fool kept driving back and forth along this road all night. I couldn't sleep a wink."

I looked around for the first time. There were about a dozen houses—cabins, really—but no vehicles in sight.

For the first time I was aware that my purse, which contained my cell phone, was missing. "I need to use a telephone," I said.

"Sure thing," Mr. Merry Eyes said. "I think the Bradleys have it."

"It's the Jamesons this week," Mrs. Crabby Face said.

"You mean there's only one phone in this place, and you're not even sure who has it?"

"We're on a religious retreat," Merry Eyes said. "We signed an agreement not to smuggle any phones in. No TVs either. Nothing but peace and quiet. We're not even allowed to bring our cars in. The organization that runs this place drives us in along with two weeks' worth of groceries. So you see, there are no excuses not to think, pray, and join in fellowship. And hopefully draw closer to the Lord."

I smoothed my clothes and straightened my prayer cap, all the while making pleasant conversation. "The no-TV rule I can see, but no phone—why, that's just plain cruel."

"I take it you're a gossip," Crabby Face said.

"Why, I never!"

"We are allowed walks," Merry Eyes said. "I find that nature nourishes my soul. My wife here, being a professional writer, finds that it stimulates her imagination."

I favored Crabby Face with a Christian smile. "My fiancé writes mysteries—at least he tries to. He's really pretty bad. What is it you write?"

"Nonfiction."

"That's my kind of writing. If you ask me, anyone can make a story up. Except maybe for Gabe. But writing something real—now, that takes talent."

"Thank you," Crabby Face said, looking not quite as crabby. "After I stopped working at *Kirkus*, I did a brief stint at *PW*, and then finally found the strength to do my own writing. Do you mind if I toot my own horn?"

"Toot away!" I cried gaily.

"Today I'm considered the number one copywriter for colonic cleansers in the country."

"For whatsis?"

"She writes instructions for enemas," Merry Eyes said. "She's working on one now called the Big Bang."

"How utterly fascinating." I rolled my eyes behind the privacy of my lids and thought desperately how to change the subject. "So, dear," I said to Merry Eyes, "what is it you do for a living—besides think, pray, and fellowship?"

He laughed. "I'm a Mennonite minister."

"Get out of town!"

"We did. We're here on retreat. Although actually, I am search-ing for a new post. The church I currently serve is looking for a younger man or woman as a draw for the youth of the community. I guess I'm just an old fossil."

"How old are you?"

"Forty-four."

I gasped in jest. "Ancient beyond description. Say, Reverend, what is your position on intermarriage?"

"I've nothing against it. God sees beyond skin color. We are all equal in His eyes."

"Let me make myself clear: I'm not talking about interracial marriage, I'm talking about a Christian marrying a Jew."

"Is this a hypothetical case?"

"Let's pretend that it is."

"Well, I require all couples to attend at least six premarital counseling sessions. I make them examine everything from finances to child-rearing. If I am convinced that they have thought things through carefully, with eyes as open as possible, I agree to marry them. So far, everyone I've married has been a professing Christian, but I see no problem with marrying a Christian and a Jew. The first Christians all had Jewish weddings."

"You're hired!"

"I beg your pardon?"

"At double your previous salary—whatever that was."

"Miss—uh—"

"Yoder. I'm on the search committee for Beechy Grove Mennonite Church in Hernia, Pennsylvania."

"Yes, but—"

"We'll take it," Crabby Face said.

Of course there were details to work out, and we agreed to a few over a quick breakfast of cornflakes, skim milk, and the weakest coffee available outside a nursing home. But first we hightailed it over to the Jamesons' cottage to use the telephone.

Ed Gingerich was apprehended just south of Charlotte, North Carolina, on his way to Florida. He was still driving the pickup filled with firewood. The authorities reported that his eyes were glazed over with exhaustion and that his first words were: "It's all Magdalena's fault."

He had the nerve to blame me for escaping and the fact that he

spent the rest of the night driving back and forth on a dirt road looking for me. When asked what he was doing on that road to begin
with, he said he'd heard on the radio that there was a roadblock up
ahead, and the police were checking cars. Ed was right about one
thing: the police were checking cars—miles away in Hagerstown,
and they were following a drug tip.

At his trial, five full months later, Ed broke down on the witness
stand and cried so many crocodile tears he nearly flooded the court-
room. Justice might have been blind, but she saw right through his
phony act, and the former farmer was sentenced to two consecutive
life sentences without parole. In a statement to the press a still sob-
bing Ed said he was only glad he didn't live in Texas, because dying
twice was bound to be twice as painful.

For the record, Agnes made a complete recovery and is just as
nosy as ever. Maybe even more so.

Chief Olivia Hornsby-Anderson sent the handsome young Chris
Ackerman to Maryland to fetch me. He brought with him the
Babester, Susannah, Alison, and Freni.

Thank heavens for my scrapes and bruises, which gave me the
right to ride up front with Chris, and no one else. My four loved
ones were squished in the backseat as tightly as Vienna sausages in
a dented can. At least, had there been an accident, Freni would not
have flown through the windshield. She was the one who elected to
go without a seat belt—there were only three back there—on the
grounds that she had the least experience with them. It should be
noted that this arrangement was totally illegal, even in Maryland.

"Hon," Babe said for the umpteenth time, "thank God you're
alive."

"Yah," Freni said. "We must thank God, but perhaps me too a little."

I tried to turn my head, but I was as stiff as an overstarched shirt.
"Excuse me?"

"When this one was little," Freni said, "she did not like to drink
her milk. Her mama, her papa, no one could make her drink. Then
one day I make the mustache on myself and say, 'Look what you can
have if you drink.' From then on she drinks milk every day—two
big glasses—and now she has bones of steel."

"Mom is awesome," Alison said proudly. "Not everyone has a mom with buns of steel."

"Ach!" Freni squawked. "I said *bones*."

"Whatever."

"Mags," Susannah said, leaning forward as much as her seat belt permitted, "you really are awesome. Yesterday morning I woke up feeling like I had the weight of the world on my shoulders, and this morning it was only Otto."

"Excuse me?"

"Well, when I woke up he—"

Sore neck or not, I whipped my head around. "Susannah, dear, may I remind you there is a child present?"

"Mom," Alison bellowed in my ear, "I'm not a child."

"Oh Mags," Susannah said, "you're always jumping to conclusions. What I was about to explain is that yesterday I was still feeling sorry for myself, you know, on account of my Shnooky Wooky was—"

"A crooky," I said.

"Right, and in jail. But then the very second I woke up this morning the phone rang, and it was Otto inviting me out on a date. Can you imagine that?"

"I imagine you told him that you're not about to start dating until your divorce goes through."

"Yeah, whatever."

"Speaking of dates," my beloved said, "you might be pleased to know, hon, that Ma and Doc Shafor are leaving this afternoon for three weeks in Bora-Bora."

"Get out of town!"

"They were going to leave this morning, but they wanted to wait until they knew you were all right."

"Right as rain!" I turned around so Gabe couldn't see my face. "While we're still on the topic of dates—although I have a slightly different meaning in mind—does anyone have plans for May fifteenth?"

"That's not the Fourth of July, is it?" Alison asked. "Because I promised this girl named Heather that I'd go with her to this stupid family picnic that she doesn't want to go to by herself on account of they're all old and yucky, but she said she'd give me twenty bucks if I went."

"I'm pretty sure it's not the Fourth, dear. Well, would anyone like to guess what I have planned for May fifteenth?"

My betrothed cleared his throat. "A colonoscopy?"

"On my wedding day? I think not!"

A chorus of gasps emanated from the backseat, and as you might expect, Gabe's was the loudest. "Hon, are you serious?"

"As serious as a blindfolded tightrope walker. Reverend Fiddle-garber—that nice man I introduced you to back there—has agreed to assume the leadership of Beechy Grove Mennonite Church. He has agreed to marry us as we are. No converting. How does that sound, dear?"

"Hon, you've just made me the happiest man in the world!"

"Yay!" Alison shrieked.

Susannah is capable of shrieking even louder. "Yahoo! Mags is getting married. Yahoo."

Freni waited until the din had died down to tolerable decibels. "Mazel tov," she said, somewhat incongruously.

We laughed most of the way home. Mazel tov indeed.